THE ONE

By the Author

THE ONE

by

C.A. Popovich

2023

THE ONE
© 2023 BY C.A. POPOVICH. ALL RIGHTS RESERVED.

ISBN 13: 978-1-63679-318-4

THIS TRADE PAPERBACK ORIGINAL IS PUBLISHED BY
BOLD STROKES BOOKS, INC.
P.O. BOX 249
VALLEY FALLS, NY 12185

FIRST EDITION: FEBRUARY 2023

CREDITS
EDITOR: CINDY CRESAP
PRODUCTION DESIGN: SUSAN RAMUNDO
COVER DESIGN BY JEANINE HENNING

Acknowledgments

My thanks go out to Michigan Humane for all their efforts to rehome so many abandoned animals. Thank you, Sandi, for feedback on my first draft and as always, thank you to the hard-working folks at Bold Strokes Books for giving my stories a home.

Dedication

To Love

CHAPTER ONE

Jody Acosta pulled another dress off the rack and held it up for her friend Ash's opinion.

"It's nice, too."

"That's not helpful, Ash. Which one?"

"Try them both on. Then you can decide."

Jody took both dresses to the tiny dressing room in the resale shop and modeled each one for her. "Well?"

"Definitely the dark green one. It makes your pretty hazel eyes sparkle."

"You think my eyes are pretty?" Jody mentally slapped herself and focused on positive self-affirmations. One of the reasons she decided to shop for a new dress to wear to the fancy fundraiser event included pushing herself to improve her self-image. "Forget I asked that. Thank you."

"You're welcome, and you're gorgeous. Wearing that dress will have every lesbian in the room drooling."

"How do you know there'll be lesbians there?"

"It's a fundraiser for an animal shelter. Do I need to say more? Besides, Nicole Bergeron is a lesbian and she's hosting the event." Ashley smirked. "If you can't decide, buy them both. The red one looks very hot on you, too."

Jody changed back into her jeans and T-shirt and took the dresses to the checkout. She had to admit she looked forward to the event, new dress or not. She'd heard about it when she'd spent the weekend volunteering at the local animal shelter and saw the lack of cleaning supplies and dog food.

"Good job," Ashley said as she started her car.

"Thanks for coming with me. I suck at shopping." Jody took a deep breath and enjoyed the feeling of accomplishment. The thrift shop was the perfect place to find bargains. For the first time since her high school prom, she looked forward to getting dressed up and going out. "So, who is this Nicole?"

"She's the daughter of the real estate mogul of the county, Daniel Bergeron. She does a lot to support the animal shelters throughout the state."

"Huh," Jody replied. "I hope this event tonight will be fun. I'm glad you agreed to go with me. I'm a little nervous."

"If it's anything like the last fundraiser she hosted, it'll be elegant and well-attended."

"Well, it's for a good cause." Jody sat up straight and took a deep breath. She could mingle with the rich and famous for one evening.

She hung her new dresses in her closet when she got home and made sure her shoes were polished. She thought about Ashley's elegant comment and pulled out her strappy sandals. Maybe she'd go for elegant, too. She was smiling when she grabbed her favorite body wash and turned on the shower. She finished quickly and stood before her full-length mirror for a minute. She'd never been obsessed with her weight or figure having always been active, so she wasn't sure why she bothered to check herself out now except she'd never been to a fancy, formal, fundraiser before. She slid into her new green dress and checked her makeup before slipping on her shoes and grabbing her clutch purse.

"You ready yet?" Ashley called from the doorway.

"I'll be right there." Jody took one last look in her mirror and went to meet Ashley at the door.

"Wow. You look amazing." Ashley grinned and shook her head.

"Thanks. You clean up pretty good yourself." Jody took her arm and tugged her to her car. The ride only took fifteen minutes and Jody watched the people streaming into the building as Ashley parked her car. It looked like there would be plenty of attendees. She followed Ashley into the brightly lit space and took in the chandeliers and crystal decanters with champagne flutes strategically placed throughout the room. "You were right about the elegance," she whispered to Ashley.

"Yeah. It's beautiful." Ashley looked distracted as she searched the area for her fiancé. "Do you see Bill? He said he'd meet us at the door."

"There he is." Jody pointed to Bill striding toward them. "He looks quite dashing. And you look stunning. Have fun." Jody sauntered to one of the tables and picked up a glass of champagne. She perused the room and her gaze landed on the most dazzling woman she'd ever seen. The beauty wore an expensive looking cream tuxedo designed to perfectly fit her solid but most definitely female form. Her thick blond hair flowed to her shoulders, and when she turned toward her, Jody found herself drowning in the depths of dark chocolate sparkling eyes. Heat followed the path as her gaze traveled from her eyes to her feet and back. Her strappy sandals were a good idea. She returned the perusal and took a sip from her glass. She never was any good at the flirting thing. She took a deep breath and released it as she watched the woman glide toward her.

"Hello. I haven't seen you at any of my events before. My name's Nicole." She never broke eye contact and gently tapped her champagne glass to Jody's.

"It's nice to meet you. This is the first fundraiser I've attended." Jody swallowed the lump in her throat when she realized she'd just cruised the event's hostess. "I volunteer at the animal shelter on Main Street, so I wanted to participate in the financial support. My name's Jody." She took another sip of the bubbly alcohol.

"I'm glad you're here, Jody. I'd offer you a drink but you beat me to it. Come on. I'll show you the plan."

Jody had no idea what "the plan" could be, but she followed Nicole. "Sounds good. Thanks." Several people, mainly women, interrupted their progress by trying to engage Nicole in conversation while shooting daggers at her, she suspected, because Nicole had taken her hand and hadn't let go.

Jody stiffened and pulled her hand away. Nicole obviously got whatever or whomever she wanted. "I'd like to see this plan you're talking about."

"It's right this way." Nicole led her across the room to a table with several photos of various shelter animals. "I found most people are more willing to donate after they see who their money is going to support." She smiled and waved at a couple standing across from them. "We have quite a few supporters who like to symbolically adopt one of these. They pick one from the pictures and donate in whatever name they decide to give them." She grinned and pointed to a picture of a Dachshund pup. "That sweetie has been adopted by seven different people and has seven different names. She's responsible for nearly half of the donations going to her shelter." Nicole took her hand again and led her to one of the small champagne tables. "Another glass?"

"Thank you." Jody's hand tingled when Nicole stroked it with her fingers as she passed her a glass. She swallowed before speaking. "How often do you hold these events?"

"I try for two or three a year. This is the first for this year, and I'm glad you're here. I'm afraid I need to leave you for a while to mingle." She glanced at her gold wristwatch. "Can we meet here later? Maybe in an hour?"

Jody's thoughts spun like a top. Jody had no desire to be the conquest of a rich playgirl, even the intriguing Nicole. And she had no doubt that was exactly what Nicole Bergeron was. "I came with friends so I need to find them." She smiled and headed to the area she last saw Ashley.

She wandered around the crowded room, smiled, and nodded to a few people while sipping from her glass. When she noted her lightheadedness, she filled one of the small plates with a few hors d'oeuvres and found a bottle of sparkling water. She settled against one of the walls and people-watched while she ate. She hadn't seen Ashley and Bill since they'd arrived, but she realized she hadn't paid attention to anyone else once Nicole had crossed into her radar. She finished eating and went to the donation table to leave the check she'd brought for her local animal shelter. She made a circuit around the room impressed with the understated but elegant décor. She had to force herself to ignore their sad eyes pleading to be taken to a forever home as she continued her stroll and checked out the photos of the animals. Once she had enough money saved to buy her own home, she'd consider adopting a dog.

Her thoughts turned to her mother alone in her house. Maybe she'd like a cat. She could talk to her about it when she saw her the next day. Thoughts of her mother reminded her of their pending wrongful death lawsuit. She had an appointment with the company representative on Monday to discuss the details. She found Ashley and Bill near the exit and she hoped it meant they were ready to leave. She'd met the beautiful Nicole and checked out the animals waiting for adoption. She was ready to go home, change into her sweats, and make a bowl of popcorn. "Have you seen enough?" she asked them.

"We have. You ready to leave?"

"Yes." Jody glanced back toward where Nicole stood talking to an elderly gentleman.

She pushed away thoughts of Nicole on the ride home. "Did you have a good time?" she asked.

"We did." Bill grinned as he spoke.

Ashley held his hand. "This is our first time at a dressy event." She leaned and kissed him. "He is dashing, isn't he?"

"Very." Jody smiled. Ashley and Bill's sister were friends and she'd met Bill at the welcome home party his family planned for him after he returned from deployment in Afghanistan. Jody had only ever seen him in his fatigues or jeans. He was a good guy and she was happy Ashley had found love. Lately she'd struggled to believe it would ever happen for her. She settled into the back seat of the car and enjoyed the memory of the warmth and gentleness of Nicole's touch when she'd taken her hand.

CHAPTER TWO

Nicole made one final tour of the room and stopped to thank the few donors and guests still present before beginning to put away the many photos and adoption documents spread across two tables. She locked away the cash and checks from the donation box and made a visual sweep of the room noting everything was in order. A stab of disappointment surprised her when she didn't see Jody and she shrugged off the unexpected feeling. A woman as beautiful as her undoubtedly had a partner or a wife. She imagined she could still feel the softness of her hand enveloped in hers and hoped she hadn't misread her interest. She helped the cleanup crew restore the room to its original state and carried the boxes of paperwork to her car. She stood next to her car for a few minutes to enjoy the pleasant evening temperature and allowed her thoughts to drift to Jody. She smiled and hoped she'd show up for the next fundraiser. She made one more walk through the room before heading home.

Nicole settled in her office to check the paperwork she'd prepared for the pending lawsuit for one of her father's companies that she managed. The information she'd collected indicated the company wasn't liable for the death of one of the employees. It was her job to inform the family, and she was not looking forward to it. She created a folder for her notes and locked it in her desk. Monday had the potential to be a difficult day. She checked the time and contemplated an evening at the local lesbian club hoping to find someone to take her mind off the fetching hazel-eyed woman in the sexy green evening gown. She changed out of her tuxedo and tied her hair back before heading to her car.

The club was packed by the time Nicole arrived and she made her way through the throng of women and smiled at a couple of familiar faces. She ordered a drink and leaned back on the bar to watch the few dancers when her gaze landed on a couple dirty dancing. She followed their impressive gyrations for a few minutes and fantasized about a remake of the movie starring lesbians. She sipped her drink, unsurprised when the woman she'd noticed at the end of the bar approached her. She'd been frequenting the lounge for a few months to help chase away the loneliness, and she'd seen the woman smile at her several times. She always stood alone and Nicole couldn't ever remember seeing her dancing.

The woman settled against the bar next to her. "Can I buy you another round?" She shifted closer so their shoulders brushed.

Nicole turned to face her. She expected to be recognized pretty much everywhere she went due to her photo being plastered throughout the pages of most magazines and newspapers whenever she attended a grand opening of one of her father's new acquisitions. "I'd like that. My name's Nicole." She waited for the brown-eyed brunette to introduce herself.

"I'm Emma. I think I've seen you here before." She passed the drink Nicole had ordered to her and turned to face her.

"You probably have. I've seen you, too. Thanks for the drink." Nicole waited for Emma to show her intentions. Too many seemingly innocent offers for company came with expectations of more when they recognized her.

"You're welcome." Emma sipped her drink. "You're very beautiful. Dance with me?"

Nicole took her hand and let herself be led to the dance floor. Emma held her close and as she relaxed in her arms, she sensed their shared need. The need that brought her to the club. The need to feel desired.

"Would you follow me home and spend the night?"

Nicole smiled at Emma's directness and shivered as her warm breath tickled her ear. "I would." She ignored memories of the feel of Jody's hand in hers as she took Emma's and walked to their cars. The drive to Emma's was a short one, and her small warm and cozy house felt welcoming.

Nicole rolled over and stretched the next morning. Emma was an attentive and tender lover and Nicole enjoyed their time together. She snuggled into her warmth and murmured when she wrapped her arm over her and pulled her closer. Emma might not be the love of her life, but she was real and Nicole had lived with *fantasy woman* for too long. She refused to give up on her belief that she'd find the one for her someday, but Emma was a pleasant diversion for one night. "This is nice." She kissed Emma lightly. "I have to get up soon, though." She nestled into her one more time before placing another kiss on her lips and swinging her legs over the side of the bed.

"I'm glad you came home with me." Emma wrapped her arms around her and pressed her breasts against her back. "I hope we can do this again." She kissed her bare shoulder.

Nicole hesitated. She didn't want to commit to anything she might not be able to follow through on. "I'd like that." It was true and she could probably make it happen. She dressed quickly and left intending to go home, but decided to stop at her brother's on the way.

"Hey, sis. I expected you later. I haven't finished the whole evaluation since you called, but this one, Emma, appears to be trustworthy."

"Thanks, brother o'mine. I appreciate you having my back." Nicole hugged her lawyer brother and accepted the glass of Old Forester bourbon he offered. She'd called him from her car after leaving Emma's house and asked him to do an extensive background check on Emma since the last woman she dated stole a hundred thousand dollars from her. She hated the intrusion into the women's lives, but she needed to know who she could trust. "I'm glad. I like this one and I'll probably see her again." She took a sip of her drink and wondered what he might find on Jody. She hoped nothing, but it was a moot point. She didn't have her last name, and she might never see her again. She checked her watch and finished her drink. "I've got to get home and review some notes before tomorrow."

"Ah. The wrongful death lawsuit. How do you think it'll go?"

"I don't know for sure, Caleb. The information I have shows no fault with the company. I'd be open to further investigation I suppose, but I doubt it'll show anything different. It's sad. He was well-liked and a good worker."

"Let me know how it turns out." He wrapped her in a hug. "And I'm glad Emma turned out to be safe."

Nicole thought about her night with Emma and smiled. She was glad Emma was safe, too. She spread her papers across her dining room table when she got home, made herself a sandwich, and poured herself a cup of coffee before beginning her review. Fifty-six-year-old Harold Acosta had been with the company twenty-five years, and his employee file indicated he was one of their top Hi-Lo drivers. It seemed odd that he'd have backed into a rack of crates causing them to fall and crush him. There was no major health issue listed in his file that could have caused him to black out. The medical examiner's report she had was preliminary, but it showed nothing except the cause and manner of death. She made a mental note to push for a copy of the final report. Whatever caused him to lose control of the Hi-Lo wasn't evident, and every one of them in the building was inspected thoroughly after the accident. No evidence of wrongdoing by the company jumped out at her.

She reviewed the maintenance schedule and planned to return to the building to re-interview the manager on duty that day. She filed all the paperwork in her briefcase and double-checked the address before washing her coffee cup and checking the time. She wanted to stop at the new animal shelter grand opening, but her late night with Emma was catching up to her and she needed to be sharp for her meeting with the Acosta family. She decided she'd have time to swing by the shelter in the morning on her way. She changed into her nightshirt and turned on the TV in her bedroom to watch a movie.

The next morning Nicole woke to an automobile commercial. She turned off the TV and stretched which reminded her of the previous morning with Emma. She disregarded the stab of loneliness and rose to start her day. She showered and dressed before making breakfast and watching the news with a cup of coffee. The trip to the shelter only took twenty minutes so she spent half an hour cleaning dog runs and filling food and water bowls. The tasks managed to distract her from the difficult confrontation with the Acostas she was certain was coming.

CHAPTER THREE

Jody hung up her dress and wrapped herself in her robe before flopping onto her bed. She'd been replaying the evening in her mind on the ride home and now she allowed her thoughts to drift to Nicole. She'd enjoyed the whole event, but warmth spread at the memory of the few minutes spent close to the hostess. She'd only dated one woman seriously after high school and before Sara. That ended when she'd moved cross-country to audition for an acting role. Jody couldn't help but wonder if she'd been practicing her acting skills with her. She sighed and rose to make a cup of tea before she settled on her couch and looked up Nicole Bergeron on her phone. She came from a wealthy family but apparently had made a name for herself by creating several charitable foundations. Nicole had never hidden her sexual orientation, even in high school. Jody continued her research and found extensive information regarding her work with animal shelters, but no mention of a wife or steady lover. She'd expected to find out Nicole had a string of girlfriends, but perhaps she'd have to revise her preconceived idea. Chances were she'd never see her again anyway so she sipped her tea and called her mother.

"Hello, dear. How was the event?"

"Hi, Mom. It went well. I was surprised at how many people showed up."

"Did you have a good time?"

Jody reflected on the evening again. "I did. It was fancy without being garish, and I think Nicole collected quite a few donations for the shelter."

"That's great, honey. Who's Nicole?"

"She's the one who organized the fundraiser. I guess she does quite a few of them."

"Are you still planning to come over Monday when the company rep visits?"

"Of course, Mom. I'll be there early."

"Thank you, honey. I love you."

"Love you, too, Mom." Jody set her phone on her charger and changed into her pajamas. She fell asleep to memories of soft hands and intertwined fingers.

The next morning, Jody woke early and recalled bits and pieces of her previous evening. She allowed the pleasant feelings to flow over her as she made herself breakfast and checked her briefcase for the inventory list she needed to take to work. She'd promised her boss she'd complete the physical count inventory and update the books. He intended to place the items that had been sitting in the warehouse for over a year on sale. She was tasked with figuring out the prices to get rid of inventory but not give it all away. She dressed and headed to the furniture store where she worked. Her boss's religious beliefs didn't allow for work on Sunday, so the building was empty and quiet when she arrived. She finished the inventory and itemized the sale items before leaving to pick up a dozen of her mother's favorite cream-filled donuts on her way to her house.

"Honey! I didn't expect you today." Jody's mother hugged her and took her hand to lead her to the kitchen. "I just made coffee."

"Thanks, Mom." Jody set the box of donuts on the counter. "I brought your favorite." She took the seat at her mother's kitchen table that she had claimed as hers when she was a child. She could see out the small window overlooking the tiny backyard. The only thing missing was the presence of her dad. His empty seat matched the empty corner of her heart. She watched her mother retrieve two donuts and neatly cut them into four pieces each. Jody had marveled as a child at her mother's ability to keep cream in every piece. She'd claimed it spread out the calories.

"Why'd you have to go to work today? Pete didn't open the store did he?"

"No. He asked me to inventory items we've had for a year. He's putting them on sale this week." Jody popped a piece of donut in her mouth and washed it down with coffee.

"I'll let Hazel next door know. She's looking for a new couch." Her mother took a sip of her coffee. "I'm a little worried about tomorrow, honey. My lawyer told me the company could contest the suit."

Jody squeezed her mother's hand gently. "We'll deal with whatever happens, Mom. Dad worked at that warehouse for twenty-five years and was the best Hi-Lo driver they had. It had to be the company's negligence that was responsible." Jody cringed at her mother's tears and stood to gather her in her arms. "I miss him, too."

Her mother hugged her and retrieved a paper towel to blow her nose. "It's been a year, and I still can't believe he won't be walking in the door, kissing me hello, and asking what's for dinner. He brought me a rose every Friday, you know?"

"I do. He loved you very much, and he was a good father." Jody swiped away her own tears. "What time is the representative coming tomorrow?"

"One o'clock."

"I'll be here by twelve thirty."

"Okay. I'll be so glad when this is over."

"Me too, Mom. Me too." Jody hugged her mother and left. She made a cup of tea before sitting to watch the news when she got home. Her phone rang as she was getting the local weather report. "Hi, Ashley."

"Hey, Jody. That was a great event yesterday wasn't it?"

"It was. I enjoyed myself." Jody didn't mention how much she enjoyed holding hands with Nicole.

"I saw you talking to Nicole. What's she like? I heard she's single."

"I don't know, Ash. She seemed nice enough, and she does a lot to support various charities."

"And she's gorgeous. You did notice didn't you?" Ashley chuckled.

"I noticed. I thought you only had eyes for Bill."

"I do, but I keep my eye out for your next girlfriend. Seriously, Jody. It's been years hasn't it?"

"I know, Ash, but I need more than just a pretty face, and I'd be willing to bet Nicole has multiple lovers all over the state."

"Okay. I'll leave you be. So, tomorrow's the meeting for your lawsuit, isn't it?"

"Yep. One o'clock."

"Good luck and let me know how it turns out."

Jody disconnected the call and took a deep breath. She rarely allowed herself to linger on her last relationship. She'd thought she'd found someone to spend the rest of her life with. She fell head over heels for Sara the summer she graduated college. They'd spent two years together and Jody was ready to take the next step. She asked Sara to marry her, and two days later, she announced she was leaving the state for an offer she couldn't refuse. Jody assumed she referred to a job, but she'd never know. She heard from a friend that she'd moved and left no forwarding address. Falling in love was too dangerous, and as lonely as she was, she was scared to let it happen again. She checked the time and decided to spend a couple of hours at the shelter. She grinned when she remembered her conversation with Ashley as she drove. She and Ashley had gone to high school together and she hadn't blinked an eye when she told her she was a lesbian. They'd been best friends ever since. She parked next to the shelter and went inside.

"Hi, Jody. I'm glad you could make it today. A man brought in a litter of abandoned newborns this morning, so all our techs are busy trying to get them fed. Could you help me clean the kennels today?"

"Whatever you need," Jody answered. She grabbed the supplies she'd need and got to work. She checked the time when her stomach let her know she'd missed lunch. "I'm making a McDonald's run. Same for everyone?"

The few workers responded with a resounding yes and Jody brushed off her clothes and left to get food. She returned within a half hour and the group settled in lawn chairs to eat. "Thanks for getting all this," Hanna said and ran her hand across Jody's shoulder and down her arm.

Jody had noticed her the first day she'd arrived and offered to help at the kennel. They'd gone to dinner a couple of times and now Jody feared she'd given her the wrong message. She'd become more familiar with her every time they worked together. She leaned away from her touch and finished eating before standing and making an excuse about the time and left with a wave.

She tossed her keys onto her kitchen counter when she got home and settled on her couch with a bottle of water to double-check the papers from the lawyer regarding the lawsuit especially the one she considered most important. The report from the medical examiner. It was labeled preliminary, but she figured the company had the final copy and it probably wasn't any different. She wiped away tears at the cause of death but took small comfort from the notation that death was instantaneous. She saw no indication of fault, and she'd make sure the company rep knew that they planned to fight against any insinuation that her father was at fault for the deadly accident. Content that all was in order, she changed into her pajamas and settled on her bed to read.

Her phone interrupted her in the middle of a sentence. "Hi, Mom. Everything okay?"

"Sorry to call so late, but I got a message from the company lawyer reminding me of the meeting tomorrow, so I called my lawyer to be here with us. I hope that's okay with you."

"It's probably a good idea, Mom. I'm bringing all the papers I have with me. I'll see you tomorrow afternoon. Sleep well." Jody liked the idea of having their attorney at the meeting. He'd know if something felt off, but she hoped it would go smoothly in their favor.

CHAPTER FOUR

Nicole took a deep breath and expelled it. Time to go inform a grieving family their lawsuit was going nowhere. The manner of death was listed as an accident. The cause was from trauma by being crushed by crates. The family would know that much from the coroner's report for the death certificate. Whatever caused Harold to apparently lose control of the Hi-Lo was unknown. She hoped she could complete more interviews with his fellow workers, but a year had flown by and their memory might be foggy. If the Acosta family pursued the lawsuit, there would be another whole investigation and she believed it would result in the same outcome. She pulled into the narrow driveway ten minutes early. She noted the neatly cut grass and trimmed bushes lining the covered front porch. They obviously took good care of the tiny house and property. She grabbed her briefcase and took the paved walk to the steps. The front door opened before she had the chance to ring the doorbell. A trim fifty-something woman with hints of gray through her brown hair answered immediately. "Mrs. Acosta? My name is Nicole Bergeron. I'm the representative of Cole's warehouse." Nicole smiled in hopes of putting her at ease but didn't believe that was possible by the look in her eyes.

"Yes, come in please. We've been expecting you. This is my lawyer, Gene Wilson." Her smile eased some of Nicole's concern.

"Thank you. Nice to meet you Mr. Wilson." Nicole stepped into the living room. Family pictures hung on the wall above a cream-colored sofa and a brown chair offset the soft beige carpet. The whole room had a warm, welcoming feel. "Your home is lovely."

"Thank you. Have a seat. Can I get you a cup of coffee or tea?"

"No, thank you." Nicole settled on the couch and opened her briefcase, surprised by her unanticipated hesitation. She'd expected the attorney present but not the seemingly warm welcome. "I'm afraid I have some bad news." She shuffled the papers and took a deep breath. "The company hasn't found any indication of being at fault for your husband's accident." Nicole watched the pain and disappointment wash over the woman and stood to support her when she paled and plopped onto the couch.

"Mom? Sorry, it took me longer to—" Jody stood in the doorway to the kitchen and glared. "You?"

Nicole kept her eye on Mrs. Acosta as she stood to face Jody. "Jody."

"So, you're the representative of the negligent company?" Jody sat next to her mother and wrapped an arm around her.

"I am. My father owns it, but I'm the manager and in charge of day-to-day operations."

"Well, my father worked there for over twenty-five years. He was good at his job and had no fault in the accident caused by your company. He's dead due to your 'day-to-day operations'!"

"Are you willing to look at my findings from our investigation? We found no reason to believe the company caused his...the accident." Nicole knew this would be difficult and she didn't want to remind them of their loved one's death. They'd never forget it. "If I could, I'd gladly go back in time and change the outcome of this. I'm so very sorry for your loss."

"Just what is it that you think caused 'the outcome' Ms. Bergeron?" Jody spit out the words. "My mother counted on my father's income and now she only has his small life insurance policy and my help. We were counting on the settlement of this lawsuit to keep her comfortable in her home. My father drove a Hi-Lo for years. He knew all the safety protocols."

Nicole took out the papers she intended them to sign discharging the company from any liability and set them on the coffee table in front of Jody and her mother. Their lawyer picked them up and reviewed them. "I'd like you to sign these and return them to me." She added a self-address stamped envelope to the pile before she stood to leave.

"Wait." Jody stepped in front of her. "My father did not cause his own death. I'm certain of it, Nicole. Is there anything more we can do to prove it?"

Surprised by her unbidden reaction to Jody so close, she glanced at her mother in tears on the couch. "We did an extensive investigation."

"Extensive? Can we do more? I'll help if you let me."

Nicole hesitated. There was nothing more to investigate. She sighed. If it was her father, she'd leave no stone unturned. Jody's plea stirred her. "I'll check with our insurance rep and if he allows it, you can meet me at the building this Sunday at nine a.m. We'll review everything I have so far and go from there. Okay?"

"Thank you." Jody wrote her phone number on a piece of paper and handed it to her.

Nicole returned to the couch and rested her hand on Jody's mother's arm. "We'll do our best to make sure we look at all the evidence again, Mrs. Acosta." She nodded to Jody and the lawyer on her way out. Raising their hopes wasn't something she wanted to do, because she knew how extensive the insurance company had researched the accident, and she couldn't question everything they found because she felt bad for the family. Or her inappropriate attraction to Jody. She sat in her car for a few minutes and made notes on her meeting with the family. Her stomach roiled at the memory of Mrs. Acosta's tears. She had to keep her personal feelings to herself in this situation. She had a job to do and everyone involved had to live with the outcome. She hoped she could keep her objectivity as she smiled at the piece of paper with Jody's number on it. She turned her thoughts to plans for the next fundraiser as she drove home and relaxed on her couch to sort the papers she had on the Acosta case. The case had the potential to linger, and she hated the thought of Mrs. Acosta suffering through years of litigation. She refiled all her information into her briefcase and noted the plan for Sunday on her calendar before she called her insurance representative.

"Hello, Nicole. What's up?"

"Hi, James. I'd like to bring the daughter of the Acosta wrongful death suit to the warehouse to help with research concerning the case. Is there any reason I shouldn't?"

"It's an unusual request, but I don't think it would be a problem. You're aware of the safety rules so make sure they're followed. I'll put a notation in the file in case anyone questions it."

"Thank you, James. I'll be careful." Nicole noted a reminder on her paperwork to let Jody know the procedure. She put her briefcase in her office, grabbed her camera, and went back to the animal shelter to check on a newborn litter she'd heard had been dropped off.

"Hey, Nicole. What brings you here tonight?" Bobbi, one of the volunteers, asked.

"I heard a litter of puppies came in this morning. I hoped to be able to photograph them for my next fundraiser." She followed Bobbi to the interior of the building to a small well-heated room and an incubator in the center. The seven squirming standard poodle puppies jostled for position as the technicians fed them formula from baby bottles. Nicole took several pictures and watched as they finished eating and curled into a pile of legs and tails and furry bodies. She took a few more shots of them sleeping before she put her camera away and helped feed the rest of the animals. She waved to the workers as she left and wondered as she drove home if Mrs. Acosta might like a puppy. She shook off the thought and reminded herself she was the Acostas' enemy now. They didn't want anything from her except the resolution of the lawsuit. She had to remember that as memories of the pleasant feel of Jody's hand in hers surfaced. She checked the time and decided it was too late for a stop at Sparks. She downloaded the pictures she'd taken when she got home and sorted them by type. The puppies would be a perfect incentive for donations and hopefully for adoption when they were old enough. She worked at her computer for an hour creating flyers with various photos of the pups. She put her favorite picture of them piled on one another in the center of the paper and seven lines for names around them. Maybe she'd make it a contest to see who could come up with the most creative seven names. She closed down her computer and picked up the book she'd been trying to finish for two days.

CHAPTER FIVE

M aybe we should accept the company's determination and move on, honey." Jody's mom looked exhausted. They'd consulted their lawyer before he left and Jody didn't feel encouraged. "It's been a year. I still have money left from the collection Harold's buddies took up, and I can always go back to work at the Laundromat if I need to."

"I don't believe it was Dad's fault. I remember how he used to talk about how driving a Hi-Lo was serious and took training and concentration. He was careful and good at his job." She began to pace.

"He was." She sighed. "That representative was nice. Kind. I hope we win the suit, but I did like her."

"I'm glad she's allowing me to participate in the review of things," Jody said. "She's the one who had that fundraiser I attended Saturday."

"Small world, I guess. Well, I'm not getting my hopes up, but at least we'll feel like we did everything we could to get to the truth. Even if it hurts."

"His loss will always hurt, but you're right, Mom. Dad would want it that way." Jody checked the time. "I have to get back to work. Are you going to be all right?"

"I'm fine, dear. I'm going to have a cup of decaf and watch the afternoon news."

Jody went back to work trying to ignore the anticipation of spending time with Nicole. "I'm back, Pete. Thanks for letting me take a long lunch." Jody settled at her desk in the back room of the furniture store. "It looks like our inventory sale is going well."

"It is. If it keeps up, we'll have all our year-old items sold soon." Pete's wide grin made him look younger than his sixty years.

Jody managed to concentrate on work for the rest of the day in between thoughts of Nicole and anticipation of their upcoming day together. She waved good-bye to Pete at five-thirty and headed home where she found a bowl of frozen spaghetti sauce in the freezer and took it to her mother's. "Hi, Mom. I brought supper." She found her mother doing needlepoint in her favorite chair in the living room.

"I didn't expect you back, honey. I got tired of watching TV and started a new project."

"I made this sauce the other day and hoped to be able to share it with you." Jody found noodles in a cupboard and filled a pot with water to boil before joining her mother in the living room. Are you doing okay this afternoon?"

"I'm fine. I'm looking forward to hearing how Sunday goes."

"Me, too." Jody set her mother's kitchen table and found salad fixings in the refrigerator. "Let's eat." She poured herself a glass of milk and her mother ice water. She'd decided to return to her mother's for dinner to check on her after the company rep's visit. When she thought about it, it was as much for herself as her mom. The visit had stirred up memories of the pain of the day they'd received a phone call from her father's supervisor informing them of the accident. The memory stole her breath and she sat in one of the kitchen chairs.

"Are you all right, honey?" Her mother rested her hand on her shoulder.

"Yeah. It's just the memories, you know."

"I do." She sat across from her at the table and began dishing noodles onto their plates. "Did you finish that inventory you told me you were working on?"

Jody appreciated her mother's attempt to distract her. "I did. We're having a huge inventory sale. Are you going to be all right?" she asked.

"I'm fine. The past six months have been healing for me. I have you and my book club friends. I know I'm not alone. Are you all right?"

"I am. I have Ashley and Bill to talk to and my fellow volunteers at the shelter. And I know I can always come to you." She finished eating and put the leftovers away. "You've got lunch tomorrow."

"Thank you. I love you."

"I love you, too, Mom. "I'll head home now. She kissed her mother's cheek. I have a new book waiting for me, but you let me know if you need anything." Jody checked the time when she got in her car and decided to stop at the shelter. She waved to a couple of people she recognized, grabbed some supplies, and headed to the dog runs. She turned the corner to enter one of the runs and almost ran into someone leaving. She began to apologize but froze when she realized it was Nicole. She wore jeans and a T-shirt that looked as good on her as the slacks and blouse she'd worn at her mother's house. "Hello again."

"Hi, Jody. I finished cleaning these two runs." She pointed with her shovel. "I'll give you a hand with the rest." She stopped talking and stood still as if waiting for permission.

"Sounds good." Jody proceeded to the next run and Nicole slid past her to the run beyond it. She finished cleaning every other space and was surprised to find Nicole leaving the last run.

"We work well together," Nicole said. She glanced at her watch. "Can I buy you a drink, or cup of coffee?"

Jody bristled. Nicole was probably used to getting whatever she wanted. Why Nicole would want to spend time with her while in the middle of settling a lawsuit didn't make sense, but she was going to be spending time with her doing research. Maybe it would be good to get a sense of who she was. She had *No, thank you* on the tip of her tongue, but what came out was, "Let me put these away." She held up the equipment she'd used and took it to the storage area. "Shall I follow you with my car?"

"It's up to you. I'd be glad to bring you back here if you want to ride with me."

Jody locked her car and followed Nicole to her Mercedes. "So, where are we going?"

"Coffee or alcohol?"

For reasons she couldn't figure out, she answered, "A glass of wine sounds nice."

"Do you like to dance?"

"Yes." Jody feared she'd gotten herself into something she might regret. "Why?"

"I know a place I think you'll like. Sparks."

"Okay." Jody definitely felt out of her element. She realized how sheltered she kept herself since she'd come out as a lesbian. Her parents had hugged her but warned that many people wouldn't be accepting. She struggled with peer pressure in high school, and her best friend had insisted it was a phase and consistently fixed her up with one boy or another for dates. She obliged her on a few occasions more to reassure herself than her friend. She thought she was done searching for love with Sara, but that turned out not to be. She took a deep breath and decided to enjoy the adventure.

"Here we are." Nicole parked in front of a building that looked like it had seen better days. She walked around to the passenger side.

Jody took her outstretched hand and allowed her to pull her to stand within kissing distance. She stepped sideways for space and followed Nicole into the building. The soft lighting, women's voices, and music enveloped her, and she didn't notice that Nicole had taken her hand and led her to the bar.

"Red or white?" Nicole asked.

"Red, please." Jody decided to throw caution to the wind for a few hours and enjoy the company of a beautiful woman. After all, she'd be spending time with her at the warehouse and this could be practice to see if they'd get along. She took the offered glass of wine and followed Nicole to one of the small tables.

"I'm glad you agreed to come with me tonight. I found this place a couple of years ago. I'm sort of surprised it's lasted this long. Lesbian bars seem to be disappearing lately."

"I've only been to a lesbian bar once about ten years ago." Jody sipped her wine and watched the few women dancing.

"We'll have to make this event extra special then." Nicole stood and held out her hand. "Let's dance."

Jody hesitated and took a drink of her wine before coming to a decision. She stepped into her arms as if she'd done it a hundred times. She'd forgotten the pleasure of holding a woman in her arms and being held by her. She followed Nicole's lead and danced until they were both out of breath. She could almost forget that Nicole held the power of her lawsuit in her hands. They fit well together, but Jody wasn't fooling herself. She'd push aside their differences only for one night.

"Would you like another glass of wine?" Nicole asked.

Jody checked her watch. "Actually, I may need to cut our evening short. I have to work in the morning."

"No problem." Nicole stood and reached for her hand. "Let's get you home."

She took one more look back at the bar and the room full of lesbians and smiled as they left. "I had a great time. Thanks for bringing me tonight."

"It was my pleasure. I know that our future will probably be strained, but I've enjoyed your company." Nicole held the passenger door open for her as she slid into the car.

Nicole was quiet on the drive back to the shelter, and Jody wondered what was going through her mind. "I'll see you Sunday."

"Do you want me to pick you up? We could ride together to the building."

"Sure. That way we could discuss any issues that come up." Jody sat in her car for a few minutes when she got home wondering how the day that started uncomfortable had turned into a very enjoyable evening. She mentally shook herself and went inside to get ready for bed. She set her phone on the charger and before she could get to the bathroom to brush her teeth, it rang. "Hello."

"I just wanted to say good night and tell you how much I enjoyed our evening." Jody recognized Nicole's voice.

"It was fun. I enjoyed it, too."

"Sleep well."

"You, too. Good night." Jody changed into her pajamas and lay on her bed wondering where her anger at Nicole had gone. Tomorrow would be soon enough to sort out her conflicting feelings.

CHAPTER SIX

Nicole pulled into her garage and smiled. What had started as a potentially difficult day had ended on a pleasant note. She was glad they hadn't run into Emma at Sparks. It definitely would have been awkward. She'd never dated more than one woman at a time, and she didn't plan to start. The idea that taking Jody to Sparks was a date hadn't entered her mind at the time, and now she wondered what message she was sending her. They had a challenging time ahead and she planned to remain neutral but open-minded about the results of the investigation. She went into her house and settled at her desk to organize her paperwork on the Acosta case, but her mind wandered to the pleasant evening with Jody. Her file gave her facts about her age, job, and schooling, but those details could fit anyone. She leaned back in her desk chair and recalled how her eyes sparkled when she smiled and the feel of her in her arms when they'd danced. Her hesitation when they'd gone their separate ways seemed to suggest she didn't want the evening to end. She turned her thoughts to Emma and their budding relationship. They'd both felt the attraction between them and desire to act on it, but she wasn't sure how much further she wanted to take things. She made a note to herself to talk to her the next time they saw each other. She made it mandatory to run background checks on anyone she was seeing, but she felt she had what she needed from Jody. She'd have plenty of time to get to know her better in the coming weeks, and she couldn't deny how much she looked forward to it. She finished her notes and went to bed.

The next morning, Nicole showered and dressed quickly. She wanted to get to the warehouse early to do some investigation before all the employees arrived. The parking lot was empty as she suspected it would be and she entered through the employee entrance. She planned to reinterview all the workers who had daily contact with Harold when she came back with Jody. She sensed Jody wouldn't be content to believe anything without hearing it herself. Nicole checked the rack that had been repaired since the accident. Photos had been taken of it and the area surrounding it after the accident and she studied them closely. She progressed to the section of the building used to park the Hi-Los and forklifts. They'd marked the one Harold had driven and she reviewed the maintenance schedule for it. She found no irregularities and put her paperwork aside while she climbed on the machine and backed it out of its parking spot. All the levers and pedals worked smoothly and she had no problem turning and parking. Whatever had happened with Harold, it didn't appear to be due to a faulty Hi-Lo. The stab of disappointment surprised her. She didn't want the company to be at fault, but she felt bad for the family. Especially since she'd witnessed Mrs. Acosta's grief. She made notes on her observations and went to her office.

"Good morning, boss. You're here early," Stacy, Nicole's office manager, said.

"Yeah. I met with the Acosta family yesterday. It was tough, so I thought I'd take another look at things. I'm bringing Harold's daughter with me Sunday, and I hope it'll give them some closure."

"Good luck. Everyone misses Harold. He was a good guy." Stacy settled at her desk and answered the ringing phone.

Nicole filed her notes from the morning in the Acosta folder and concentrated on the work of the day. It was six o'clock before she left for the day and headed home. She was almost to her house when she decided she needed a distraction. She pulled into Sparks' parking lot and all thoughts of work and Harold Acosta fled. She walked through the door and was immediately swamped with memories of Jody's smile as she took in the place and her firm body pressed against her as they'd danced. She ignored the thoughts and searched for a familiar face. She didn't see Emma right away, but movement at the bar drew her attention. Emma sipped a drink as she stood within the arms of a busty platinum blonde. Nicole stepped back and bumped into the door before turning and walking back to her car. She sat behind the wheel and took several deep breaths. She had no claim on Emma. Her disappointment at seeing her with another woman was totally unwarranted. They'd made no promises and apparently she'd invested more in their night together than Emma had. She shook off her disillusionment and drove home. She was halfway there when she decided to stop at her brother's.

"Hey, sis. You okay?" Caleb asked.

"Yeah. I'm fine." Nicole sat on her brother's couch and leaned her head back. "Have you ever heard the saying about repeating the same behavior and expecting different results? Or something like that."

"I have. What's up?" He settled next to her and put his arm over her shoulders.

"Remember the woman I had you do a background check on?"

"Yeah. Emma."

"I saw her tonight in the arms of a woman at the bar, and it bothered me a lot." She sighed deeply. "It seems I'm not able to be as detached as I thought. Do you have any more of that bourbon?"

Caleb poured them each a glass and sat next to Nicole. "I get it. It gets old being alone."

"Well. I'm going to have to be more careful. No more jumping into bed with anyone I haven't spent time with. Thanks for listening, and for the drink." She swallowed the last of the bourbon in her glass and went home. She considered her options as she drove. Maybe she could pretend she never saw Emma with that woman. A million thoughts scrolled through her mind, but she landed on the truth. She'd never settle for sharing. She needed a lover who wanted her. Not her money or the prestige of being with her. She wanted someone who wanted her for her or she'd be better off alone. She ordered dinner from her favorite Chinese takeout and ate while watching television. She finished and stretched out on her bed with a book, but a few minutes later, she set the book aside, picked up her phone, and called Jody. She justified the call by telling herself she needed to let her know about the bit of investigation she'd done that day.

"Hello, this is Jody."

"Hi, Jody. It's Nicole."

"Hi, Nicole. What's up?"

"I wanted to tell you I looked at the Hi-Lo today that was assigned to your father. I didn't find anything wrong with it."

"We're not going to dismiss our lawsuit. I hope you realize that. Are we still going together Sunday?"

"Oh, yes. I hope it'll put your mind at ease. That's all I'm concerned about, Jody. I'm not trying to force you to drop the suit. If the company was at fault, so be it." Nicole hesitated. She wanted to say more but couldn't think of another excuse to keep her on the phone except that she wanted to hear her voice.

"Okay. You all right?"

"Sure. I know you're looking for answers, and I want you to know I'll do everything I can to help."

"Thanks, Nicole. I appreciate it. Are you at home?"

"Yes. Why?"

"I thought maybe you went to Sparks."

Nicole cringed at the memory. "No. I stopped by my brother's earlier, but I'm home reading a book."

"Reading a book?"

"Yeah." Nicole objected to the question in Jody's voice. "Why do you sound surprised?"

"I'm not surprised. Well, maybe I am. I guess I figured you'd be out with…someone."

Nicole considered Jody's words. Her reputation in the tabloids as a playgirl could account for Jody's idea. "Actually, I spend quite a few nights at home reading."

"So, what're you reading?" Jody's voice held a smile.

"It's my favorite author's latest romance novel." Nicole liked that Jody seemed to enjoy their talk.

"I'm going to work early tomorrow, so I better say good night."

"Sleep well." Nicole put her phone away and went to bed. The next morning, she woke and smiled at memories of her phone conversation with Jody as she made breakfast. She wasn't naive enough to believe they wouldn't run into tension once they began the investigation regarding her father's death, but she'd enjoy her company before anything hit the fan. She stopped at the animal shelter on her way to work and spent an hour feeding the animals and cleaning the kennels then she left with a promise to return and a wave to the other volunteers. Stacy was at her desk waiting for her when she arrived at work. "Hey, Stacy."

"I received more paperwork from the Acostas' attorney this morning. He's pushing for closure on this case." She placed the papers on Nicole's desk.

"Okay. Thanks. Interesting. He was at the meeting with the family and he didn't say anything about more papers. I'll take a look at them now." Nicole went over the new papers carefully. There wasn't anything she could find different than the originals except a request for a timely resolution to the case. She leaned back in her chair. It made sense after Jody's comment about her mother living on her help and life insurance. They needed the money from a suit Nicole was certain they couldn't win. She'd have a better idea of a timeline for the lawyer after she and Jody began their investigation. She called to leave a message for the attorney and explained her plans for further research before filing away the new papers and making her daily tour of the building.

CHAPTER SEVEN

Jody plopped onto one of the two small couches that hadn't sold and grinned at her boss. "We did good, Pete. Our extra stock is gone. We'll need to begin to restock next week. I'll check with our supplier tomorrow."

"Thanks for your hard work on this, Jody. I was beginning to wonder if I'd have to carry this supply for another year. This is for you." Pete handed her an envelope.

She opened it and gasped. "Wow. Thank you! I didn't do anything special." She looked again at the check made out to her.

"I couldn't have done it without you, and I want you to know how much I appreciate you."

She hugged him before stepping out of his arms and speaking. "Thank you, so much. This will help a lot since it doesn't look like we're going to win the lawsuit against Cole's."

"You go home and get some rest. Tomorrow we'll see about ordering some new stock."

Jody drove straight to her mother's. "Hey, Mom. I have good news." She went to the living room and found her mother watching TV.

"Hello, honey. Good news?"

"Yes. Our sale went well and Pete gave me a bonus." She waved the check in front of her mother before taking it to the kitchen table, finding a pen, and signing the back of the check. "It'll cover six months of mortgage payments." She handed the check to her mom and hugged her.

"Thank you, dear, but you earned this. You don't have to give it to me."

"Mom. I'll be getting a paycheck next week. I'm fine. I want you to have this."

Her mother stood and pulled her into a full body hug. "You're a good daughter," she spoke with tears in her eyes.

"I'm going to check on the shelter before I go home. Do you want me to fix supper for you first?"

"You go, dear. I've got a tuna noodle casserole to finish. Do you want some before you go?"

Jody's first thought was to decline, but if her father's untimely demise had taught her anything, it was to make the most of the time she had with her parents. "Sure. That sounds great, Mom."

Jody finished eating and helped her mom clean up before leaving. She decided it was too late for the shelter so she headed straight home. She was half-way there when she changed her mind and turned down the street she remembered Nicole had taken to Sparks. She considered what she'd say to Nicole if she was there, but she'd had a good day and a huge part of her hoped she'd meet a nice woman to dance and share a drink with. She took a deep breath before she entered the club and headed for the bar. She ordered a glass of wine and turned to scan the room. Her heart rate settled when she didn't see Nicole. A nice-looking platinum blonde winked at her and sauntered toward her. She knew she was totally out of her element, but Jody decided being friendly was safe enough. She smiled when the woman introduced herself as Delia.

"May I buy you something more interesting than wine?" Delia stroked Jody's arm as she spoke.

"Thank you, but I'm good with wine." Jody sipped her wine and scrambled to figure out what else to say. Why was talking to Nicole so easy? She decided to go with what she knew. "Have you ever volunteered at one of the animal shelters?"

Delia narrowed her eyes and stared at her as if she didn't understand the question.

"I enjoy it very much. There are several in our area. I can show you, if you'd like?" Jody set her half-empty wine glass on the bar and waited for a response. Delia turned and hurried to a table where a lone woman sat. She pulled her out of her chair, into her arms, and onto the dance floor.

Jody rushed for the door. So much for a night out at the club. Maybe she'd try one of the online dating sites. She plopped onto her bed when she got home and told herself Delia wasn't her type anyway. Nicole's smile flashed through her mind, and she shook off the startling reaction. She went to her desk to check on the papers and notes she'd collected on the lawsuit. She didn't care that she was being obsessive. She knew her father hadn't been negligent and she planned to prove it. She packed everything in a briefcase that had belonged to her father. It struck her as appropriate that it would contain proof that his untimely death wasn't his fault. The next morning she turned her thoughts to the job of replenishing Pete's inventory as she drove to work. She spent the day talking to suppliers and studying furniture trends on the internet. By the end of the day, she'd arranged for enough inventory for the year. She gave Pete the list of items for his review, left for the day, and smiled as she drove to her mother's.

"Jody. I didn't expect you today." Her mother hugged her as she spoke. "It's Saturday night. Don't you have a date or something? You're too young to spend Saturday night with your mother."

"I don't have a date, and I like spending time with you."

"Well, since you're here, I made meat loaf and mashed potatoes. Sit and we'll eat."

After dinner, Jody stopped at the animal shelter to say hello to the workers before heading home. She relaxed and finished the book she'd started before drifting into sleep.

Jody woke Sunday morning to her phone ringing. "Morning, Nicole."

"Good morning. Were you planning to meet me at the warehouse?"

"I was, why?"

"I thought I could pick you up and we could stop for breakfast before we begin."

Jody hesitated. Spending time with Nicole away from the task before them sounded nice but unwise. There might be tension later though. "Okay."

"I need an address."

Jody gave her address to Nicole and went to take a shower and dress. She finished making coffee when her door buzzer sounded. "Just in time," she said as she opened the door for Nicole.

"For?"

"Coffee. Freshly made." Nicole grinned as she stepped into the room and Jody's breath caught. Her designer jeans hugged her extremely nice ass and she would have preferred a couple more than only two top buttons on her long-sleeved shirt be unbuttoned.

"Thank you." Nicole took the offered cup and sat on the end of the couch. "Are you ready for this today?"

"I'm looking forward to it. I'm certain we'll find proof that my father wasn't at fault."

"I hope it'll give you and your mother some closure. I'm sure it's not easy losing a father and husband. We'll start with the Hi-Lo today and I'll map out the route that he would have taken and the location of the racks he was assigned to. I'll do my best to cover all the bases for you." Nicole rested her fingers lightly on Jody's arm.

"I appreciate that." Jody put her coffee cup in the sink. "Shall we go?" She was anxious to see things for herself.

Nicole was quiet as she drove to the restaurant so Jody studied her profile. Her thick blond hair looked to be naturally wavy, but it was possible she used a curling iron. Her skin was smooth, and Jody couldn't tell if she wore foundation or if she was one of those natural blondes with flawless skin. She clenched her fist to keep from stroking her cheek to feel its softness. She followed Nicole into the restaurant when they arrived and sat across from her at the small table. The atmosphere was cozy and people looked relaxed. They both ordered omelets and bacon and didn't linger over coffee. Jody wanted to get to what they were after.

Nicole pulled into a parking lot marked *Private* and parked in a reserved spot, then turned to face her. "We'll go to my office first, and I'll show you all the information I have there." She stepped out of the car and Jody followed.

"Wow. Nice office." Jody took in the plush dark gray carpet and light gray wingback chairs. The mahogany desk sat with the swivel chair overlooking a large window with a view of the warehouse floor. Nicole could watch the goings-on throughout the day.

"Thank you. I don't see any sense in being uncomfortable when I spend most of my workdays here." She opened a small refrigerator tucked under a counter against the wall and pulled out two bottles of sparkling water. "The files are in the next room."

Jody followed Nicole to a large closet with file cabinets lining three walls and a small table in the center. She pulled out several files and set them on the table and moved two chairs from the corners. "Ready to begin?"

"I am." Jody took a deep breath and settled in the chair across from her. She picked up the first file. It was her dad's personnel file. There were no issues with the information regarding him and his family. She found no discrepancies or misinformation. She continued reviewing all the files Nicole handed her and found no disciplinary actions or other work-related issues. Her final conclusion, and what she already knew, was that her dad was a hard worker and an exemplary employee. "I don't see anything in his file that indicates he was careless or irresponsible."

"No. Neither did I. Let's take the rest of the information and do a walkabout on the floor."

Jody took a deep breath and followed Nicole.

CHAPTER EIGHT

Nicole led the way to the Hi-Lo parking area. "This was the machine your father was using that day." She watched Jody touch the joystick as if hoping to feel a trace of her father's touch. She swiped a tear off her cheek and turned to her.

"Was it driven by anyone else?"

"Yes. We only have a certain number of them and a few forklifts, so they're used as needed by several different employees. This is what I want to show you." Nicole led Jody to the back of the Hi-Lo. "This dent and these scratches were made when Harol—your dad, ran into the rack full of crates."

"Do you have the maintenance record for it? How often is it inspected? Maybe the brake failed."

"I do." Nicole handed the schedule to Jody. "This was the accident report." She pointed to the date of Harold's death. One she was certain Jody would never forget. She waited for Jody to review it and hand it back to her. "As you see, we have regular inspections for the equipment. Shall we go look at the rack?"

"Okay," Jody whispered.

"Are you all right? We can take a break if you'd like." Nicole rested her hand gently on Jody's lower back.

"You know? I would. Can we go back to your office for a cup of coffee?"

"Sure." Nicole resisted taking Jody's hand.

"I'm sorry. I had no idea how I'd feel seeing the last place my dad was alive." Jody took a drink of coffee. "He was always so careful." She wiped away a tear. "It's too hard to believe the accident was his fault. I know how cautious my dad was. He insisted I review all the rules and recite them to him when I was learning to drive. He was never careless. I just can't accept that this was just a freak accident. It could be that the crates were improperly stacked on the shelves. Maybe they fell off because someone didn't secure them properly and it was my dad who happened to be working there when they slid off the rack."

"It's okay, Jody. I know I'd feel the same way. We can continue in a couple of days. I'll plan on Wednesday evening. Would that be okay for you?" Nicole ached to wrap Jody in her arms and chase away her pain. She clasped her hands in her lap to keep herself in her seat.

Jody looked up and smiled. "Thank you. I'll plan to meet you here after work. About six okay?"

"That'd be great. I can come and get you if you'd rather. We could have dinner on the way."

Jody looked at her for a long moment. "It might be better to keep things uncomplicated."

"Okay. Whatever you're comfortable with." Nicole put away all the files they'd taken and locked the office before following Jody to the car.

Jody paused. "Thank you for this morning and for not pushing me. I had no idea I'd feel so sad."

"It's okay. You take as long as you need."

"I'd been to the warehouse twice. Dad took Mom and me to the company open house. I'd gotten to see where he worked and the Hi-Lo he drove. That was quite few years ago." Jody sighed.

Nicole parked in front of a buffet restaurant and turned to face Jody. "I have a carryout order to pick up, but would you like to stay and have something to eat?"

"I could go for a cup of tea."

Nicole chose a table away from the buffet and the crowd of people seated nearby. "This okay?" she asked.

"It's great. I've never been here before." Jody surveyed the room. "I like it."

"It one of my favorites. They have a fantastic Sunday brunch buffet, too." Nicole ordered their drinks when the server stopped at their table. Jody looked much calmer and even smiled.

"Thank you for this." Jody sat across from her and sipped her tea.

"You're welcome. You look like you're feeling better." Nicole liked that she was part of making Jody feel better. She liked it a lot. Nicole sat back in her seat and wrapped her hands around her coffee cup.

"I'm going to bring my mom here. I think she'd love it." Jody gazed around the room.

"I can attest to the Sunday meal. Scrambled eggs, bacon, waffles, and fruit."

"So, when is your next fundraiser?" Jody asked.

"I'm working on a plan for two weeks. It'll be at the same venue as the one you attended. I should know by the time I see you on Wednesday.

"Do you live near there?"

"I have a house on Main Street at the north end of town."

"Any siblings?"

"Yes. I have a younger brother. His name's Caleb." Nicole surprisingly didn't feel like she was being grilled as she did with many of her dates. Her past experiences usually put her on the defense. She wasn't fooling herself that time spent with Jody felt like a date. She had no idea how Jody felt, but she seemed to be beginning to relax with her and they were getting to know each other. She feared losing their tenuous connection once they got further into their research regarding her father's death. She took a deep breath and relaxed as they discussed different animal shelters and Jody's experiences with them.

"Would it be all right if we went back to the warehouse now?" Jody asked.

"Sure. You must feel more settled."

"I do, and I'd like to get an idea of what happened."

"Okay. But Wednesday we can talk to a few of the workers who witnessed the event."

"I've been obsessing over it for a year. Can we just look at the rack you mentioned and then we can go?"

"Sure." Nicole understood Jody's distress over the pending lawsuit. If evidence of the company's fault was found, her mother would receive a substantial settlement. She only wished she could cushion the blow when they saw what the outcome would be.

"Are all the racks the same?" Jody asked when they returned to the warehouse. She ran her fingers over the frame.

"In this area, they are. We had to replace the one damaged in the accident, but I have pictures in my office I can show you." Nicole cringed at the memory of the Hi-Lo and Harold buried under the pile of crates filled with scrap metal. She was grateful she wasn't present when the paramedics had pulled Harold out and pronounced him dead. The pain of any one of her employees being injured lingered for her. She posted all OSHA safety regulations throughout the building and suspended any worker ignoring them. She shook off the memories and followed Jody as she ran her hands over the racks. She wanted to wrap her arms around her and protect her from any hurt to come. Any hurts from anywhere she realized. She shook off the unfamiliar feelings and stepped next to Jody. "Do you want to see the pictures today or wait until Wednesday?"

"Let's look at them Wednesday." Jody took a deep breath and released it. "At least I know where it started and ended." She smiled a weak smile.

"Okay. Let's go." Nicole stopped herself from reaching for Jody's hand. She was probably dealing with some deep feelings. Nicole drove Jody home and turned to face her after parking in front of her apartment. "Are you okay?" She gave in and rested her hand on hers.

"I am. Thanks. I'll go see Mom later and fill her in, but I think I need some down time first. I'm looking forward to doing more research Wednesday." She smiled, squeezed her hand, and got out of the car.

Nicole decided to stop at her brother's on her way home. "Hey, Caleb. You busy?"

"Never too busy for you, sis. Coffee?"

"Sure. Thanks." Nicole accepted the mug of steaming coffee and took a sip. "How'd you learn to make such good coffee?"

"I dated that barista, remember? So, what's up that you'd stop in on Sunday afternoon?"

"I took Jody Acosta to the warehouse so she could see where her father died. It was hard on her." Nicole took a drink of coffee. "It was hard on me to see her relive the pain of losing him, you know?"

"I imagine it was. Your dad goes to work as usual and never comes home. Not something I want to experience." Caleb sliced pieces of coffee cake as he spoke and set a plate in front of Nicole.

"Thanks." She took a bite and a sip of coffee. "We're going back on Wednesday. I'm going to talk to a few employees who witnessed the event."

"Have you shown her the papers from the insurance company?" Caleb took a bit of coffee cake.

"She has copies of everything I have and there's nothing indicating fault anywhere. With us or Harold. The only issue it states is driver error."

Nicole pinched the bridge of her nose and squeezed her eyes shut. "I don't want to hurt her if something does come up." She raised pleading eyes to her brother.

"You care about her, don't you? Like really care about her."

"We've only known each other a couple of weeks, but…yeah, she's gotten to me. She wants to spend time with me and doesn't care about my money or my name."

"It sounds nice. I wish I could find someone that down to earth."

"What happened to Jamie? I though you two were pretty tight?"

"She told me she 'needed some space' and wasn't interested in 'getting serious' with anyone." Caleb shrugged. "I'm giving her 'some space.'"

"Sorry, bro. Looks like we're both on our own."

CHAPTER NINE

Jody made herself a cup of green tea and sat in her recliner while she contemplated what she'd seen at the warehouse. There had been nothing that indicated cause for her father running into the rack and knocking it over on top of him. She feared Wednesday would only bring more questions. She wondered if there might be confidential files that she wouldn't be able to see, but she'd push as far as she could for answers. She considered the accident report she'd read. It only described the event and indicated *driver error* as the cause. She sighed. Shouldn't it have been the company's responsibility to assure the rack could withstand being bumped into? Those Hi-Los were driven back and forth all day. There must have been a few accidental bumps. She had to admit that the dent in the Hi-Lo had to have been caused by more than only a bump, but she made a mental note to question Nicole about it. She finished her tea and called her mother.

"Hi, dear. Are you back from the warehouse?"

"I am, Mom. I was going to come over and give you an update. Such as it is."

"I'd love to see you, update or not. I'm making a pot roast with carrots and potatoes for dinner. Can you stay?"

"I'll be over in a little while." Jody retrieved a pound cake from her freezer and changed before heading to her mother's. Her thoughts drifted to Nicole as she drove. She'd appreciated her sensitivity and she could still feel her gentleness when she'd taken her hand. Whatever her investigation turned up, she was certain Nicole would do what she could to help.

"Hi, honey." Jody's mother kissed her cheek.

"I brought dessert." Jody handed her the pound cake.

"My favorite. Thank you. Dinner will be ready in ten minutes."

"Do you want to hear about the warehouse before dinner?"

"You can start now and we'll finish while we eat."

Jody sat on the couch next to her mom. "We only looked at the Hi-Lo that Dad drove. It had a major dent in the back and looked like he'd rammed it hard. The company had replaced most of the rack, but I saw the scratches he made on part of the frame."

"So, that was still there after a year?"

"Yeah. It wasn't damaged like the rest of the rack. I guess he knocked the whole thing over and all the crates fell off on top of him."

Her mother visibly shuddered. "Come sit at the table. I'm hungry." She set the roaster in the center of the table and took a seat. "The paramedics said it was quick. I'm grateful he didn't suffer." She used her napkin to dab at the tears in her eyes.

"Yeah. Me, too, Mom." Jody filled her plate and sat back in her chair. "It was difficult for me to see the last place he stood. Nicole's meeting me there on Wednesday after work. We may never know all the details, but I hope to get more information then. Nicole is open and honest with me, so I'm hoping to have answers. I hope she doesn't think we'll withdraw the lawsuit by being so cooperative."

"After you finish with her, we'll talk to our lawyer and see what else we can do." Her mother took a bite of carrot and remained quiet.

Jody finished eating and made a pot of decaf coffee to have with the pound cake. "We're going to talk to some of Dad's co-workers Wednesday. Maybe they'll remember something to give us more insight into the event." She set a cup of coffee in front of her mom and cut two pieces of cake. "I just can't believe Dad could have caused an accident like that." Jody blotted tears with her napkin.

"I know, honey. Maybe he was tired. He worked a lot of overtime around that time. Or maybe he was distracted. Maybe talking to a coworker or something." Her mother sighed and sipped her coffee. "Your father was always liked by the guys he worked with. Remember when we had that backyard get-together for his work buddies and their wives?"

"I do. Dad was so proud to show us off."

"I want this suit resolved, but he's been gone a year. I want to heal and live with cherished memories."

"I know, Mom. I do too. But, I want to be sure the company takes responsibility if we can prove it."

"He's gone, honey. We can't bring him back. Does it matter who's at fault for his death?"

"I don't want to put you through any more grief, but I think it's important to find the truth." Jody took a deep breath. Maybe she should accept his death and move on. She was feeling the stress and probably making it harder on her mom. "I'll talk to Nicole on Wednesday."

She stayed with her mother another hour and steered the conversation to her job and her mother's book club. She helped her with the dishes and remembered the cat question. "I just remembered, Mom. Would you be interested in adopting a cat? There's a real sweet tabby at the shelter that needs a home. He's a neutered male and seems to be friendly "

"I'll think about it. It might be nice to have a pet to care for."

"There're plenty of small dogs, too if you'd prefer. Let me know and we can go pick one out for you one day." She rose and put their cups and plates in the dishwasher before kissing her mother on the cheek and leaving. She drove home contemplating what she'd found out so far. Her dad's death certificate listed his death as an accident caused by trauma due to being crushed by crates. If it weren't for her mother's financial situation, she'd give up and accept what she couldn't change. She made herself a cup of chamomile tea when she got home and called Ashley.

"Hey, Jody. Everything okay?"

"Yeah. We haven't talked in a while and I miss you."

"So what's new? Oh, are you dating Nicole?" Ashley's voice rose as she spoke.

"No, Ash. I've been going to her warehouse to research my father's death."

"Wow. I thought that was all settled."

"No. Mom has a wrongful death lawsuit pending, and I'm trying to get Nicole to admit it was the company's fault."

"I knew about your lawsuit, but I didn't know it was Nicole's company."

"Yeah. It's a warehouse she manages for her father."

"Ah. It sounds like we need a girls' night out. Shall we meet somewhere?"

Jody's first thought was Sparks. "How would you feel about a lesbian club?"

"Sure. I'll expand my horizons. When do you have in mind?"

"How does Friday sound?"

"Perfect. Bill works late that day. We'll have fun."

Jody smiled at her enthusiasm. "We will. You be sure to let me know if you're uncomfortable, okay?"

"Sure. This isn't some kind of kinky S&M place is it?"

"No, Ash. It's a bar where we can dance and have a few drinks."

"Okay. I'll come by your place and you can drive since you know where we're going."

"Perfect. See you Friday about eight?"

"I'll be there."

Jody finished her tea and refused to think any more thoughts of the lawsuit. It took longer to push away thoughts of Nicole and where she might be that night. She shook off the unexpected thought. It was none of her business where Nicole was or who she was with. Why would Ashley ask if they were dating? Did Ash see something she was missing? She'd only seen them together at the fundraiser. Maybe it was time to finish the investigation and keep her distance. She lay on her bed and allowed herself the anticipation of going out with Ash. She picked up the book she'd been reading.

She woke the next morning with the book next to her. She rolled over and went to make breakfast and dress for work. The new supply of furniture would arrive that morning and she needed to inventory everything.

"Morning, Pete," she called to her boss when she arrived. She settled at her desk and began to sift through the pile of shipping receipts. She entered each piece of furniture into her computer and organized the lot by type. It looked like they'd be stocked for at least six months. She priced everything and closed down her computer to take her lunch break. She walked across the street to a small coffee shop and sat at one of the two-seater tables by the window. When she finished her sandwich and relaxed with a cup of coffee, she watched the passersby outside. The Mercedes came into her peripheral vision and she watched Nicole park and walk around to the passenger side to take the hand of a striking redhead. The woman was about Nicole's height, dressed to the nines in what looked like an expensive and short form-fitting dress. She laughed at something Nicole said and Jody certainly saw what Nicole must be attracted to. The scene reinforced her speculation about Nicole's playgirl status. Jody finished her coffee and waited until Nicole and her friend disappeared into one of the stores before leaving to go back to work. She spent the rest of the day inspecting and cataloging the inventory before heading home. She decided to swing by her mother's at the last minute so she gave her a quick call. "Hey, Mom. I'm on my way home and thought I'd stop in to say hi."

"I'd love to see you, honey. I'll put the tea on."

Jody sat in her mother's driveway for a few minutes to collect herself. She had absolutely no reason to be unsettled by Nicole's beautiful friend, but she had to be honest with herself. It bothered her. She went inside to spend time with her mother.

"Is everything all right, dear?"

Jody smiled at her mother's question and shook off the disquiet that had settled in her chest since seeing Nicole with her girlfriend. The pleasant feel of being in her arms while they'd danced now felt like a punch to her gut. "Yes. I've had a long day, Mom. We got six months of inventory delivered today so I was swamped." She managed another smile as she listened to her mother tell her about her latest book club meeting, then she finished her tea and went home.

CHAPTER TEN

Nicole took a seat outside the dressing room door. After ten minutes of waiting, she began to regret her offer to help her cousin pick an outfit for her upcoming gala event. She had no idea why she'd asked her for help, but Nicole's mother had insisted that she assist her for no other reason than she didn't want her showing up in tattered jeans like she had at the last one. As far as Nicole was concerned, she looked terrific in the dress she'd worn for the shopping expedition. She pulled out her phone while she waited and looked up Jody. She hadn't asked Caleb to do a background check on her, and she didn't plan to, but curiosity got the better of her. She'd graduated from the local community college with a degree in finance, and she'd been employed by a local furniture store since her graduation. She put her phone away deciding she'd rather get to know Jody on a face-to-face basis. Her cousin stepped out of the dressing room in a beautiful sparkling light beige gown that highlighted her smooth bronze skin and deep brown eyes. She smiled and Nicole grinned. "That is perfect for you!"

"Thank you, Nicky. I like it, too." She twirled and batted her eyelashes.

Nicole hated being called Nicky, and she blamed her brother for calling her that when they were kids. Their cousin picked it up and Nicole had been Nicky to her ever since. "Ready to go home?" Nicole was done with shopping. She dropped her cousin off at home and headed to Sparks for company. It was too early for many dancers, but several women sat at tables and a few lined the bar. She didn't see anyone familiar so she ordered a drink and found a good vantage point from where to watch the room. She sipped her drink and began to relax. She'd nearly finished her drink when the platinum blonde she'd seen with Emma ambled through the door. She watched her scan the room and grin when their gazes met. Within a minute she was beside her at the bar.

"Can I buy you a refill?" Her warm breath tickled her neck when she leaned close to whisper the request.

Nicole's curiosity got the better of her. She wanted to know who this woman was. "I'd like that," she whispered back. She finished her first drink and set the empty glass on the bar.

"What's your name?" The blonde pressed her breast against her arm.

"Nicole. What's yours?"

"Delia."

Nicole stepped back from Delia's gyrating breasts against her arm. She looked at her watch and feigned surprise. "Oh, I'm so sorry. I'm late for an appointment. We'll continue this another time." She rushed to her car and didn't look back as she drove out of the parking lot. Now she knew who busty Delia was. *Nothing compared to Jody.* She drove home, changed into leggings and an oversized shirt, and plopped onto her couch with a cup of hot chocolate. She picked up a book and stretched out with her feet up. After reading a few pages, she put the book down and went to her computer to update her notification for the next animal shelter fundraiser. She printed out the advertising flyer as she did with every event to check for errors. Then she reserved the venue, contacted the caterer, and wrote herself a note to check all the local animal shelters for models. She closed down her computer and went back to her book. Her phone interrupted her before she finished a chapter. "Hi, Jody."

"Hi, Nicole. I wanted to let you know that there is a week-old litter of poodle puppies in the shelter on Main Street. I thought they might make a great photo spread for your next fundraiser."

Nicole grinned at Jody's enthusiasm. "Thanks for letting me know. I actually had heard about them already. I think you're right about the photos."

"I thought we could stop on Wednesday on the way home if you'd like to take some pictures."

"Let's plan on it. Thank you for suggesting it."

"Okay." Jody was quiet for a heartbeat. "Did I interrupt your reading?"

"I'm kind of distracted tonight anyway, so no problem."

"Distracted? God, I'm sorry. You're probably not alone."

"No, Jody, it's okay. I'm alone. My mind keeps wandering for some reason."

"Chamomile."

"What?"

"Whenever I can't sleep or shut my mind off, I make a cup of chamomile tea. Works every time." Jody's voice held a smile.

"I'll give it a try. Thanks." Nicole knew she didn't have any chamomile tea, but she did appreciate Jody's suggestion.

"Okay. I'll let you go. I wanted to let you know about the pups."

"Thank you. I'll see you Wednesday." Nicole hesitated. She wanted to keep Jody on the phone for some unknown reason. Wednesday could develop tension between them and she wanted to hang on to the pleasant feeling of this call.

"Good night, Nicole." Jody disconnected the call.

Nicole went back to reading her book surprised at how much more settled she felt after talking to Jody. She made a mental note to buy some chamomile tea on her next shopping trip. She set her book aside and was smiling as she drifted into sleep.

The next morning Nicole rose early to head back to the animal shelter to get more shots of the poodle pups. She hoped to find Jody there, but she was probably at work. She ate breakfast and filled a travel mug with coffee before heading out the door.

"Hi, Nicole," one of the volunteers called from the puppy room.

"Hey, Hanna. How are the new ones?"

"Great. You here for pictures?"

"I am." Nicole could swear the puppies had doubled in size overnight. "They're growing like crazy."

"I know. They're a bunch of cuties, though."

Nicole followed Hanna to get a closer look at them. She'd often thought of adopting a dog, especially since she knew firsthand how many were tossed into shelters, abandoned to a life trapped in a cage. It was also why she donated money to have fenced runs installed in many of the shelters. At least they could have some time outdoors in the sun and fresh air. Maybe she'd consider one of these as soon as they were old enough to be adopted. "Have you started to take dibs on adoptions yet?

"You can be the first. Dr. Meyers will be back today to check on them, but she told me yesterday that they all looked plenty healthy."

Nicole watched the pile of pups crawling over each other. One sat quietly off to the side, its bright brown eyes beseeching her to give it a home. "I think I've been chosen." She pointed to the puppy.

"That's one of the three females. She's going to be one of the bigger ones in Dr. Meyers's opinion." Hanna held out her hand but the puppy's gaze never wavered. "Her vision seems to be clearing faster than her siblings."

Nicole smiled and squatted to be able to look closer. "What do you think, little one? You want to spend your life with me?" She watched as the tiny tail moved slightly. It was probably gas, but she took it as a sign and turned to Hanna. "She's mine. Please let me know when Dr. Meyers says she's old enough to bring home."

"Absolutely and congratulations. You're a mom." Hanna registered the adoption on the paperwork the shelter kept on all their animals. "Name yet?"

"For now, let's call her Tiny." Nicole took a few close-up shots of her new dependent and swore she was posing as she tilted her head when Nicole cooed at her. "I'll see you later, little one." She waved to Hanna as she went to her car. If she stayed any longer she might take home the whole litter. As she drove to work, she made a mental list of puppy items she'd need when she brought Tiny home. She grinned as she drove, surprised that a helpless puppy could bring her such happiness. She couldn't wait to share her news with Jody and that thought startled her. Jody was an animal lover. That's all it was. She called her before going in her building.

"Hi, Nicole."

She scrambled to come up with a logical excuse for calling. "I got to work and I was thinking I'd take a look at all the paperwork

I have on your father's accident. If you have your copies I thought maybe we could compare them at lunchtime."

"I'm at work and I don't have them with me, but I could stop at home and get them and meet you somewhere."

"Am I wrong to presume I have more flexibility as far as how long I'm gone for lunch than you do?"

"No, but I can take an hour and a half."

"Okay. Can I invite myself over to your place? I think we'll have more room to spread out." Nicole held her breath and waited.

"Sure. We'll use my dining room table."

"Great. I'll see you about twelve fifteen." Nicole put her phone away and forced herself to concentrate on work.

Chapter Eleven

Jody tried to remember if she had any clothes or dishes strewn around her apartment but decided it didn't matter. Nicole invited herself over so it would be what it would be. Ashley called her a neat freak, so she relaxed and concentrated on pricing the inventory she'd been working on. She checked the time and wondered if the clock had stopped, so she double-checked it on her computer and it matched. She mentally shook herself and wondered how she'd come to a point of looking forward to spending time with Nicole. The first time she'd seen her across the room at the fundraiser, she'd immediately caught her eye, but she was a beautiful woman. Now that she knew who Nicole was, she ought to feel angry and push her away. She was looking forward to scrutinizing all the evidence of the accident, but wasn't fooling herself that she was also looking forward to spending time with her. She checked the time again and grinned. Ten more minutes. She finished what she was working on and let Pete know she was leaving for lunch before heading to her car. She mentally scrolled through the items in her refrigerator as she drove. Nicole would probably have her own lunch. If not, Jody hoped she liked tuna. She parked and her phone chimed just as she walked through her door. She squashed the disappointment that surged when she thought it might be Nicole canceling and answered it. "Hello."

"Hi, Jody. Do you like pizza?"

"Yes. Very much."

"Vegetarian okay?"

"Perfect. Thank you."

Five minutes later, Nicole was at her door carrying two pizza boxes.

"That smells divine. Get in here quick." Jody stepped out of her way and closed the door before rushing to get plates, silverware, and napkins.

"I'm glad it's okay with you. I figured since I invited myself over, the least I could do is feed you." Nicole set the boxes on the table and opened them.

"I've got Coke, water, or 7 Up." Jody stood with the refrigerator door open.

"Coke please." Nicole was piling pizza on two plates.

"Mmm. Where did you get this pizza?" Jody reminded herself to chew. "This is the best pizza I've ever had."

"It's kind of a neighborhood secret. A tiny mom-and-pop place half a mile north of town. They've been there for years." Nicole took a bite, chewed, and swallowed before continuing. "My brother found it one day and my whole family has been getting pizza there since."

"Thanks for bringing it. I'm not sure I want to find it. I'll be three hundred pounds by the end of the year." Jody grinned but knew the truth of her words. It had taken her years to lose the extra weight she'd carried throughout high school. She cleaned off the table when they finished eating and retrieved her paperwork. "Hopefully, this paper shuffling won't give us indigestion. I'm stuffed."

"Yeah. Me, too. But it was worth it." Nicole grinned and leaned back in her chair. "Oh. I have something to tell you. Well, I want to tell you because I'm excited about it. I have someone new in my life. Her name is Tiny."

"Your girlfriend's name is Tiny?" Jody worked to keep the disappointment out of her voice as the scene of the attractive woman crawling out of Nicole's car flashed through her mind.

"Girlfriend? I don't have a girlfriend. I'm adopting one of those poodle puppies." Nicole smiled and took a sip of Coke.

"A puppy. That's great. I'll have to stop by the shelter tonight and see her." Jody hoped her relief didn't show. "What made you decide to adopt a puppy?"

"She picked me."

Jody chuckled.

"Honest. She did. I took some pictures and she sat off to the side staring at me."

"I see." Jody grinned, but she understood. "And her name?"

"Hanna told me that Dr. Meyers told her she'd be one of the biggest of the litter, so Tiny felt appropriate."

Jody shrugged. "Makes sense to me." She broke out laughing and Nicole joined her.

"Let's look at the papers we talked about." Jody spread her copies out in front of her.

Nicole did the same and they matched up each group. "It looks like you have the same information I do." She compared both copies of the medical examiner's report. "I'll request the final copy of this when I get back to my office. I don't think it'll be any different but it can't hurt."

"I thought the same thing. Why didn't we get the final copy right away?"

"Who knows? Bureaucracy? I think it goes through several hands before it's finalized, and in accident cases, they want to get cause and manner of death released as soon as possible so the family can get the death certificate. I'll check on it."

Jody refilled their glasses and reviewed all the other papers. She read the incident report carefully. It didn't seem possible that her father had lost control of the Hi-Lo and crashed into the rack, but that's what the report said. "Did you say we're going to talk to workers who were there?"

"Yes. I notified them already and they're more than happy to help." Nicole collected her papers and put them into her briefcase. "If I stay a few more minutes will it make you late?"

Jody checked her watch. "Nope. I told my boss I'd be an hour and a half."

"Did your dad ever talk about having a locker at work?"

"Not that I remember. I can ask Mom. Why?"

"I don't have a record of him having one, but I know the guys share them sometimes." Nicole finished her glass of Coke. "I'll double-check today. We can check it out on Wednesday."

"Sounds good. Thank you for the pizza. I enjoyed it and your company. I don't think I've told you how much I appreciate you letting me participate in the review of the information."

"No problem. I can't imagine how awful it must have been for you and your mom. I hope we can find a definitive answer for you."

"Me, too. Mom is tired and wants to move on." Jody turned to hold Nicole's gaze. "Do you think I'm being unkind by pushing for resolution?"

"I can't know how difficult it must be to try to move on from a tragedy like that, so I understand your need for closure. Your mother seems like a strong lady. She'll probably let you know when she's had enough."

Jody sighed. "Yeah. I just want to know what happened, you know?"

"I do, and I'll do my best to help." Nicole touched her hand briefly. "I'll let you get back to work." She stood and took her glass to the kitchen sink. "Thanks again for meeting me today." She smiled and left.

Jody squelched her disappointment. She'd hoped for something. Anything that would prove her father's innocence in the accident, but she wasn't going to give up. Not yet. She went back to work and turned her attention to pricing inventory. She finished the day and decided to swing by the animal shelter on her way home.

"Jody! It's good to see you," Hanna said. "Are you here to see the puppies? They've brought more traffic through here than I've ever seen."

Jody laughed. "I'm only here to see Tiny. I heard she was adopted."

Hanna laughed with her. "Nicole Bergeron claimed her yesterday. I'm glad at least one of the litter has a home. So, you want one?" Hanna looked expectantly at her.

"I'm not ready yet, Hanna. I don't even think my apartment complex allows pets. I'm waiting until I have a little house." Jody watched the puppies for a few minutes and waved at Tiny after Hanna introduced her before leaving. She stopped at her mother's on the way home. "Hi, Mom," she called from the doorway.

"Hi, honey. Come on in. I'm in the living room."

Jody found her mom in her usual chair with her needlepoint. "You're making progress." She kissed her mother on her cheek and settled on her couch.

"I am. I found this larger project this morning. Hazel and I are getting together once a week with another lady from my book club to have a needlepoint day. It's fun." She set aside what she was working on. "So, how are you doing, honey?"

"I'm good. I met with Nicole today to compare paperwork regarding Dad's accident. We have the same ones as she does."

"Ah. Is there anything more that she can do for us? This can't linger forever I suppose."

"She's following up on the medical examiner's report. She has the same preliminary copy as we do." Jody sighed and turned the conversation to her mother's friends and the book her club was reading. If there was any new information from the suit, she believed Nicole would update her. "How do you feel about leftover pizza?"

"Sounds yummy!" Her mother stood and followed Jody to the kitchen.

Jody reheated the leftover pizza and sat across from her mother. "Have you thought anymore about adopting a pet?"

"I have, actually. My friend Jeanie is looking for a home for her Main Coon. He's a sweet cat but her husband has become allergic to him. She's willing to give me all his toys and litter box. What do you think?"

"I think it might be nice for you. Does he have a name?" She thought of Nicole's Tiny.

"Jeanie calls him Mr. Grumbles. I guess he makes grumbling noises when he wants to eat."

"Makes sense." Jody finished her pizza and wrapped the leftover pieces in foil for her mother. "I'd like a dog someday I think. Not until I have a house though. I guess I'll head home." She kissed her mother's cheek. "Call if you need anything." Jody drove home with her thoughts bouncing between a puppy and a kitten.

CHAPTER TWELVE

Nicole left work with a wave to Stacy and headed to the animal shelter. Tiny and her littermates were sound asleep when she entered the building to check on them. She watched them sleep for a few minutes before collecting cleaning supplies and working on the dog runs. Her mind wandered to Tiny and how she'd be able to balance her puppyhood with her job. She could probably make an area for her in her office, but potty training would a challenge. Maybe it was a bad idea to adopt a puppy. She second-guessed her decision several times until she went back to check on them and Tiny bounced toward her. Her tail worked a little better than the previous day and her eyes seemed to focus on her. She realized it was going to be a long few weeks until she could bring her home. "Hey, Tiny. You've got a permanent home when you're old enough to leave your littermates. We're going to have a great life together." Nicole continued to talk and Tiny never wavered with her gaze. "I'm going to go home now and begin puppy-proofing my house. You be a good girl and finish all your food so you'll grow up to be big and strong." Nicole turned to head to her car and nearly bumped into Hanna.

"You are going to make a great puppy mom," she said.

"Thanks. It'll be a learning experience for us both." Nicole grinned and pushed aside the minor embarrassment at getting caught talking to a week-old puppy. "I'll see you tomorrow." She stopped on her way home to look at doggy beds and bought four. She took the examiner's report out of her briefcase when she got home and reviewed it before writing a formal request for the final copy. She put it in an envelope with plans to drop it off at the post office the next day. She couldn't imagine it would be any different than what she had, but it would put Jody's mind at ease. Hers too she realized. She placed each of Tiny's new beds in different rooms. Once she brought her home, they could be moved if necessary. She ate dinner, changed, and headed out the door. It had been a while since she'd been to Sparks, and she looked forward to some female company and maybe some dancing. The bar was crowded when she walked in, so she stood by the door and scanned the room. She didn't see Emma or Delia anywhere, but it didn't mean anything. The place was full of lesbians and there had to be a few single ones in the group. She ordered a drink and stood at the bar watching the few dancers. She noticed a couple leave and went to claim the table. She relaxed and enjoyed the atmosphere while she sipped her drink. Her mind wandered to Tiny, and she acknowledged a sliver of apprehension at the responsibility she was about to take on. She shifted in her seat and turned toward the door as a familiar face appeared. She suppressed her surprise and smiled when Jody turned to approach her.

"Is this seat taken?" Jody asked.

"It is now." Nicole stood. "Red wine?"

"Yes. Thank you."

Nicole took a deep breath while she waited at the bar for Jody's wine. They had quite a bit more of the facts in her father's death case to review and spending social time together might be ill-advised, but she couldn't ignore the pleasure that flowed through her when she'd seen her enter the room. "Here you go." She set Jody's glass in front of her.

"Thank you." Jody took a sip and set the glass down. "I wasn't sure I'd see you here."

"I was here a few days ago, but I didn't stay long. I've been stopping at the shelter after work to check on Tiny."

"She's a cutie. I think she'll be a good companion for you." Jody took a swallow of her wine. "Would you dance with me? I mean since we're both here…"

"I'd like that." Nicole stood, took Jody's hand, and pulled her to the dance floor. "Since we're both here and all," she whispered in her ear as she held her.

"I think I find myself in an awkward position." Jody moved to put a small space between them. "It feels wonderful to dance with you, but we're in the middle of a dispute over the cause of my father's death."

"I get it." Nicole led Jody back to the table. "I have an idea."

Jody looked at her but remained silent.

"I think we should declare Sparks a neutral zone. While we're here, there'll be no talk of lawsuits or anything related. Okay?"

Jody smiled. "I think that sounds perfect."

Nicole smiled back. It did sound perfect. "So, do you want to dance some more?"

Jody stood and reached for her hand. "Let's."

Nicole checked her watch when they sat back at the table. "How long can you stay tonight?"

"I should head home pretty soon. I'm sort of celebrating finishing up recording our new inventory today."

"Time for another wine?" Nicole knew she was pushing but couldn't stop.

"One more," Jody said.

Nicole went to the bar and returned with Jody's wine and a ginger ale. "Here you go." She set the glass in front of Jody.

"Thank you. I visited Tiny today. She's growing fast. They all are." Jody sipped her wine.

"I visit her every day. I went to buy her a bed yesterday and bought four of them. I'm afraid she's going to be a spoiled puppy." Nicole took a drink of her ginger ale.

"Let's dance one more time before I go, okay?" Jody asked.

"Sure." Nicole stood and reached for Jody's hand before drawing her into her arms. She held her close as they moved to the music and reluctantly released her when it stopped.

"Thanks for the lovely evening," Jody spoke softly as she stepped back.

"I'll walk you out." Nicole followed Jody to her car and waved as she drove away. She took a deep breath and reminded herself she needed to keep her distance. At least until this lawsuit was resolved, but she was smiling as she drove home.

She grabbed a sparkling water from her fridge when she got home and downloaded the pictures from her camera to her computer. It was too late to start creating flyers, so she organized them by group and closed down her laptop. She checked her calendar and circled the date she'd planned for the next fundraiser before heading to bed.

She woke the next morning to her phone. "Morning, Caleb. What's up?"

"I wanted to update you on the gala party, thingy, whatever Mom is calling it this year. She wants it to be 'super fancy.'"

"That doesn't sound any different than previous years." She climbed out of bed and put on her robe while she switched her phone to her other hand.

"Maybe you ought to give her a call. I think she has the idea that you're in charge of it. Are you?"

"Hell, no. I don't even want to be there. It was enough I had to take our cousin shopping for a dress. This yearly event is Mom's baby. Let her be in charge." Nicole began to pace.

"I have a feeling she'll be calling you soon, so be warned." Caleb disconnected the call.

"Damn!" Nicole made coffee and mentally reviewed the work she had planned for the warehouse the coming week. Most importantly, Wednesday with Jody. She ate breakfast, showered, and headed to work.

"Good morning, Stacy." Nicole went into her office and checked the stack of work orders in her in-box. She booted up her computer and began the work for the day. She took a break after an hour and went to make her daily walk-through on the warehouse floor. Satisfied that everything was in order, she went back to her office. "Would you please put this in today's mail, Stacy?" She handed her the envelope addressed to the medical examiner. "Thank you."

"Are you okay this morning?" Stacy asked.

"I'm fine, why?"

"You seem distracted."

Nicole sighed. "My mother's planning her yearly *world-renowned* fancy social event and it sounds like she wants me to take over planning it."

"Ah. I suppose I could help. Maybe. If you think I'd be helpful," Stacy's voice trailed off as she offered.

Nicole smiled at her office manager. She was phenomenal at her job, but she hated parties. "Thank you for the offer, Stacy, but I have a party planner in mind if Mom forces this on me. I'll let them do their thing. By the way, the envelope I gave you is a request for the final coroner's report on the Acosta case. Please bring it to me as soon as it arrives."

"Will do."

Nicole went back to her office and forced away memories of Jody and their evening together. She worked until noon and ordered a pizza lunch for the workers. That reminded her of the lunch she'd shared with Jody at her apartment. She took a walk on the warehouse floor to distract herself. She passed the Hi-Los and thought of Jody as she touched the one her father had driven. She walked around the rack they'd stopped to look at and had caused Jody's tears. She gave up and went back to her office to turn her thoughts to payroll. She finished and collected all the information she had on Harold Acosta's case. She couldn't find anything new and put it all away until Wednesday. "I'm going to head home, Stacy. I'll see you tomorrow." She headed to her car and decided to skip a visit to Tiny and had a hard time suppressing her anticipation at seeing Jody on Wednesday.

CHAPTER THIRTEEN

Jody finished cleaning the last dog run and put away the cleaning supplies. She'd taken her time hoping Nicole might show up to visit Tiny, but it was near dark so she gave up and went home. Nicole had no reason to seek her out, but Jody held out hope that she would. She needed to reset her expectations. They were going to investigate her father's accident on Wednesday and things could get tense. She focused on her paperwork when she got home and sat to watch the news. When she rose to make herself a cup of tea, she noticed a message on her phone. She returned Ashley's call.

"Hey, Jody. Thanks for calling me back."

"Sure."

"I wanted to make sure we're still on for Friday night."

"Absolutely. I'm looking forward to it."

"Me, too. Do you want to stop to eat on the way?" Ashley asked.

"Good idea. Do you want to meet at the restaurant?"

"That sounds good. See you about seven?"

"Yeah. How's Bill?"

"He's great. We went to the church today to make reservations and talk to the minister."

"Wow. Time is flying. Have I told you how happy I am for you two?" Jody squelched a stab of regret for not keeping in closer touch with her. "Let me know when we need to go for fittings." Jody smiled and stifled an image of her and Nicole dancing at the wedding.

"We can talk about it Friday," Ashley said.

"Good. I'll see you Friday." Jody put her phone away and went to bed. The next morning, she stopped at her mother's to check on her.

"Good morning, honey. Is everything okay?" Her mother looked worried.

"Yes. Everything's fine, Mom. I wanted to say hello and make sure you were doing all right."

"Do you have time for a cup of coffee?"

"Sure." Jody sat in her seat and took a bite of one of the chocolate chip cookies her mother set in the middle of the table. "These are good," she mumbled with her mouth full.

"Hazel made them. They're leftovers from our book club meeting. Is there anything new with the warehouse?"

"We're going to talk to dad's fellow workers tomorrow. I don't know if we'll find out anything new, but it's worth a try."

"Let me know what happens."

"You know I will, Mom." Jody sipped her coffee.

"I know you will. I'm just a little anxious."

"We might not find anything, Mom, but I appreciate Nicole letting me stay involved."

"Are you two getting along all right?" Her mom looked worried.

"Oh yeah. No problems." Jody smiled at the memory of holding Nicole while they danced. "No problems at all." Jody hugged her mother and left for work.

Jody finished updating the store's books by noon and left for lunch. She settled in the small restaurant she'd been in when she'd seen Nicole and the beautiful woman. She reminded herself that Nicole probably had beautiful women falling at her feet everywhere she went. She'd said she didn't have a girlfriend and Jody shook off the feeling that she was probably one of many women to have fallen under her spell. She finished her sandwich and took a 7 Up to go back to her office. She finished the afternoon and stopped by her mother's on the way home. "Hi, Mom," she called from the door. She stepped inside and nearly tripped over a huge furry cat. "Mr. Grumbles I presume." She ran her hand over his back as he rubbed against her leg.

"Hi, dear. I see you've met Mr. Grumbles." Her mother leaned against the kitchen wall and grinned.

"He's a friendly one, isn't he?" Jody continued to pet him.

"I never realized how much joy a pet could be. He's been curled in my lap all afternoon after Jeanie dropped him off."

"I'm glad, Mom. I'm sure Jeanie misses him." Jody had to admit the warmth of his body and his purring was calming.

"I have a chicken roasting if you're interested," her mother said.

"Yum." Jody sat on her mother's couch and smiled when Mr. Grumbles settled in her lap.

"Are you nervous about tomorrow, honey?"

Jody thought for a moment. "Not nervous, but it sounds like the company did a thorough examination of everything, so Nicole is probably only appeasing me by letting me look at things."

"It can't hurt to review things, I suppose. Let's eat." Her mother stood and Mr. Grumbles jumped to take her place on the couch.

Jody followed her mom to the kitchen and helped her cut the chicken into pieces.

"Are you and Nicole getting along all right, honey? I worry."

Jody hesitated. "We are." Memories of them dancing, working together at the shelter, and Nicole's sensitivity when she'd faltered after touching her father's Hi-Lo. "She's letting me go at my own pace, and I hope we find answers." She helped her mother clean up after dinner and watched her cuddle with Mr. Grumbles before she left. She spread out all the papers she had regarding her father's death on her dining room table to review them before putting them in her briefcase. No matter how many times she looked at the same information, she couldn't give up the hope of finding some answer. It might be futile, but she allowed herself the anticipation of possibly learning something new about her father's death and couldn't deny the flutter in her belly at the thought of spending time with Nicole. She fell asleep to thoughts of her smile and gentle touch.

Jody woke early the next morning with her thoughts already on the task with Nicole. She finished her workday and stopped at the animal shelter for half an hour before heading to the warehouse. She checked her watch and realized she was still early, so she sat in her car and listened to the radio for a few minutes before going into the building.

"Hi, Jody." Nicole's warm welcome put her at ease.

"Hi. I'm a little early…"

"No problem. Let's stop in my office before we begin." Nicole picked up a pad of paper and a pen before turning to her. "Ready?"

Jody took out a pen and the folder she'd put in her briefcase. "Let's do this." She followed Nicole to the warehouse floor and took a deep breath as she passed her dad's Hi-Lo and turned away from the rack she'd touched.

"These are the lockers I told you about." Nicole waved at one of the workers. "Hey, Jack. This is Harold's daughter, Jody. Do you know if Harold used a locker?"

"Hey, Nicole. I'm sorry about your dad, Jody. He was a great guy." Jack shuffled his feet.

"Thank you, Jack. He was," Jody said.

"I think he shared one with Phil til the renovations are done." Jack pointed to one of the lockers. "Number twenty-two."

"Thanks, Jack." Nicole opened the locker and motioned to Jody to look inside.

"Is that a vodka bottle?" Jody asked.

"It is." Nicole made a note on her pad of paper and picked up the empty bottle.

"It couldn't have been my dad's. He didn't drink." Jody searched her memory and didn't come up with a time she ever saw her father with alcohol.

"I'll talk to Phil tomorrow when he gets in. It's probably his." Nicole rested her hand on Jody's shoulder. The only other things in the locker were a pair of boots and a work shirt. "Let's go talk to his supervisor."

Jody followed Nicole to a tiny office in the corner of the warehouse floor. A burly fortyish man sat at a metal desk.

"Hey, Roger."

"Hi, Nicole. What brings you to my little corner of the world?" He smiled.

"This is Harold's daughter, Jody. She requested I take a second look at details of the day of the accident."

Roger nodded to Jody. "We were all real sorry 'bout losing your dad. I'm sorry for your loss."

"Thank you," Jody replied, holding back tears.

"I know it's been a year, but is there anything more you can remember about that day? Whether Harold was feeling ill, or tired. I'm hoping to find out what made him lose control of that Hi-Lo."

Nicole rested her hand on Jody's lower back as if recognizing her anguish.

"Sorry, Nicole. Everything I know I put in the report that day. Harold was one of my best workers."

"Okay, Roger." She set the empty vodka bottle on his desk. "This was in Phil's locker. If I find out anyone has been drinking on the job, they're fired on the spot. Please keep an extra eye out."

"No problem, Nicole. I'll keep an eye on all the lockers. Thanks for letting me know."

Jody followed Nicole to one of the loading docks. She pushed a button on a two-button control dangling from the ceiling and the large metal door rolled up. The early evening breeze rustled her hair, and she looked over the expanse of the semi-truck parking area. "Is this where the Hi-Lo loading and unloading happens?" Jody asked.

"It's one area. We have three, but this is the one your dad used most. It takes finesse to get the Hi-Lo in the right position for ease of loading. Your father was extremely good at his job." Nicole closed the roll-up door and led the way back to a spotless large-windowed room. "Would you like to sit for a minute? Have a cup of coffee or something?"

Jody sat next to her on the bench of one of the long folding tables. "This is the cafeteria, isn't it?"

"Yes."

"Dad used to talk about the Friday chicken and dumplings." Jody's tears welled.

"We have a cook that comes in Fridays. The rest of the week the employees bring their own lunches."

"Can we go back to your office now?" Jody stood and took a deep breath before following Nicole.

CHAPTER FOURTEEN

Nicole set a bottle of sparkling water on the table when they got to her office. Jody took a drink and seemed to relax a little.

"I thought I was stronger than this." Jody sniffled. "I mean, I've accepted my dad's death, but it still hurts, you know?" She propped her elbows on the table and rested her face in her hands.

Nicole took a seat next to her and rested her arm over her shoulder. "I'm so sorry, Jody. I wish I could change things." Her heart ached and her insides twisted at Jody's pain.

"Sorry." Jody sat up straight and took a deep breath. Her smile looked forced.

"It's okay, Jody. I'd be a puddle if my father died. Would you like to come back during lunch hour? Tomorrow or Friday? We can talk to your dad's buddies. The ones he ate lunch with."

Jody finished her bottle of water and stood. "I'll let my boss know I'll need a longer lunch Friday. Is that okay with you?"

"It's great. Friday it is." Nicole walked Jody to her car. "Be careful driving home. I'll see you Friday." Nicole gently stroked Jody's cheek before she stepped away from her car and watched her drive away. She went back to her office and checked the schedule on her computer before she blocked off Friday afternoon in case Jody needed her and left. She got halfway home and decided to stop and visit Tiny. She picked up cleaning supplies on her way inside and squatted at the entrance to the puppy room and called Tiny softly. When she waddled away from her littermates and pushed her tiny nose against the bars, Nicole gently stroked her head and was rewarded with a tail wag. Tiny was growing fast and her eyes were wide open. Her hearing would come soon. "Hey, Tiny. You're going to be a beautiful dog. I'm going to buy you a food and water bowl soon. I have to go clean the runs now. You go eat and grow big and strong." Nicole stood and went to begin her cleaning duties.

"Hi, Nicole," Bobbi spoke from the run next to her.

"Hey, Bobbi. How're you doing?"

"Great. Your little puppy has become popular with all the volunteers. She'll be missed when you take her home."

"She is a cutie, and she's growing so fast. I'll admit I'm a little nervous. I've never had a dog before." Nicole shrugged.

"If you need any help, ask any of us here. We have a lot of experience."

"Thanks, Bobbi. I'll remember that." Nicole went to finish cleaning and headed home. She made dinner and sat to eat while watching TV, but her thoughts kept wandering to Jody and her palpable grief. She checked the time and gave in to her longing and called her.

"Hi, Nicole." Jody sounded groggy.

"I wanted to check on you and see if you were feeling any better."

"I am. I stopped at Mom's and gave her an update, then came home and crashed. I'm planning to go to bed early."

"I won't keep you. I needed to make sure you were okay."

"Thank you. I appreciate your concern. I'll see you on Friday."

"I'm looking forward to seeing you. Good night, Jody." Nicole put her phone away and enjoyed the burst of pleasure at the thought of seeing Jody in a day. She shut off her television and went to bed. The next morning, Nicole arrived at work early.

"Good morning, Nicole," Stacy spoke from her desk.

"Hi, Stacy. Would you please get Roger on the line for me?"

"No problem."

Nicole went to her office and reviewed work schedules while she waited for Roger's call. The call came within minutes.

"Morning, Nicole. What's up?"

"Hi, Roger. Please send Phil to my office when he gets in this morning."

"Will do. Is there a problem?"

"No. I have a question for him. Thanks." She disconnected the call and went back to work. She was interrupted twenty minutes later by Stacy letting her know Phil had arrived.

"Hey, boss. You need me for something?"

She pulled out the empty vodka bottle from her drawer and set it on her desk. "Is this yours?"

Phil shifted foot to foot. "No."

"I found it in your locker."

"There're several of us that share that locker."

"Roger told me you shared it with Harold. Could this have been his?"

Phil shrugged but didn't answer.

"You're not in trouble, Phil. Harold's daughter is looking for answers, and I'm trying to help her. She said Harold didn't drink. Do you know different?"

Phil shifted foot to foot again. "Not for sure."

"Who else shares that locker?"

"I'll get a list for you today, okay?"

"Okay. Thank you."

Phil left and Nicole made a note to herself to follow up with him later that day. She finished her workday, checked the time, and headed to Roger's office.

"Hi, Nicole. What brings you to my corner of the world twice in two days?"

"Hey, Roger. I was looking for Phil. He was going to let me know who shares the locker with him."

"Ah. I know that Harold was one, but they're not assigned by name so it could be anyone else too. Is this about the vodka bottle?"

"Yeah, partly. I'm going to put in enough lockers so no one will have to share."

"Actually, it's more of a social thing. The guys meet at the lockers and talk in the morning and during breaks. They have a locker decorating event on Christmas. They'd probably share lockers even if they didn't have to."

"Thanks, Roger. Maybe they can change it to a decorating contest. I'm going to post a memo about this, but I'm starting a policy of unannounced locker checks and no more sharing. I don't want anyone thinking they can hide alcohol and get away with it." Nicole went back to her office and composed the memo on her computer. She emailed copies to Roger and human resources before printing out two copies. She tacked the copies to the walls in the locker area, left for the day, and headed to the shelter.

"Hi, Nicole," Hanna called from one of the dog runs.

"Hi, Hanna. Haven't seen you in a while."

"My hours at work changed, so I've been here later in the day. How're you doing? I heard you adopted one of the poodle pups."

"I did. I'm nervous, but I'm looking forward to taking her home."

"Let me know if I can help." Hanna waved and went back to the run.

Nicole spent time with Tiny before she went home with nonstop thoughts of Jody. It made sense to her that she'd be on her mind due to the lawsuit, but the protectiveness and serenity she felt when they were together puzzled her. She shook off her confusion and went home to change. An evening at Sparks would set her back on track. She settled at the bar when she arrived and ordered a drink as she watched the crowd. Several familiar people danced and smiled at her as she watched. One woman gave her a long perusal and winked before making her way through the group to her side.

"I'd like to buy you a drink." Her voice was vaguely familiar.

"I already have one." Nicole lifted her glass and took a sip. She couldn't place the woman but was certain she'd met her before. Something niggled in the back of her mind. She didn't trust her.

"If you won't drink with me, how about a dance?" She grinned and held out her hand.

Nicole smiled but recognition hit her hard. She was the newspaper reporter famous for looking for dirt on her family. Truth didn't matter to her. Only the notoriety of reporting on the rich and famous. "I'm late for a very important event." Nicole set her half full glass on the bar and walked out the door. She sat in her car for a few minutes to settle the bubbling anger. It had been a long time since she'd had to worry about being recognized and exploited. She took several deep breaths before starting her car. She checked the time and changed her mind about going home. She pulled into Caleb's driveway ten minutes later.

"Hey, Nicole. You okay?"

"I'm fine. I'm sorry for dropping in like this but I know you're usually up late." She plopped onto his couch.

"You look like you could use this." Caleb handed her a glass of bourbon.

"Thanks." She took a drink and stared into the golden liquid.

"So, what happened?" Caleb sat in a recliner across from her.

"Doreen happened."

"Damn. I thought she'd moved out of state. New York or somewhere."

"Nope. She was at Sparks tonight. She tried to get me to dance with her."

"Like the last time?"

"Yep. The woman is evil. She takes anything anyone says and turns it around to her advantage. The only thing she's interested in is getting a story and making a name for herself. Truth or not." Nicole stood and paced trying to remember what she'd said to Doreen. "I didn't say anything she could twist into something scandalous." She continued to pace.

"Okay, sis. Sit down. Tell me exactly what she said and you said." He grabbed a pad of paper and pen off his desk.

"She asked to buy me a drink. I told her I already had one. Then she asked me for a dance if I wouldn't drink with her. I told her I was late for an event and I left."

"I don't hear much to believe she'd have anything to put a negative spin on, but I'll check with our lawyer tomorrow."

"Thanks, Caleb. She's a sneaky bitch. I'll be at home tonight and in my office all day tomorrow." She hugged her brother and went home.

CHAPTER FIFTEEN

Jody shook off her drowsiness and poured a second cup of coffee. She immersed herself in the inventory and updates to the sales figures when she got to work. The furniture store was doing well, and she was proud to be a part of its success. "I'm going to stop at Mom's for lunch, Pete." She smiled at his wave of approval and left.

"Hello, dear. I have homemade chicken noodle soup for lunch," her mother said when Jody entered through the back door.

"Thanks, Mom." Jody sat at the table and pondered what to say to her mom about her day with Nicole.

"How did it go yesterday?"

Jody smiled. "It went well, but we didn't find anything new. I talked to Dad's friend Phil. Dad shared a locker with him, and there was an empty vodka bottle in it."

"Vodka?" Her mother looked pensive.

"Yeah. I told Nicole that Dad didn't drink and she was going to talk to Phil. We talked to Roger, too."

"I remember Roger and Phil. I met them at one of the open houses. You were just a kid."

"Anyway, we didn't find anything new, and I'm going back at lunchtime tomorrow to talk to some of his co-workers. I'm not sure what to expect, but I'm not too hopeful." She finished a bowl of soup and directed their conversation to talk of Mr. Grumbles and the animal shelters. She helped her mother clean up after lunch and kissed her cheek. "I'll talk to you tonight. Thanks for lunch." Jody went back to work and contemplated her mixed feelings which bounced between looking forward to seeing Nicole and anxiety that they wouldn't find any evidence of wrongdoing by the company. She finished her workday and headed to the animal shelter.

"Hi, Jody," Hanna called from the building.

"Hi, Hanna. How are the puppies doing?"

"They're growing like weeds and starting to be noisy. Dr. Meyers just left. She gave them all a clean bill of health."

"Good." Jody collected cleaning supplies and spent an hour cleaning dog runs. She stopped to say good-bye to Hanna before she left and thought about Tiny and Nicole while she drove. She couldn't deny she'd hoped Nicole would have been at the shelter visiting Tiny. She reflected on the first time they'd met and her preconceived idea of who she was and who she knew her to be now. Jody was certain Nicole cared about the outcome of their research and was willing to accept whatever the result turned out to be. She respected her for her honesty and admired her compassion. She was a beautiful woman which explained her allure. Unfortunately, Jody knew she wasn't the only lesbian who'd fallen under her spell if the stolen glances at her by the shelter volunteers were any indication. She let herself into her apartment and grinned at the memory of Nicole bringing pizza to share. She made herself a cup of chamomile tea and settled on her couch to watch TV. Her phone interrupted the evening news. She looked at the readout. "Hi, Nicole."

"Hi, Jody. I wanted to check on you. Are you doing okay?"

"I'm at home stretched out on my couch watching television with a cup of chamomile tea. That seems okay to me. I appreciate you checking on me, though."

"That does sound pretty comfy. I'm sitting up in bed reading."

"Another romance novel?"

"Absolutely. It's one of my favorites."

Jody took a deep breath to keep from expressing her first thought. That she wished she were sitting next to her. "That sounds pretty comfy, too."

"I won't keep you. Enjoy your tea, and I'll see you tomorrow."

"See you tomorrow, Nicole." Jody put her phone on her charger and finished watching the late news before going to bed. The next morning Jody finished breakfast and obsessively rearranged her paperwork before going to work. She grinned at the memory of her conversation with Nicole the night before and squashed the inappropriate tingle of desire when she thought about sharing a bed with her. She poured herself a cup of coffee to go and drove to work.

Jody settled at her desk and began her work for the day. She was in the middle of reviewing the previous day's sales when Pete interrupted her.

"Today is the lunchtime review with Cole's isn't it?" Pete asked.

"It is. I might be a little late coming back."

"Don't worry about it. I want you to take the afternoon off. Who knows what you'll run into, and I'm concerned about you. You take your time and don't even think of coming back to work. Okay?"

Jody held back tears. She stood and pulled Pete into a hug. "Thank you, Pete. I appreciate it." She made a mental note to stop at the store and pick up a package of his favorite cookies. She finished what she'd been working on and left.

Nicole was waiting for her at the door when she arrived. "Come on in. I let the guys know we'd be in to talk to them." Nicole took her hand when she passed her.

"It'll be nice to see my dad's friends, and I hope they have some insight into what happened."

"Me, too. I ordered a few pizzas for lunch, and I've got bottled water and Coke."

"Thanks for thinking of that." Jody followed Nicole to the lunchroom where the group of employees sat at long tables. Several smiled and waved when they arrived.

"Hi, Jody." Phil stood and hugged her. "You doing okay? How's your mom?"

"Thanks, Phil. We're all right. I'm hoping you or some other of dad's friends might be able to help figure out what happened."

"It was a horrible accident." Phil went back to his seat.

Jody sat next to Nicole and talked to a few workers while she ate then stood to address the group. "Thank you all for being here. I find it difficult to believe that my dad did anything to cause the accident. If anyone can remember anything about it, I'd appreciate you letting Nicole know." She returned to Nicole's office with her after lunch.

"I hope you feel a little better, Jody," Nicole said when they were seated in her office.

"I guess." Jody sighed. "It didn't sound like anyone had more information. I feel sort of deflated."

"There're a few more things we can look at. I'll get the information together and we can review it together."

"I appreciate it, Nicole. I'd sure like to bring some good news back to my mom."

"I'll contact our insurance company and get with Roger for the daily incident reports. Maybe there'll be something we missed there."

"Thanks. I don't mean to be a pain in the ass about this, but I can't believe Dad was at fault." Jody stood and paced.

"Do you think you'd like a little distraction tonight?" Nicole asked.

"What do you have in mind?"

"Maybe a night at Sparks would help."

"Actually, I'm going with my friend Ashley tonight. She wanted a girls' night out so I suggested Sparks." Jody wasn't going to abandon Ashley.

"Okay. Maybe another time?"

Jody wasn't sure if Nicole was asking her out or only being friendly. She didn't like being unsure. "Are you asking me out?"

Nicole was quiet for a minute. "How about a sociable encounter?"

Jody smiled. "We'll probably be there about eight." She turned and left.

"Hi, Mom," Jody called from her mother's doorway. She went inside and nearly tripped over Mr. Grumbles. "Hey, big kitty." She scratched under his chin and he followed her into the living room. "I'm going to have to remember you're here when I walk through the door."

"Hi, honey. How did things go today?" Her mother lifted the book she was reading to make room for her cat in her lap.

"There was nothing new. Dad's buddies were sympathetic but didn't have any new info. I see he's settling in nicely." She pointed with her chin and grinned at her mother as she shifted to give Mr. Grumbles room and leaned to kiss his head.

"I had no idea I'd be so attached to an animal. He's made himself right at home."

"I'm glad, Mom." Jody thought of Nicole and Tiny. She'd be bringing her home soon. Would she ever see Nicole again after that? She shook off her disappointment at the thought. She'd asked her out today. Jody was certain. And she had another fundraiser coming up that Jody planned to attend in her new red dress. "I'm going out with Ashley tonight, so I better get home and change. Do you need anything before I go?"

"You go have fun, honey. I'm fine. I have a pot roast baking, and I made some rice pudding. There'll be plenty for leftovers tomorrow."

"Sounds good. See you tomorrow." Jody mentally scrolled through her wardrobe as she drove and called Ashley when she got home.

"Hi, Jody. We're still on for tonight aren't we?"

"Oh yes. I'm looking forward to it. I'll be at the restaurant by seven."

Jody chose a pair of new black jeans and a long-sleeved cream colored silk blouse. She left the top three buttons unbuttoned and regarded herself in her full-length mirror. Satisfied, she grabbed her brown leather coat and went to her car.

The restaurant was crowded when she arrived, and she saw Ashley waving to her from a table. She squeezed through the crowd and hugged Ashley when she stood to greet her.

"Damn, girl! You look hot." Ashley held her at arm's length as she spoke.

"Thanks. You look pretty good yourself." Jody hung her coat over the back of her chair and sat across from her. After dinner, Jody led the way to her car.

Loud music and women's voices drifted out as Jody opened the door to Sparks. This was going to be a fun night "Over there." Jody pointed to an empty table.

"Is it always this crowded?" Ashley asked.

"I'm not sure. Probably because it's Friday night. I only found out about this place recently." She shivered at the memory of Nicole's arms around her as they'd danced. "Wine?"

"Yes, please."

Jody returned to their table with two glasses of wine and checked her watch as she sat to watch the dancers.

CHAPTER SIXTEEN

Nicole finished her workday and stopped to check on Tiny. The shelter was unusually quiet and she called out to Hanna. "Oh, hi, Nicole." Hanna stepped out of one of the runs. "Are you here to help tonight? Bobbi couldn't make it and I haven't heard from Jody or the other volunteers."

Nicole picked up a shovel and broom and grinned. "I'd love to help." She worked with Hanna until her empty stomach grumbled. "We're done here. How does dinner sound?"

"I won't turn that offer down." Hanna put away the cleaning supplies and followed Nicole to her car. "McDonald's?"

"Sure." Nicole drove to the fast-food restaurant wishing she were on the way to Sparks with Jody seated next to her.

"You're going to be able to take Tiny home pretty soon, aren't you?"

"Another week or so according to Dr. Meyers. I'll talk to her tomorrow and see if I can bring her home earlier, but she still needs her mom and littermates." She took a bite of her fish sandwich. "I have to admit, I'm a little nervous. I bought a few books on puppy rearing, and I've been puppy-proofing my house."

"You'll do great." Hanna patted her hand. "Let me know if I can help."

"Thanks. Ready to head back?"

"Yep."

Nicole dropped Hanna off at the shelter and debated stopping at Sparks on the way home. It wasn't lost on her that Jody had mentioned what time she and her friend would be there, but interrupting their evening didn't feel right. She fantasized that there would be another time she and Jody could go together as she pulled into her garage. A sociable encounter indeed. She laughed at herself, but her growing feelings for Jody were inappropriate and worrisome. She changed into her nightshirt and settled on her bed to read. The next morning, she picked her book up from the floor and made breakfast. She was dressing after her shower when she noticed the text message on her phone.

We had a great time at Sparks. Danced and drank too much, and Ashley enjoyed herself very much. Maybe next time you could join us?

Nicole considered her reply as she drove to work. She and Jody still had incident reports to review and the results could be difficult for her. This was not the time to get too close. She settled at her desk and gave in to her curiosity. She logged onto her Facebook page and searched for Jody. She'd already googled her, but she admitted she wanted more personal information. She cringed at her invasion of privacy, but social media wasn't private. She looked at a few of her posts and the pictures of her with her parents and friends. The latest post was from the previous night. A selfie of her and Ashley seated at their table with raised glasses. She logged out and switched to Twitter and Instagram searches. She wondered if Jody had looked for her and she realized how unexciting her life had become since she'd quit seeing anyone on a regular basis. Her recent posts consisted of her fundraisers, and lately, of Tiny. Animals and a puppy. At least keeping a low profile kept her out of the tabloids and away from Doreen. She quit her searching and concentrated on work for the rest of the day. "Nothing from the medical examiner on the Acosta case yet Stacy?" she asked.

"Not yet. Do you want me to contact them?"

"Yes, please do that. Tell them I'm following up for our files. Thanks." Nicole went to check with Roger and walked through the building before heading to her car. She looked at Jody's text again before putting her phone on the holder and driving home. She picked up Thai food for dinner and relaxed on her couch to eat and compose a text to Jody. *Glad you had a great time and got home safely after you "drank too much." When do you want to go over the incident reports?*

Nicole set her phone on her end table and propped her feet up to watch TV. Her phone pinged ten minutes later.

Whenever you're available. I can come by after work. Tomorrow?

Nicole shook off the pleasure at the simple text and replied.

Tomorrow sounds good. See you then.

She grinned and went to bed looking forward to the next afternoon.

The next morning she woke to a feeling of anticipation. She picked up breakfast sandwiches for herself and Stacy on her way to work and settled at her desk to review invoices. She worked until noon and went to talk to Roger.

"Hi, Nicole," Roger greeted her and stood at his desk.

"Hi, Roger. I had an idea this morning and thought you could help me. I'd like to re-create the Acosta accident. I don't want anyone to get hurt, but I'll drive the Hi-Lo and back it into the rack. I'd like to see how well we have it secured to the floor."

"I'm not sure that's a good idea." Roger looked nervous. "What if you get hurt?"

"I don't plan to have full crates fall on me. I calculated the weight of what was on the rack that day, and I think we can secure weights to the rack so they don't fall off."

Roger looked hesitant. "If you're insistent on doing this, let me drive the Hi-Lo."

"I can't ask anyone else to do this, Roger, but I appreciate your offer. It's my idea and my risk."

Roger remained quiet for a minute. "I'll go along with this if you promise to wear a helmet."

"Okay. Would you help me set it up for tonight? Jody's coming to review incident reports with me."

"I'll have the rack set up this afternoon." Roger walked away shaking his head.

Nicole knew her plan probably wouldn't be approved by the insurance company, but she hoped it would give Jody further proof that the company wasn't at fault. She went back to her office to finish her workday. The closer it got to the time she expected Jody, the more nervous she got. Maybe her little experiment wouldn't work. Maybe she'd be hurt. She picked up the phone to call Roger to cancel and hung up as a solution occurred to her. She went back to talk to him.

"Now what?" Roger smiled as he spoke.

"I don't think I actually need to ride the Hi-Lo. We know Harold hit that rack at full speed. I can set it up to hit the rack after I hop off." Nicole relaxed the rest of the day as she waited for Jody.

"I'll see you tomorrow," Stacy called from the door.

"Good night, Stacy." Nicole walked her to the door as Jody pulled into the parking lot. She held the door open for Jody and forced herself not to grab her hand. "Good to see you."

"It's good to see you, too," Jody said.

Nicole led the way to her office thinking about how she'd tell Jody about her Hi-Lo idea. "I've got all the reports spread out on the table." She retrieved two bottles of water and set one in front of Jody. "I didn't find anything, but these are the incident reports before and after." She didn't see the need to remind Jody of the before and after.

"Thanks for doing this." Jody reviewed one of the reports. "So, why am I reading these?"

"I wanted you to know that our safety record is exemplary. There aren't any incidents of negligence by the company." She sat next to Jody but didn't touch her. "We—I—take safety seriously."

"I believe you, Nicole, but I knew my dad. He was so careful." Jody took a deep breath and looked to be holding back tears.

Nicole gave up resisting and rested her hand over Jody's. "I know. I have a little experiment with the Hi-Lo if you're up for it."

"Experiment?"

"Come on. I'll show you." Nicole held Jody's hand and led her to the area she'd set up. "I thought I'd run this Hi-Lo into the rack we set up with weights. It simulates the full crates that were there that day."

Jody looked at the rack and reached to touch it. She turned to face Nicole with tears streaming down her cheeks. "I can't. It's—"

Nicole reacted the only way she could. She gathered Jody in her arms and held her as she cried. "I'm sorry. This was insensitive of me. Of course you don't want to see this." She held back her own tears as she and Jody went back to her office. Why did she think this would be a good idea? "If you'll forgive my thoughtlessness, I'm starving. Can I buy you dinner?"

Jody sniffled and offered a small smile. "Yeah. I'm pretty hungry, too."

Nicole locked the doors behind her as they left. "Do you want to ride with me or take your own car?"

"If you don't mind bringing me back after we eat, I'll ride with you."

Nicole relaxed when Jody smiled. She needed to convince Jody that the company wasn't at fault for Harold's death, but she wanted to do it without hurting her. She concentrated on where they were going for dinner. She pulled into the restaurant parking lot and turned to Jody. "Okay?"

"Yeah. Thanks." Jody stepped out of the car.

Nicole breathed a sigh of relief. It seemed her inconsiderate actions were forgiven and she might get a chance to redeem herself. She followed Jody into the restaurant and slid into a booth across from her.

"I saw Tiny yesterday. She's growing like a weed," Jody said.

"I know. Dr. Meyers said I could take her home pretty soon. I'll find out more this week." Nicole relaxed a little more but vowed to remain more sensitive to Jody's loss even if she couldn't change it.

CHAPTER SEVENTEEN

Jody plopped onto her bed when she got home. Nicole was trying to help, she knew that, but there was no way she could stand watching her re-create the event of her father's death. She rolled to her side and wiped away a tear. Her growing feelings for Nicole troubled her. They'd spent a lot of time together and looked at so much evidence regarding her dad's death that her head was spinning. Nicole remained open to further research, but she'd begun to wonder if it would make any difference. She appreciated Nicole's efforts to appease her torment over her father's death, but maybe it was time to accept the inevitable. She went to the kitchen for a bottle of water and settled on her couch to compose a text.

Thank you for your efforts to find answers for me. I'm sorry I fell apart today.

She sent the text and turned on the evening news. The next morning, Jody stopped by her mother's on her way to work.

"Morning, honey. What brings you here so early?" Her mother poured her a cup of coffee.

"Thank you. I wanted to check on you."

"Are things going okay with Nicole? Did you find anything important?"

"No, Mom. So far, there's no evidence of blame on either side. It looks as if it had to have been a horrible accident."

"I'm sorry, honey. I was hoping you'd find something."

"I'm going to talk to Nicole today. She might have an idea of the next step." Jody hugged her mom and went to work. By lunchtime, she gave in and called Nicole.

"Hi, Jody. I got your text yesterday. Sorry I got busy and didn't reply, but you have nothing to apologize for. I should have realized how upsetting it would be for you."

"Well, is there anything else we can do?"

"I'm waiting for a copy of the final examiner's report. I don't suppose it will be any different than what we have, but I'll be glad to have it."

"Yes. Thank you. I'd like to see it."

"Of course. Your mom will get a copy. Are you planning to come here after work?"

"Are there more things to look at?"

"I'll think about it today. Would you come over for dinner tonight?"

"To the warehouse?"

"No. To my house. Do you like Chinese food?"

"I do."

"Please come to dinner tonight. I'll text you my address."

Jody hesitated. She wanted to say yes, but if this was a date, it would change the dynamics of their relationship. It was only dinner. They had to eat. "Okay." The first thought she had after the call was what would she wear?

Jody checked the Google map on her phone and found Nicole's house easily. She pulled into the driveway of a modest Cape Cod. She'd expected an elaborate mansion but as she sat in her car reflecting on what she knew about Nicole, it fit. She was honest, down-to-earth, and straightforward. She didn't put on pretense, and Jody bet the interior was comfortable without being pretentious. She stepped out of her car and Nicole opened the front door.

"I'm glad you came." Nicole held the door open for her to pass into the living room.

"Nice." Jody took in the tall ceiling and comfortable looking furniture. The cushy love seat drew her to sit, but she wanted to curl up on it with Nicole. She followed Nicole to the dining room table and sat across from her. "This is a lot of food." She pointed to the array of Chinese food boxes and bags.

"I probably should've asked you what you liked, but I didn't, so I got a little of everything." Nicole set plates and silverware on the table. "Help yourself."

Jody had never seen Nicole look uncertain before. "It's perfect." She squeezed her hand gently. Nicole's grin and the warmth of her hand stirred the butterflies in her belly. This whole evening was new ground for them. She'd been alone with Nicole at the warehouse and in her office, but they were totally alone now in Nicole's home. The intimacy of the situation wasn't lost on her, and she decided she liked it. She filled a plate with the various options and took a bite. "Mmm. This is great."

"It's from my favorite restaurant. I'm glad you like it." Nicole filled her plate. "I'm glad you came over tonight."

"I'm glad you invited me." Jody smiled at their formal attitude. Maybe Nicole was as nervous as she was. She decided to face the question floating in the room head-on. "I'm considering this a date and I hope you are, too." She shoved a forkful of food in her mouth.

Nicole swallowed before she spoke. "You are? Then I guess I will as well. I like you, Jody, and I wanted to have an evening away from work and the issues we're dealing with."

"I appreciate it. This is nice." Jody finished what she'd piled on her plate and sat back in her chair. "I'm stuffed."

"Me, too." Nicole retrieved two sparkling waters from her refrigerator. "Sorry, I just thought of these. Can you tell I don't entertain often?"

Jody grinned. "No problem. I'd rather sip on this while we relax on the couch after dinner." She helped Nicole put the leftovers away and retrieve two wine glasses.

Nicole filled the glasses with their water and carried them to the living room. "I have a great movie, if you're interested." She picked up a DVD to show her.

"*Imagine Me and You*," she read the title. "Oh, I like it!" Jody squirmed in her seat at one end of the couch. "Another water?" She went to Nicole's refrigerator and returned with two bottles.

"Thanks." Nicole started the movie and settled next to her on the couch.

Jody stood and clapped and sang at the ending, surprised when Nicole joined her. She leaned into her and swayed to the music as they sang, then plopped back on the couch laughing. "That is a great movie."

"Yes, it is. I've seen it a hundred times and enjoy it more every time. It was fun to share it with you." Nicole grinned and finished her water. "Another water? I have wine, too."

Jody checked her watch. "I have to go to work tomorrow. I should head home. Thank you for a lovely evening." She stood and took her empty bottle and glass to the kitchen. "It was nice to spend time with you away from…everything."

"It was nice. I'd like to do it again whenever you're available." Nicole held her hand and walked her to the door.

"Thanks again for tonight. Maybe I can cook for you next time."

"I look forward to it." Nicole took a step back. "Be careful driving home."

Jody waved as she walked to her car. She locked the doors when she got in to keep herself from rushing back to grab Nicole into a kiss. She settled down as she drove and told herself she could wait until their second date. She tossed her key fob onto the kitchen counter when she got home and sat on her couch to review the most pleasant evening she'd had in a long time. She began to debate calling Nicole to let her know she got home safely when her phone rang.

"Hi, Ash."

"Hey, Jody. I wanted to touch base and see how you and your mom were doing."

"We're good. I'm not sure how much more Nicole and I can do about my dad's case. I've been there a few times and Nicole's been forthcoming with everything. So far, it looks as if it was a terrible accident."

"So, how's it been working with the beautiful Nicole?"

Jody grinned. "It's fine. She's been open and honest with me about everything. She's sensitive, patient, and gentle."

"Huh. Sensitive? Gentle? Sounds like you're doing more than just looking at Hi-Los."

"No, Ash. I went to dinner at her place tonight. It was her attempt to distract me from the stress."

"Okay. So you went to her house for dinner and she distracted you from stress by being patient, sensitive, and gentle?"

Jody objected to Ashley's insinuation. "Nothing is going on between us. We had a friendly dinner and watched a movie. That's all."

"A movie, too? We need another girls' night out so I can hear all about this gorgeous, sensitive, gentle, and patient wealthy woman."

"Sure, Ashley. How about next Friday?"

"Good. I'm looking forward to getting all the details."

Jody put her phone away secretly hoping she'd have details to tell. She changed into her pajamas and lay on her bed before retrieving her phone and calling Nicole.

"Hey, Jody. Everything okay?"

"Yeah, everything's good. I wanted to let you know I got home safely and to tell you how much I enjoyed our evening."

"I enjoyed it very much, too. Glad you liked the movie."

"I guess I'll be talking to you."

"I'll be at the shelter tomorrow night visiting Tiny."

"I'll see you then. Good night, Nicole."

"Good night, Jody."

She put her phone away and drifted into sleep smiling.

CHAPTER EIGHTEEN

Nicole rolled over in bed replaying the pleasant evening with Jody. A twinge of concern worked its way into her belly. Would last night complicate their easy connection? No. They only had dinner and watched a movie. She needed to keep her temptation to Jody to herself. At least until the case was resolved. She rose and got ready for work. She'd miss Jody's presence, but there might not be anything more to show her so she turned her thoughts to payroll and renovations. The new lockers would be installed that week, and she wanted to check every one of the existing ones for contraband. She greeted Stacy when she arrived and went directly to Roger's office.

"Morning, Nicole. You're here early." Roger looked at her expectantly.

"I need to check all the lockers this morning. The new ones will be in this week. Would you please assign one to each employee and copy me on the results?"

"No problem. I'll let you know when they arrive."

Nicole inspected each locker and walked to the rack that Harold had hit and tried to shake it a few times. "Solid." She went to her office and opened Harold's file on her computer. She reviewed all the details for what felt like the hundredth time. She'd do it a thousand if it would help Jody, but she saw nothing new. She pulled out all the hard copies and compared them to the electronic files. She wanted all her bases covered before she presented the liability waiver forms to release the company of all claims against it in Harold's case. She saved all her files, both electronic and paper. As soon as she received the final medical examiner's report, it would be done. She only wished it wasn't Jody who could be hurt by it. She went to talk to Stacy. "Nothing from the medical examiner yet, Stacy?"

"Not yet. I'll give them another call this afternoon. Do you want me to go pick it up if it's ready?"

"That might be faster than waiting for the mail. If you don't mind, I'd appreciate it. I'm going to lunch. I'll be back in an hour. You have my cell."

Stacy waved and went back to her computer.

Nicole stepped outside into a beautiful summer day. Her intention to eat inside changed to an outdoor picnic. She took out her phone and called Jody.

"Hi, Nicole. Everything okay?"

"Yes. I left for lunch and discovered a beautiful day. Would you like to meet me for an outside picnic lunch?"

"Where are you?"

"In your parking lot. I see a picnic table amongst the trees."

"I'll be right there."

Nicole took a blanket out of her trunk and spread it over the dirty picnic table and wiped off the seats before she sat and waited for Jody.

"It is lovely out here." Jody sat across from her.

Nicole opened the insulated bag she'd brought and pulled out bottled water and sandwiches. "I only have tuna, peanut butter and jelly, and egg salad."

"Only? You're a regular Girl Scout. Always prepared." Jody smiled. "I'll take a tuna sandwich, and thank you."

"You're welcome. I'm glad you were here. I was afraid you'd gone to lunch already."

"No. I'd planned to eat at my desk today, so I'm glad you called. I had no idea it was such a pleasant day. It was raining when I came to work this morning."

Nicole wanted to tell Jody about the new lockers and her new request for the examiner's report, but it was so peaceful and sunny, she didn't have the heart to bring it up. "Do you eat out here often?"

"I do, actually. It's a good place for quiet time."

"Would I be intruding on your quiet time if I met you here, say, on Fridays?"

"I'd like that."

"Okay. If it rains on Friday, I'll come on Monday. How does that sound?"

Jody grinned. "And if it rains on Monday?"

"I'll come inside and find you!" Nicole laughed. Nicole told Jody about Tiny and how she'd doubled in size, and the lunch hour flew by.

"I suppose I should get back inside. Thanks for stopping by. It was nice," Jody said.

Nicole packed her insulated bag and tried unsuccessfully to ignore the feel of Jody's fingers when she'd rested them on her hand before she left. She drove back to work smiling.

"Hi, Nicole. I'm glad you're back." Stacy spoke as she walked to her desk. "The examiner's office told me we already have the final report for the Acosta case. I showed them the *preliminary* copy we had and was told they'd look for the final copy. I was also reminded that it'd been a year. I disregarded the griping and thanked them before I left. Sorry."

"Thanks for trying. Hopefully, they'll 'find' it soon. I'll follow up with it if we don't get the copy by next week." Nicole settled in her office and concentrated on the work for the day. Her thoughts drifted to Jody enough to keep a smile on her face. She went to check in with Roger and the new lockers being installed.

"Hi, Nicole. Things are going smoothly out here," Roger said.

"Great." Nicole watched the workers for a few minutes before going to talk to Roger. "Please call a group meeting for this afternoon. I want to review the rules."

"Will do. Three o'clock okay?"

"Perfect, thanks, Roger." Nicole went back to her office to compose the notice she planned to post regarding the new lockers. She managed to ignore thoughts of Jody most of the rest of the day. They hadn't found any clues as to what caused Harold to crash into the rack and she couldn't come up with anything else to look at. There was no longer a reason for Jody to spend time here and that thought saddened her. She checked the time and gathered her information to take to the meeting. She checked on the progress of the new locker installation, pleased with the results. She reviewed the company policies with the group before leaving for the day.

"Hi, Nicole. I think Tiny's waiting for you." Hanna grinned.

"Thanks." Nicole peeked into the shelter before entering. Tiny sat at the door. She stood with her little tail wagging when Nicole approached her. "Hey there, little one. It looks like your eyes are open and maybe you can hear me." Nicole entered Tiny's area and sat on the floor with her in her lap. "Hi, Nicole," Dr. Meyers spoke from the doorway.

"Hi, Dr. Meyers. How's my little girl doing?"

"First of all, please call me Jaylin, and Tiny is doing quite well. I think you can probably take her home in a few days. I'll have an instruction sheet and a list of the vaccinations she's received ready for you to take home with her."

"Thanks, Jaylin. I'm looking forward to having her home, but I'm nervous. I've never had a dog before." Tiny squirmed in her lap once and fell asleep. "I guess she's comfortable with me." She lifted her to kiss her little head.

"You call me if you need anything, and bring her to my office when she's six months old for more shots and a checkup." Jaylin went to check on the rest of the litter.

"Soon you'll have a permanent home, Tiny." She gently set Tiny next to her littermates and went to help clean the dog runs. She drove home mentally reviewing preparations for Tiny. Her fenced in yard would be perfect for her and she pictured a doghouse and a training area. She forced away her feeling of inadequacy and gathered all the books she'd collected on puppies. She had a lot of studying to do.

She heated a bowl of chicken soup for dinner and reviewed her plans for the upcoming fundraiser. The timing would be perfect to try to get the remaining puppies adopted. They were days away from being old enough to live apart from their littermates. She put her spoon and bowl in the dishwasher and went to her computer to design the notice. She printed the picture of the pile of newborn pups and arranged several other various photos on a board she planned to display on the donation table. She made copies to post at various shelters and checked the time. Not too late to stop in at Sparks for a drink.

She scanned the room when she arrived for any signs of Doreen before heading for the bar and ordering a drink. She watched the dancers for a few minutes and began to relax when Emma walked through the door. She caught her eye, smiled, and walked toward her. Nicole scrambled for an excuse to avoid going home with her. It wasn't fair to avoid her without an explanation.

"I was hoping we'd see each other again." Emma leaned on the bar with their arms touching.

"Hi, Emma. I've been busy dealing with work issues lately. I pretty much go home and crash." Nicole told herself it wasn't a total lie.

"How about a dance?"

Nicole had no reason to refuse just because she'd rather be dancing with Jody. Jody wasn't here and they'd made no promises to each other. She accepted Emma's outstretched hand and let her lead her to the dance floor. Emma held her close and she relaxed as she followed Emma's steps. Her mind wandered to the one time she'd held Jody when they danced. It wasn't fair to Emma, and she pointed to an empty table. She went to the bar for drinks and returned to sit and watch the dancers.

"I'm glad you're here tonight. I've looked for you often after our lovely night together. I'd like a repeat." Emma ran her hand over her shoulder and down her arm to clasp their hands.

Memories of her patience and gentle touch tugged at her, but the one time feel of Jody in her arms overrode them. "I'm sorry, Emma. I'm afraid I wouldn't be good company tonight." She kissed her softly and left.

CHAPTER NINETEEN

Jody finished cleaning the last dog run and continued to the area with the poodle puppies. Tiny was definitely the largest of the group. She smiled at the thought of Nicole talking to the puppy. She looked forward to seeing her the next day for their lunch meeting, but had hoped she might be at the shelter. She finished her tasks and thought about stopping at Sparks but changed her mind and headed to her mother's.

"Hi, honey. You're just in time for dinner."

"Hi, Mom. I'm afraid I come empty-handed."

"You know I love it when you come by. You don't need to bring anything." She set the table and Jody filled water glasses before they sat to eat. "So, how are things going with you and Nicole?"

Jody grinned knowing her mother didn't mean what she was thinking. "We've pretty much exhausted the options regarding Dad's accident. There's no evidence of wrongdoing by the company. I'm afraid it may turn out to have been an awful accident."

"Well, honey. It is what it is, I suppose. Are you all right?"

"I'd like something definitive, but I'll have to accept the outcome."

Her mother sighed and took a bite of her food. "No date tonight, huh?"

"No, Mom." She squelched thoughts of Nicole.

"I'm not the reason you're not dating anyone am I?" Her mother looked sad.

She stood and pulled her mom into a hug. "No. Absolutely not. I'm picky I guess. I can't see going out with someone for the sake of going out. I want more than a convenient get-together."

"You'll let me know if I'm in your way, won't you, honey?"

"You'll never be in my way, Mom. You come first in my life even if I find someone special."

"So, is Nicole single?"

"Yes, she is."

"Good." Her mom took another bite of dinner and smiled.

Jody wondered what might've shown when she spoke of Nicole. Her mother was probably only holding out hope she'd find love one day. "Speaking of Nicole. She's adopting a puppy from the animal shelter."

"That's a good thing. I've grown so used to having Mr. Grumbles that I can't think of a reason I'd give him up. Maybe you could adopt one of the pups."

"I'm not ready for one yet. I'd like to have a house first. I think it'd be great to have a little fenced yard before I commit to a dog."

"Okay, honey. I'll leave you be. Why don't you bring Nicole over for dinner one night?"

"Are you sure, Mom?"

"You haven't found anything wrong with her have you?"

"No. Nothing wrong with her. She's gentle and kind, but she's also in charge of the company you're suing."

"I get the impression that it's difficult for her." Her mother looked contemplative.

"I'm having lunch with her tomorrow. I'll ask her if she'd be interested."

"Okay. Let me know and I'll make something special. In fact, ask her what her favorite food is."

"I will, Mom." Jody finished her meal and helped her mother clean up before leaving. She considered her mother's request and realized there was a lot about Nicole she didn't know. What was her favorite food? Maybe Chinese. They needed another date. She took her phone out of her pocket and called her.

"Sorry I missed your call. Please leave a message after the beep."

Jody left her a message to call her back and put her phone away. She scooped herself some ice cream and sat on her couch to watch television. Her phone rang within half an hour. "Hi, Nicole."

"Hi there. You called?"

"I did. I had dinner with my mom today, and she wanted me to invite you to dinner one day."

"That's nice of her and I'd love to. Let me know when, and I'll be there."

"What's your favorite food?"

Nicole laughed. "It's easier to tell you what I don't like. Liver. I never could stand it."

"Okay." Jody laughed, too. "I'll let Mom know."

"So, what's your favorite food?"

"I pretty much like anything. Including liver. But I'm not fond of lamb."

"I'll remember that. Not that I've ever cooked lamb, or plan to."

"I'm looking forward to lunch tomorrow."

"Me, too. I miss our meetings at work, even though it was a little stressful. Are you doing okay?"

"I am."

"And your mom?"

"She invited you to dinner, didn't she?" Jody chuckled.

"I suppose you're right. I hope the hard feelings don't come between us. I mean you and me."

"I'll see you at noon tomorrow. Good night, Nicole." Jody put her phone on her charger and decided she needed a cup of chamomile tea. She analyzed her feeling as she thought about Nicole. She liked her a lot. And it sounded like the feelings were mutual, but what it meant going forward confused her. She'd talk to her at lunch. She finished her tea and went to bed.

The next morning, Jody stopped at her mother's on the way to work. She was met at the door by Mr. Grumbles. "Hey, big boy. Where's Mom?"

"I'm right here." Her mom came into the kitchen in her nightgown and robe.

"I stopped by to let you know I talked to Nicole. She'd love to come to dinner. The only thing she doesn't like is liver."

"Thank you for rushing over to let me know." Her mother laughed. "A cup of coffee before you go?"

"Thanks, Mom." She sat at the table. Pete would understand if she was late.

"So, you talked to Nicole last night? Or did you see her?"

"We talked on the phone." Jody sipped her coffee. She knew her mom wanted the best for her and liked Nicole. "I had dinner and watched a movie with her at her house last weekend."

"I'm glad. I worried, you know. It couldn't have been easy to spend time with her at the warehouse."

"Actually, it wasn't too bad. Disappointing for me, but Nicole was gentle and caring." She checked the time. "I better get to work."

"Say hello to Pete." She kissed her cheek.

Jody settled at her desk when she got to work and labored to keep her mind on her job. She kept checking the clock as it got closer to noon. Finally, she stood and let Pete know she was leaving for lunch.

Nicole was already seated at the picnic table, and she smiled and stood when Jody approached. "It's good to see you." She took her hand and pulled her into a hug.

"Nice greeting." Jody lingered in her arms and reluctantly stepped away.

"I brought pizza!"

Jody smiled. "Sounds great. Thank you." She grabbed a piece and took a bite.

"I saw Dr. Meyers yesterday. She said I'd be able to bring Tiny home in a couple of days."

"Cool. I look forward to visiting her. Are you ready?"

"As ready as I can be. I have books and she's going to give me some instructions. I bought a couple of baby gates to control her before she's potty trained."

"I hope the rest of the litter finds homes as good as Tiny's."

"Me, too. I made some pretty nice flyers for my next fundraiser. I hope it sparks interest in them." Nicole took a bite of pizza and shrugged.

"When is the fundraiser?"

"Next weekend. Saturday."

"I'll plan on it." Jody took a drink of water.

"I was hoping you'd be there. It's at the same place as the last one." Nicole reached for her hand and squeezed gently. "I have something else I'd like to ask you."

"Okay." Jody smiled.

"My mother is having this thing. It's a fancy gala, party, event…I don't know. She does this every year to keep up with the socialites. I have to attend, and I'd love it if you'd go as my date."

Jody froze. The "date" part didn't scare her, but the "fancy gala" did. "I—"

"You don't have to give me an answer right this minute. Honestly, I'm still trying to figure out a way to get out of it. Caleb told me she wanted me to organize it. I don't even want to go." Nicole ran her fingers through her hair. "I even had to help my cousin find a dress this year." She took a deep breath and released it. "Anyway. Think about it, please?"

"When is this thing?"

"In June."

"Huh. It gives me time to shop." Jody frowned, torn between delight that Nicole had asked her to be her date, and anxiety over what she would wear.

"Is that a yes?" Nicole beamed.

"You helped your cousin find a dress, will you help me?"

"Absolutely."

Jody relaxed as they talked and finished the pizza. She checked the time and reluctantly stood to go back to work. "I'm glad you came today and thanks for the pizza."

"You're welcome." Nicole stood and stepped close before wrapping her in a hug. "I miss you." Her breath was warm on her ear. Nicole stepped back but held eye contact until she slowly turned to collect the empty boxes.

Jody sat at her desk for a moment to collect herself. She was certain Nicole was going to kiss her, and she'd wanted her to. But they still had the pending lawsuit between them to resolve. She finished her workday and drove directly to the animal shelter.

"Hi, Jody. Glad you could make it today. We got a Great Dane and two other big dogs in today. Need I describe the large size poop to clean up?" Hanna laughed.

"Great Dane? That's unusual. I guess we have our work cut out for us tonight." She smiled as she grabbed the large sized pooper scooper.

CHAPTER TWENTY

H ey, little one. Are you getting ready to come home with me?" Nicole watched Tiny wrestle with her littermates. She could see why they needed each other for a few weeks before being separated. She watched the bunch for a few minutes before starting to clean. She shoveled and swept for half an hour and moved to the second building. She opened the sliding door and slipped through it, closing it behind her. She turned and stood face-to-face with Jody.

"Twice in one day. This is a nice surprise." Jody grinned.

"It is. I came to see Tiny and stayed to help clean. Hi, Hanna." She waved. "Is there anything left to do here?"

"There's a Great Dane pooping in the second run. We cleaned it but you can check."

Nicole laughed at Hanna's description. "I'll go check." She smiled at Jody and hoped she'd follow her to the run. "Wow. You're a big boy," she said to the dog. "Where'd you come from?" So many strays were animals people got as puppies unknowing they'd grow into giants. She went back to where Hanna and Jody stood. "He seems like a nice dog."

"He does," Jody said. "I have to wonder where he came from. He's neutered so someone cared about him."

"Is the shelter putting up *dog found* signs?"

"Yeah."

"If he's still here by Saturday, I'll take his picture and post it at the fundraiser. I think we're done here. Want to come by for a drink or water or something?"

"My place is closer. I probably don't have the options you do, but I have water, tea, coffee, and I think I have a bottle of wine." Jody shrugged.

"I'll follow you."

Jody led the way to their cars, and Nicole smiled as she followed her.

Nicole remembered the apartment where they'd shared pizza for the first time. She parked and followed Jody inside.

Jody opened her refrigerator. "Sparkling water, orange juice, plain water." She opened a cupboard. "Coffee, tea, hot chocolate." She opened another cupboard. "Red wine."

Nicole stepped to within a foot of Jody. "Will you have a glass of wine with me?" She was rewarded with a smile, and Jody opened the bottle.

"It's nothing expensive, but I like this brand." Jody filled two glasses and handed one to her.

"Thank you." Nicole took a sip. "This is good." She sat on the couch and Jody settled next to her.

"Sorry I don't have any movies, but we can turn on the news if you'd like."

"It feels nice to just relax with you." Nicole took a drink from her glass and leaned her head back.

Jody mimicked her pose. "I appreciate that you're willing to shop for a dress with me, but my friend Ashley would probably do it and she's good at shopping. She's getting married next month, and I'm her maid of honor."

"A May wedding. Nice. It's up to you. I wouldn't mind helping if it's you." Nicole switched her wine to her other hand and rested her arm around Jody's shoulders. She sighed when Jody leaned into her. "This is nice, too."

"It is. I have popcorn. You interested?"

"Sure." She nearly shivered at the cold breeze that replaced the warmth of Jody pressed against her. She stood to shake off the disturbing feeling. "Can I help?"

Jody chuckled as she opened yet another cupboard and retrieved a large canister. "Buttered, caramel, and Parmesan cheese." She set the tin and two bowls on her coffee table along with a pile of napkins. "Help yourself."

"I thought you'd be popping the popcorn." Nicole filled one of the bowls from the caramel covered section.

"Last year, I joined one of those big box stores and found this." She held up the container. It's much easier and takes less time. My favorite is the Parmesan cheese, but I also like to mix them." She filled her bowl with a little of each flavor.

Nicole smiled at Jody's enthusiasm. "I like it." She sat back on the couch thrilled when Jody settled next to her again. "I might have to join that store." She wrapped her arm around Jody again content to stay there all night. "I'm pretty cozy here. You're going to have to kick me out. What time do you get up for work?"

Jody turned to face her. "It doesn't matter," she whispered.

Jody was kissing close and Nicole wanted to kiss her more than anything. She took a breath and held herself back, but stroked her cheek. "Do you plan to be at the shelter tomorrow?"

"I do but I'll stop by Mom's first."

"Is she doing okay? I know she was hoping our research would come up with answers, too."

"She is okay. In fact, she's more okay with this than I am, but we're grateful for your help."

"Well, I have to say I'm grateful that it brought you into my life, but if I could go back and change things and bring your father back, I'd do it in a heartbeat." She raised Jody's hand to her lips and kissed it.

"Thank you." Jody took a sip of wine and set her glass on the end table.

Nicole drained her glass and turned to Jody. "I'll see you tomorrow at the shelter. Sleep well." She stood and took her empty wine glass to the kitchen before going to the door.

"You sleep well, too." Jody stood and followed her. Before she opened the door, Jody grabbed the front of her sweatshirt, pulled her close, and claimed her lips with hers. Nicole's back was against the wall and Jody held her upright when her knees went weak. She'd kissed and been kissed by many women, but Jody's handling of her had her insides molten. She gave in to her bubbling desire and retuned the kiss. Jody moaned and Nicole held her close until their breathing became normal. "I doubt I'll be able to sleep at all after that kiss." Nicole cupped her chin, brushed her lips with hers, and left.

She sat in her car for a few minutes to let her libido settle down. She'd wanted to kiss Jody since the first time she'd seen her across the room at the fundraiser, but she knew firsthand what could happen from moving too fast. And the final ME's report regarding Jody's father was still in question. She had no business kissing Jody, but her body still tingled from the feel of her pressed against her. God, she could kiss. She blew out a breath and started her car.

The next morning, Nicole decided to stop at the ME's office on her way to work. She carried her briefcase inside in case she needed to show the preliminary copy of the Acosta report.

"Can I help you?" the desk clerk asked.

"I'm Nicole Bergeron from Cole's Warehouse. I need the final copy of the ME's report on Harold Acosta."

The clerk went through a door behind the desk. She returned within ten minutes. "Do you have the date of the incident?"

Nicole handed her the preliminary report and waited while the clerk reviewed it.

"This was a year ago!"

"I know. That's why I'm here instead of waiting for the mail." Nicole worked hard to keep the anger from her voice.

The clerk read the copy and nodded slowly. "I vaguely remember this…" She held up a finger in a wait a minute signal and went back through the door. She returned in five minutes. "I'm sorry, Ms. Bergeron. The final copy of this has been filed away with hundreds of others. We'll begin going through them today. I'm dreadfully sorry for the delay."

"Can you at least tell me if there's a toxicology report?"

"Oh, yes. Tox screens are standard for us in accident cases."

"I suppose that's been 'filed away' also."

"Yes. I'm sorry. I'll get it to you as soon as we find it."

"Thank you." Nicole left and made a note regarding the new information before driving to work.

"Morning, Stacy." Nicole went directly to her office and put away her new information in the Acosta file. By lunchtime, her nerves were jangled and she had a hard time concentrating. Jody and their kiss kept invading her thoughts. She'd never been so consumed with memories of a kiss. She waved to Stacy as she left the building. She had no excuse for interrupting Jody at work, but she needed to know if she was as affected by the kiss as she was. It wasn't Friday, but it was a beautiful sunny day, so she hoped Jody would be at their picnic table. She sat on the same side she sat on before and waited.

"This is a nice surprise." Jody sat on the seat across from her.

"I needed to see you." Now that Jody sat across from her, she was at a loss for words.

"I'm glad. I've been thinking of you all day. All night, too." Jody blushed.

"Yeah. Me, too. That was quite a kiss."

"Are you okay with it? You're not upset are you?" Jody looked spooked.

"Oh, no. I'm not upset. In fact, I wouldn't mind a repeat." She watched Jody's hazel eyes darken.

"That definitely can be arranged." She grinned. "But probably not right now." She looked at her watch. I've got a ton of work to finish before the end of the month. Will you be visiting Tiny tonight?"

"I plan to." Nicole stood and held out her hand. "Can I walk you back to the building?"

Jody stood and took her hand. "I'm going to stop and say hello to Mom before I go to the shelter. So, I'll see you there."

"Oh. That reminds me. I stopped at the medical examiners office. They're searching for your dad's final report. I guess they moved to a new building last year and completely revamped their computer system. Many of the existing clerical staff retired or moved on and the newbies mislabeled files. I'm told nothing was lost and they're reorganizing everything. The last thing the clerk told me was that it was filed away with hundreds of others."

"Ah. Thank you for following up with that." She squeezed her hand before going into the building.

Nicole took her time going back to work. She felt calmer after seeing Jody. Her feelings with Jody were new for her. She thought of Emma and their one night. It didn't even come close to what she imagined with Jody. All she knew was that their kiss was just a kiss, and she really wanted another one.

CHAPTER TWENTY-ONE

Jody didn't even try to suppress her smile for the rest of the afternoon. She hadn't stopped thinking of Nicole all morning and seeing her waiting for her at their picnic table thrilled her. Knowing she'd see her at the animal shelter that night had her watching the clock. She headed to her mother's at the end of her workday.

"Hi, honey." Her mother hugged her and pulled her into the living room. She pointed to the recliner where her dad used to sit. Mr. Grumbles lifted his head to blink at her and meowed. "I think Mr. Grumbles might sense that's your dad's chair. He's trying to comfort me. To let me know I'm not alone." Her mother wiped a tear from her cheek.

Jody went to her mom and put an arm around her. "I believe animals have a sense of how we feel. I've been comforted many times while at the animal shelter after Dad's death. It might be me, but I'm not sure. I think they have a sixth sense about things."

"Can you stay for dinner?"

"Of course, Mom. Can I do anything?"

"I made a cauliflower casserole. Hazel gave me the recipe. Sit."

Jody worked to sound excited. "Great." She wanted to get to the shelter as soon as possible. Nicole might be there.

Her mother scooped a mound of the casserole onto her plate and one on her own.

Jody took a bite, surprised that it was good. "This is good." She shoved another forkful into her mouth.

"I'm glad you like it. It's easy to make. I'll give you the recipe."

Jody's first thought was that she could make it for Nicole if she came over for dinner. "Thanks, Mom, and thank Hazel for me." She finished eating and visited with her mother for a while before hugging her and leaving. Her thoughts turned to Nicole as she drove. Would they have another opportunity for a kiss? Would Nicole want to? She pushed away her uncertainty and thought about the Great Dane needing his run cleaned.

"Hi, Bobbi," Jody called when she arrived. "Everything quiet?"

"As quiet as a building full of barking dogs can be. I'm glad to see you tonight. It sounds like we may be the only ones here. Hanna has a dentist appointment and everyone else is usually here by now."

Jody squashed her disappointment. Scenarios floated through her mind. Nicole didn't want to see her. She regretted their kiss. She'd found someone else to kiss. She shook her head to try to dispel her anxiety and picked up a shovel and broom. She and Bobbi finished cleaning and began the task of feeding everyone. They washed bowls and filled water buckets before sitting on the floor with the poodle puppies. Tiny reminded her of Nicole's absence. The puppy was the largest of the litter as Dr. Meyers had predicted, and she led the group in chases and jumping exercises. She checked the time and decided she might as well go home. "I'm heading home now. Thanks for being here tonight, Bobbi."

"I love it here. I'll probably see you tomorrow."

"I plan to be here." Jody checked her watch again and slowly pulled out of the parking lot and headed home. She plopped onto her couch and turned on the TV. She found a stray popcorn piece in between the couch cushions and threw it across the room. Had she pushed Nicole away? She'd come to see her at noon, so maybe she was just busy tonight. Maybe she was busy with someone at Sparks. Nicole was beautiful and rich. Why she thought Nicole would want her made no sense. And they still had the wrongful death lawsuit hanging in the air. Just when she had herself convinced she'd never see Nicole again her buzzer sounded. She pushed the intercom button to ask who was there. She'd never used the thing before so she hoped she pushed the right button.

"It's me. Nicole."

Jody hesitated for a second and pushed the buzzer to unlock the outside door. She checked her hair in the bathroom mirror and straightened her clothes before she opened the door. "Hi, Nicole."

Nicole stepped into the room and closed the door behind her before standing close and placing her hands on her hips. "May I please kiss you?"

Jody cradled Nicole's face in her hands and whimpered when their lips met. Nicole pulled her against her body and Jody's nipples ached at the feel of her breasts against Nicole's.

Jody broke their connection first. "I missed you at the shelter today." She ran her hands up and down Nicole's arms to assure herself she was actually standing in her apartment kissing her.

"We had an outgoing shipment today and the semi driver backed into one of our doors. It was a mess, but I'm glad no one was hurt. I stayed until it was cleaned up and arranged for a new door to be installed tomorrow." Nicole took her hand and led her to the couch.

"I have some of that wine left." Jody stood and poured them each a glass.

"Thank you." Nicole took a sip. "Did you see Tiny today?"

"I did. She's grown so much she's the largest in the group." Jody sipped her wine and leaned against Nicole. "The Great Dane that came in the other day has become one of the favorites. He's so friendly I can't believe someone isn't looking for him."

"I'm too tired to stop by tonight. I'll plan on checking him out tomorrow." Nicole shifted and put her arm around her.

Jody nestled closer. "I'll be there after I visit Mom."

"Is she doing all right? I haven't even checked on her after my visit."

"She's good. We both miss Dad, but life goes on and we'll always have memories of him." Jody sighed, grateful Nicole had asked about her mother. "Did you have dinner?"

"No. I came over right from work. Why?"

"I have popcorn left." Jody reminded herself to keep more real food in her fridge from now on.

"Is it too late for me to take you to dinner?"

"Actually. Do you like spaghetti?" Jody remembered she had a batch of sauce in the freezer.

"Sure."

"I made a bunch of sauce the other day and took some to Mom's." She put the frozen sauce in a pot and turned the stove on low before checking for noodles.

Nicole stood behind her and wrapped her arms around her waist. She rested her chin on her shoulder and whispered in her ear. "Thank you."

Jody leaned back against her and her knees nearly gave out when Nicole kissed her neck. She managed to stay standing and wondered what Nicole would do for a four-course meal. She dished out the spaghetti onto plates and set her tiny two-seater table. She wasn't hungry but she didn't want Nicole to feel odd by eating in front of her.

"This is great. Do you cook often?" Nicole spoke in between bites.

"Not too often, but I like to try new recipes. I got one today for a cauliflower casserole that I want to make."

"I volunteer to be your taste-tester. Anytime."

"Do you do much cooking?"

"Not much. We had a full-time cook growing up, and Mom never liked to cook. I guess I got that from her. I find it easier to order from my favorite Chinese restaurant." Nicole pushed her chair slightly away from the table and sipped her wine. "I'm glad you had a little left of this wine."

"Me, too. It went well with spaghetti." Jody mimicked Nicole's pose. "I'm glad you came over tonight."

Nicole turned to face her and set her glass on the table. "I was hoping it would be okay. I wanted to see you." She hesitated for a moment. "I like spending time with you."

Jody sensed Nicole's uncertainty. "I like spending time with you, too." She rested her hand on Nicole's. "I know we still have issues to resolve, but you've become special to me."

"Yeah. Same with me. I don't want you to think I'm taking advantage of our situation. I don't know how things are going to turn out, but I look forward to getting to know you."

Jody grinned. "Don't think you're getting out of taking me to that fancy-shmancy party of yours."

"Oh no. You're committed now. I am not going alone!" Nicole laughed.

"I'm actually looking forward to it," Jody said.

"Yeah, well you haven't met my family yet." Nicole finished her wine.

"I'm looking forward to that, too." Jody carried their dishes to the sink.

Nicole followed her with their empty glasses. "Thanks for the meal and the company." She stood in the doorway to the kitchen. "I needed a kiss when I got here, and now I need another in order to leave." She waited in the doorway.

Jody set the dishes aside and sank into Nicole's open arms. "You don't ask for much." She rested her arms on Nicole's shoulders planning a slow exploration, but Nicole stepped her back until she was pressed against the kitchen counter before covering her lips with her own. Her intended unhurried adventure turned into impassioned probing tongues and total body contact. She broke contact long enough to catch her breath and create some space between them. When she caught her breath, she gently lifted Nicole's hand to kiss her palm. "Be careful driving home." She walked Nicole to the door and pushed aside the stab of loneliness as she disappeared through the outer door.

CHAPTER TWENTY-TWO

Nicole sat in her car for a few minutes to let her bubbling desire settle. Jody had somehow become an important part of her life. In spite of the tragic accident and pending lawsuit, they'd managed to spend quality time together and feelings she never expected were beginning to emerge. Thoughts of her surfaced in the middle of her workday. She missed her when they were apart, and her world settled when they were together. She gave up trying to figure it out and smiled all the way home.

The next morning, Nicole organized all the material she had for the upcoming fundraiser. She downloaded the pictures she'd taken of the Great Dane and other dogs at the shelter and created flyers for them. She sent emails confirming the time and date before leaving for work.

"Good morning, Stacy," Nicole called as she passed her desk. "I'm heading to the back to check on our new door. Do I have any messages?"

"One. An odd one. She asked to please let you know that 'she hasn't forgotten your shopping offer.'"

Nicole grinned. "Okay. Thank you." Jody was thinking of her, too. She checked the new door and talked to Roger before going back to her office and concentrating on work. She checked the time and left for lunch.

"Hi there." Jody's welcoming smile eased Nicole's concern over her showing up unannounced. She settled on the picnic table bench and rested the McDonald's bag on the table.

"I'm glad you were out here." She removed fish sandwiches from the bag. "I worried you might not be today."

"It's gorgeous today, and I kind of hoped you'd show up." Jody picked up a sandwich and took a bite. "Thank you for the fish sandwiches."

"It is a lovely day and you're welcome." Nicole tipped her face to the sun for a minute before taking a bite of her sandwich. "I got your message and I haven't forgotten that we're going shopping." Nicole didn't say how much she was looking forward to seeing Jody in the new dress. She had no doubt she'd be stunning.

"You may be off the hook. Ashley told me she was excited to help me. Anyway, is your fundraiser still on for this Saturday?"

"Yes. I printed out the flyers this morning. I hope we'll find someone who wants the Great Dane."

"Me, too. He's a sweet boy." Jody finished her sandwich and checked her watch.

"Do you need to get back?"

"Soon. I'm glad you came. This is becoming our thing."

"Is it okay?"

"It's great as far as I'm concerned. It's supposed to rain tomorrow, so I'll probably stay in."

"I'll plan to see you Friday for lunch. Rain or shine. I have several umbrellas." Nicole took Jody's hand and squeezed gently before stuffing their empty wrappers into the bag and leaving. She checked the time and sent a reminder text to Stacy that she'd be late getting back from lunch. She pulled into the parking lot of Hairs Unlimited, took a deep breath, and went inside. An hour later she waved to her stylist and went back to work.

"I'm back, Stacy." Nicole went to her office to review work schedules and payroll. She automatically reached to push her hair behind her ears, startled by the lightweight feel of it. She'd wanted a change for a while, and it was no longer hanging down her back, but her hair feathered to her shoulders. She liked it and she hoped Jody would, too. She reminded herself it would grow if she didn't. She booted up her computer hoping for the medical examiner's report but shut it down after checking her email and finding nothing. She was checking invoices when Stacy interrupted her.

"You got your hair cut!" Stacy tipped her head side to side and reached to touch her hair. "It's beautiful. I love it."

Nicole smiled in relief. "Thanks, Stacy. I'm nervous about it, but it's something I've wanted to do for a long time."

"You have beautiful hair, but the cut took away the heaviness and accents your lovely face."

"Thank you." Nicole could tell she was blushing. The ringing of her phone interrupted them.

"Hey, sis. I'm calling to check on you," Caleb said.

"Hi, Caleb. I'm fine. Just working."

"Mom wants to know if you've planned her gala event yet."

"And why doesn't she call me if she wants to know?"

"I don't know. I'm out of it now. I did my duty."

"All right. Thanks. I'll talk to her and see what the hell she wants me to do." Nicole ran her hand through her hair startled by the lightness of it. "Take care. I'll see you soon."

Nicole debated calling her mother now or waiting until she got home. She decided to get it over with and dialed her number.

"Hello, dear. Your brother must have called you."

"He did, Mom. I guess you haven't gotten anyone to plan your event yet."

"I want you to do it. You do such a good job with those doggy things."

"They're fundraisers, Mom. Not parties."

"Whatever. Please do it for me."

Her mother disconnected the call and Nicole sighed. Her mother was used to getting what she wanted, so Nicole searched her contacts and found the event planner she'd been referred to. She called her and made an appointment. Her mother didn't need to know who planned her social event. She'd be happy as long as it was fancy and she didn't have to do it. She checked the time and let Stacy know she was leaving for the day. She took a deep breath as she pulled into the Acosta driveway. She hoped Mrs. Acosta would let her in the house, but it would be her call. She rang the bell.

"Hello, Nicole. Come in."

Nicole could see where Jody got her manners and gentle nature. "Thank you, Mrs. Acosta." She entered the neat living area.

"Would you like a cup of coffee or tea?"

She looked nervous and that was not Nicole's intent. "No, thank you. I stopped by to see how you were doing. I've talked to Jody several times, but are you okay?"

"Have a seat, dear." She patted the area next to her on the couch. "It's still hard. I miss Harold every day. But he's gone. I have to accept that. I don't suppose you and Jody found anything new, did you?"

"No. I'm sorry we haven't, but Jody probably told you we're waiting for the final medical examiner's report."

"She did. She told me about the computer snafu. I honestly can't get my hopes up. It was so hard to accept when it happened, and I don't ever want to go through that again."

"I'll leave you alone. I just wanted to check on you." Nicole patted her hand and stood to leave.

"Thank you for checking on me. Jody will be home shortly. Would you like to stay for dinner?"

"Thanks, Mrs. Acosta, but I need to get home. You take care and call if you need anything." Nicole drove home a little more settled. She turned her thoughts to her own mother's party she needed to make happen. She changed her mind at the last minute and turned to head to the shelter. She missed Tiny and she hadn't even had her home yet.

"Hi, Nicole," Hanna called from the doorway. "Glad you could make it. Bobbi will be late so I'm the only one here so far."

"Hi, Hanna." Nicole picked up cleaning supplies and headed to Tiny's area. "Hey, little one. You're getting to be a big girl. You ready to come home with me soon?" Nicole sat on the floor for a few minutes to enjoy the feel of her puppy in her lap.

"When are you taking her home?" Hanna asked.

"I'll check with Dr. Meyers tomorrow. I've got my house as ready as I can."

"Hey, Hanna?" Jody called from the parking lot.

"Sounds like help has arrived." Hanna went to meet her.

Nicole gently removed Tiny from her lap and stood. She grinned when Jody walked to her and touched her hair before running her hand over her shoulder and down her arm to her hand. "Very nice."

"Thanks. I'm glad you like it." Nicole relaxed.

"Mom told me you stopped by to check on her. That was nice. Thank you."

"You reminded me of my negligence. She was incredibly gracious."

"Shall we get this place cleaned up and relax? I replaced that bottle of wine we finished."

"Let's get to it then." Nicole went straight to the Great Dane's run and Jody started in the one next to her. She noticed a couple of new dogs and mentally reminded herself to get shots of them for her fundraiser table. She put away her cleaning supplies and waited for Jody by her car.

"Ready?" Jody asked.

"Yep." Nicole followed Jody home flooded by memories of their first kiss. She took a settling breath before stepping into her apartment.

Jody poured them each a glass of wine and settled on the couch. "So, what made you decide to cut your hair?"

"I've wanted to do it for months. I saw a woman on TV who had hair similar to mine with this cut." She pulled the ends of her hair on one side. "I liked it a lot, so I tried it."

Jody took a sip of wine, set her glass on the end table, and clasped Nicole's face in her hands before kissing her. "I like it, too." She kissed her again before picking up her wine glass.

Nicole took a drink and a deep breath wishing she'd cut her hair a month ago.

CHAPTER TWENTY-THREE

Jody relaxed on her couch to watch the news after Nicole left. She allowed her mind to wander to the first time she'd seen Nicole and her preconceived idea of her. She reflected on how their relationship had evolved and her growing feelings for her. A niggle of worry surfaced and she didn't push it away. If Sara had taught her anything, it was to examine her feelings and be open and honest about them. Trusting Nicole came easily, so she cautioned herself to go slow. She picked up her phone and called Ashley.

"Hi, Jody. You're up late."

"Nicole left, so I was watching the news. Do you have time to talk?"

"Sure. Sleep's overrated sometimes. Nicole? As in beautiful, rich, gentle, all those other things, Nicole?"

"Yep. We've sort of been seeing each other."

"Wow. What does 'sort of' mean?"

"Just spending time together. That's all." Jody paused. "And lately, doing a lot of kissing."

"Whew. I think we may need another night out."

"Are you and Bill planning on going to the fundraiser Saturday?"

"Yes. Do you want to ride with us again? Are you going to wear that new red dress?"

Jody chuckled. "Yes to both."

"Great. We'll talk more then. And, Jody?"

"Yes?"

"Be careful."

"Thanks, Ash. I'm doing my best." Jody put her phone on her charger and went to bed.

The next morning she stretched and allowed herself memories of Nicole's kiss and the heat of her body when they'd snuggled on the couch. She thought back to Sara and their last intimate time together. She smiled at the memory. As nice as the memory was, she knew it would be many times more intense and explosive with Nicole. Ashley's warning to be careful resonated with her. She wasn't ready to take their relationship there yet. She rose and ate breakfast before heading to work. She settled at her desk and worked until noon and waved to Pete as she rushed out the door to the picnic table. Nicole stood and waved her arm toward the bench as if it were a fancy restaurant. The table was covered with various pizza boxes.

"Thank you," she said as she sat.

Nicole sat across from her and handed her a paper plate. "It's good to see you." She put a piece of pizza on her plate.

"It's good to see you, too. I talked to Ashley last night after you left. She and Bill are going to the fundraiser, so I'll ride with them."

"I think it'll be packed. My brother is doing extra advertising for me." She took a bite of pizza.

"I'm looking forward to it." Jody finished two pieces of pizza and relaxed with her face to the sun. "We've lucked out with the nice weather."

"Yes, but like I said, I have many umbrellas in case it rains." Nicole smirked. "I like spending time with you. Rain or shine."

"Me, too." Jody rested her hand on Nicole's across the table.

"I'm bringing Tiny home on Monday. I talked to Dr. Meyers this morning."

"Great. Now the fun begins. I've never housebroken a puppy, but I've heard tales. Some good, some not so good." Jody smiled.

"We'll see. I hope to be able to take her to work with me."

Nicole looked worried, and Jody took her hand and kissed it. "You'll do great." She checked her watch and sighed. Lunch hour ought to be called lunch minute. "I should get back to work."

"Will I see you at the shelter tonight?" Nicole spoke as she picked up the leftover boxes.

"I plan to be there." Jody stood. She wanted to kiss Nicole good-bye like lovers do. She shook off the response. "See you later, and thanks for the pizza." She reluctantly turned and walked back to the building.

Jody checked the clock for the fifth time that afternoon, relieved to see it was almost time to leave. She finished what she was working on and called to Pete on the way out. "See you tomorrow."

She pulled into the shelter parking lot and immediately looked for Nicole, and then mentally shook herself and went to collect cleaning supplies.

"Hi, Jody," Bobbi called from the building. "Come see what just came in."

Jody went to see what Bobbi was talking about and stopped short when she reached the door. "Oh my." She grinned at the mama cat nursing eight tiny kittens. "Wow. We haven't had kittens in here for a while."

"I know," Bobbi replied. "They're so small."

"They're cute." Jody thought of her mother and Mr. Grumbles.

"Good. Here's Nicole. She can take pictures of them for her fundraiser." Bobbi hurried to meet her at her car.

Jody grinned at the sight of Bobbi grabbing Nicole's arm and pulling her toward the kittens. She went to start cleaning the Great Dane's area. "Hi there, big boy. You might have a forever home after Saturday." She spoke as she scooped his poop and mopped. "I'd take you home in a minute if I had room, but I'm in a small apartment. You'd take up the whole living room." She grinned at his thumping tail as he followed her movements with his eyes. She filled his food and water bowls and moved to the next run. She finished cleaning and filling bowls and went to look for Nicole. She found her along with Bobbi photographing the squirming baby felines. She rested her hand lightly on Nicole's lower back enjoying the tensing of her muscles when she moved, but pulled her hand away when Nicole turned and handed her a squirming kitten. "Are we supposed to be touching these newborns?"

"They're not newborns," Bobbi said. "They've been here for two weeks already. Someone moved them to this area."

"They are cuties." Jody set the kitten next to its littermates.

"Anyone up for McDonald's?" Bobbi asked.

"Sounds good," Jody and Nicole spoke together.

Bobbi returned with the food and they settled on lawn chairs to eat.

Jody finished eating and enjoyed the company of her friends before she headed to her mother's.

"Hi, honey. Is everything okay?"

"Yes. I wanted to stop and say hello. And"—she held up a take-out bag from McDonald's—"a fish sandwich and chocolate shake."

"Oh, my favorite! Thank you." Her mother grabbed the bag and set it on the table. "Do you want half?"

"It's all yours, Mom. I already ate." She made herself a cup of tea and sat with her mother while she ate. "How do you like living with a cat?"

"It's calming. He sits in my lap and purrs. Why do you ask?"

"There's a litter of kittens at the shelter, and for a fleeting moment, I thought about adopting one of them."

"Mr. Grumbles is six, so I can't compare him to a kitten."

"Well, I wanted to see how you were doing and bring you the fish sandwich and shake."

She kissed her mom's cheek and went home. She tossed her keys on the counter and went to her bedroom to change into sweats as she shook off the melancholy threatening to seep in. How could she get so used to evenings with Nicole so quickly? She missed her. She retrieved the popcorn tin but immediately returned it. It reminded her of Nicole. She sat on her couch to watch television and turned her thoughts to the upcoming fundraiser. Maybe she'd wear her hair up for the event. Nicole's new haircut was sophisticated and sexy. Maybe she could try for something besides wash-and-wear. She wrote herself a note to make a hair appointment. She watched a few more minutes of television, shut it off, and picked up her phone.

"Hi, Jody. What's up?" Ashley asked.

"Is it okay if I bring a date to your wedding?"

"Of course it is. You're my maid of honor. You can bring whomever you want. I sort of hope it'll be Nicole. It is isn't it?"

"Yes. I didn't want to ask her until I cleared it with you."

"I'm looking forward to seeing you two at the fundraiser Saturday."

"She'll be busy doing stuff. I may not get to see her much."

"You want to though, don't you?"

"Yeah. I really do."

"I don't mean to put a damper on your infatuation or whatever it is, but what about the lawsuit? Didn't you say you were working with her to find answers?"

"I did. We haven't found anything yet, but we don't have the final medical examiner's report yet."

"Huh. Well, I hope it all works out for you. We'll pick you up about six on Saturday."

"Thanks, Ash. I'll see you then." Jody disconnected the call, turned off the TV, picked up a book, and propped her feet up on the coffee table. She read for half an hour before heading to bed.

The next morning Jody called for a hair appointment on her way to work. She spent the morning wondering if Nicole would show up for lunch and left at noon intending to stop at her favorite restaurant downtown if Nicole wasn't there. She pushed down her excitement when she saw her seated on the bench facing her. Her heart rate soared and her breathing accelerated when she felt the heat of Nicole's gaze scan her. "I'm glad you made it today."

"I thought we could go out to eat today. Would that be okay with you?" Nicole asked.

"Sure. That's where I was headed if you hadn't been here." She followed Nicole to her car, and she pulled into the parking lot of the restaurant Jody had planned on. "This okay?"

"Perfect. I like this little place." Jody thought about the day she'd watched Nicole with the sexy woman across the street. She shoved that thought away. She was here with her today. She picked up her menu and smiled.

CHAPTER TWENTY-FOUR

Nicole checked the time and took a deep breath. Her mother would never let up on the pressure regarding her party, gala, whatever it was. She pulled up her contacts on her phone and called her mom.

"Hello, dear. This is a nice surprise."

"Hi, Mom. I wanted to confirm some details with you about the gala you want me to plan."

"Oh, thank you for volunteering, honey!"

Nicole sighed and shook her head. "Do you want the same venue as last year? And do you have a theme in mind, or can it just be fancy?"

"I think the hall last year will do. But make sure it's properly decorated. I don't want any of those crepe paper things or God-awful balloons."

"Okay, Mom. You want elegant and expensive."

"Exactly! I knew you'd do a great job. I'm thinking maybe soft pastels."

"I'll do my best. Will Saturday the eighteenth work for you?"

"Perfect. Let me know if you have more questions." Her mother hung up.

Nicole called her party planner to update her and made an appointment with her to review details. She pushed aside thoughts of Jody and concentrated on final plans for the Saturday fundraiser. She collected everything she planned to take to the hall and piled it on her dining room table. She looked forward to this fundraiser more than usual. She wasn't fooling herself. Jody being in her life was the cause. She settled on her couch with one of her puppy books to study but finished one chapter and decided she'd have time to make a visit to Tiny before dark.

She parked in the shelter parking lot twenty minutes later and went to the puppy room. "Hi there, Tiny. You look sleepy." She watched Tiny raise her head and wag her little tail once before her eyes drifted closed. The room was warm and the lights were dimmed. Nicole watched her sleep for a few minutes before whispering good night and leaving. She went home and back to studying the puppy book. She took a break and filled a glass with sparkling water as she debated training Tiny to ring a bell to let her know she needed to go out or just standing by the door. She walked through her house making notes about locations for doggie gates and most convenient exits. She'd already chosen a spot for her food and water bowls. She looked at the list she'd gotten from Jaylin and planned to shop for puppy food the next day. She finished her water and got ready for bed.

The next morning Nicole reviewed all her notes on the fundraiser and stopped by the venue on her way to the puppy food store. She set up the tables she'd use for pictures and donations and set out the small round tables along the walls for champagne glasses. The rest of the decorations could wait until Saturday. She left in search of puppy food.

The My Pet store downtown was crowded when she arrived. She checked her list and picked out several bags of each kind of food Dr. Meyers had suggested along with a puppy crate for her car. On her way to the checkout, she spotted a whole aisle of chew toys and treats. The checkout clerk grinned as he rang up her purchase. "New puppy?"

"Yeah." Nicole knew she'd probably overdone things, but she didn't care. Her new little dependent was going to have the best of everything. Content that she was prepared to bring Tiny home, she made one last walkthrough of her house and left to meet Jody for lunch. She found her already seated at the picnic table.

Jody smiled when she saw her. "I wasn't sure you'd make it today."

"I went shopping for puppy stuff." She grinned.

"Ah. Monday's the day huh?"

"Yep. I think I'm ready. Still nervous, though."

"You'll do great." Jody opened a bag and pulled out sandwiches and bottled water. "It's not pizza, but I hope you like egg salad sandwiches."

"I do. Thanks for bringing them." Nicole told Jody about the food she'd bought and toys she'd picked out for Tiny.

"I can't wait to come over and see how she settles in." Jody grinned.

"Ha. Me either." Nicole pushed down her uncertainty.

"Are you ready for the fundraiser tomorrow?" Jody took a bite of her sandwich.

"I am. I stopped by and dropped off pictures and things. I'll bring the champagne and hors d'oeuvres tomorrow. You're still going to be there, aren't you?"

"I wouldn't miss it." Jody took her hand and squeezed.

"I'm going to the shelter this afternoon to check on her and make sure all the animals I have pictures of are still available for adoption." A chill replaced the heat from Jody's touch when she released her hand and stood.

"I've got to get back to work. Will I see you at the shelter tonight?"

"I'll be there. Have a good afternoon." Nicole stood and stepped close to Jody blocking her way. "I have to do this." She cupped her face in her hands and kissed her. "See you later." She walked back to her car smiling.

Nicole pulled into her reserved parking spot when she got back to her building and headed to her office. "Hey, Stacy."

"Hi there. I didn't expect you in today."

"I wanted to check on the examiner's report. Any word?"

Stacy checked her email and shook her head. "Sorry. Not yet."

"Okay. I'll check my email before I leave." Nicole went to her office and logged onto her computer. She checked her email and responded to a few requests from Roger before shutting down her computer and leaving. She went home and loaded everything except the champagne and hors d'oeuvres into her trunk. Then she dusted, vacuumed her living room, and mopped the kitchen floor. Nicole was used to being at work all day and wondered what people who didn't work did. She turned on her television and flipped through all her channels before shutting it off and going to change.

She arrived at Sparks an hour later. It was early enough there were only a few couples at the tables and no one at the bar. She ordered a drink and watched a couple dance for a few minutes while she finished her drink then decided to go visit Tiny.

"Hi, Nicole," Hanna called from the building. "Your Tiny is growing fast."

"Hi, Hanna. I know. I'm taking her home Monday. I bought food and all kinds of stuff today." She squatted in front of the cage and watched Tiny bounce with her littermates. "She's going to miss her brothers and sisters."

"Yeah. But she'll have you." Hanna grinned and went to clean one of the runs.

Nicole entered the room with the puppies and cradled Tiny for a few minutes. She squirmed in her arms and chewed on her fingers. "Ouch, you. No biting." Nicole gently pushed her head away from her fingers like she'd read about doing in one of her books. "We're going to have a great life together. You have a lot to learn and a lot to teach me." She set her back on the floor and went to help Hanna with the cleaning.

"Hey all," Jody called as she went to collect cleaning supplies.

"Hi, Jody." Hanna waved. "There're three of us tonight. We should get done early."

Nicole stepped out of the building and stopped to say hi to Jody on the way to get her cleaning supplies. "I'm glad I stayed long enough to see you."

"Me, too." Jody smiled.

"We may not be here long tonight. Would you like to go to Sparks with me?"

"Did I hear Sparks?" Hanna asked from next to them. "I love that place."

"It's a date." Nicole laughed. "It'll be fun." She finished cleaning one of the runs and helped with the others before putting away her supplies. "You two want to follow me?"

"Sure," Hanna said.

"Okay," Jody answered.

Nicole led the way to Sparks wishing she'd offered them both a ride. She consoled herself by hoping Jody would dance with her. She held the door open for them and lightly touched Jody's back when she passed her. "Can I buy you ladies a drink?" she asked.

"I'd like a beer. Whatever they have on tap," Hanna said.

"I'll have a red wine, please," Jody said.

Nicole handed them their drinks and followed them to an open table. She watched Emma enter the building and make a beeline for their table. She took a deep breath and scrambled for an explanation to Jody about Emma.

Emma offered a smile to the table but focused her attention on Hanna. She held out her hand and Hanna took it and followed her to the dance floor.

"I guess it's you and me," Jody said.

"I guess so." Nicole took a sip of her drink before speaking again. "Would you like to dance?"

Jody grabbed her hand and tugged her to the dance floor. "I'd love to," she whispered in her ear.

Nicole relaxed and lost herself in Jody's heat, the scent of her, and the feel of her in her arms. She noted Hanna and Emma a few feet away wrapped in each other and sighed with relief that Emma would probably not be interested in her anymore.

CHAPTER TWENTY-FIVE

Jody called to her mother from the door.

"I'm in the living room, honey."

She grinned when she saw her mom on the couch trying to brush Mr. Grumbles. "I see he's not happy about this."

"Jeanie told me he needed brushing every week or he gets mats." She stood when he jumped off the couch and escaped into the kitchen. "I have coffee. Have you had breakfast?"

"Yes. I'm fine, Mom."

"How are things going with Nicole, Honey?"

"I think we've gone about as far as we can with our investigation. So far, it looks to have been a terrible accident."

"Has it been difficult working with her?"

Jody suppressed a smile at thoughts of being with Nicole. "Not at all. She's honest and fair and willing to look at everything regardless of the outcome."

"We'll be all right, honey." Her mother sighed, and Mr. Grumbles rubbed against her legs.

"I'm going to another one of her fundraisers tonight. She does a lot of good for the animal shelters." Jody kissed her mother's cheek before she left.

"Have fun." Her mother's voice followed her out the door.

She stopped at the animal shelter on her way home. "Hi, Bobbi. How're things?" She picked up a shovel and broom. Bobbi looked upset.

"The big boy has quit eating. Dr. Meyers is on her way this morning to look at him."

"Does his run need cleaning?"

"I finished it. He looks sad to me."

"Maybe he is." Jody went to talk to the Great Dane, but he looked at her and continued to pace.

"Hi, Jody," Dr. Meyers spoke as she stood next to her. "Has he been like this long?" She went into the run and put her stethoscope on his belly.

"I don't know. I just got here. Bobbi told me about him."

"Would you mind finding out if he's been eating?" She continued her examination.

Bobbi spoke from behind her. "He ate last night. I came to feed him this morning and he wouldn't touch his food. He drank a little water, but he's been pacing and retching for a while now."

"I hope we've caught this in time. He's bloated. It happens in the large breeds and it can be deadly. He needs surgery, and I'll take him to my clinic immediately." She pulled out her phone and made a call.

"Can you do it in the clinic here?" Bobbi asked.

"I'd rather have him close to keep an eye on him in recovery. Kristen, my tech, is on the way with our van to transport him. You all did a great job catching this. He'd have been beyond help by the end of the day. Bloat happens when a dog's stomach fills with gas, food, or fluid. If it twists, gastric dilatation volvulus develops which obstructs blood supply to major organs. They call it GDV. There's a surgery called gastropexy where the stomach is sutured to the diaphragm to keep it from happening again." Jody put her arm around Bobbi's shoulders when she saw her tears. "He'll be okay. You can visit him anytime you like." Jaylin waved Kristen to the run and they carried him to the van.

Jody cleaned the run after they left and went to talk to Bobbi. "He's in good hands."

"I know. I've grown close to him. He knows me." Bobbi wrung her hands. "I'm going to visit him as soon as he's out of surgery."

"I think that's great, Bobbi." Jody continued to clean runs and went to check on Tiny. "Hi there, little girl. Your mom is going to take you home soon." She cleaned the puppy's area and watched them play for a while before going home. She tamped down her excitement at the thought of seeing Nicole that night. She took a shower and put on a button-down blouse before heading to the hair salon. The process took longer than she expected so she hurried to get dressed and wait for Ashley and Bill.

"Hey, Jody. You look fantastic. I love your hair." Ashley grinned.

"Thanks, Ash. I thought I'd give it a test try for your wedding. I have another fancy event in June, too."

"Well, you look great. Let's go drink champagne." She took Bill's arm and led the way to their car.

Jody spotted Nicole immediately as they walked into the room. She wore the same sexy tuxedo she'd worn for the last fundraiser. Nicole held her gaze as she walked toward her, and by the time she reached her, her knees were weak.

"You look stunning." Nicole touched her hair lightly.

"I'm practicing for Ashley's wedding. You're invited, by the way." She grinned at Nicole's confused look. "As my date."

"I'm honored." Nicole smiled and took her hand.

"Hi, Jody," Hanna called as she approached holding Emma's hand. "You look beautiful. I love your hair." She grinned and wrapped her arm around Emma's waist.

"I'm glad you two could make it tonight," Nicole said.

"It's a great event," Emma smiled and stroked Nicole's cheek.

Jody stepped next to her and glared. She shook off her unbidden response and lifted their joined hands to kiss Nicole's. "She does an excellent job fundraising for the shelters." She watched Emma shrug and Hanna smile and walk away. "Sorry if I interrupted, but I don't like the way she looks at you, or touches you." Jody took a breath. It was no business of hers if Nicole and Emma had something going, but it didn't feel right.

Nicole squeezed her hand. "It's okay. We met at Sparks a few months ago."

Jody released her hand and cradled her face with her hands and kissed her. "I don't like her."

"Come on. I want to show you the pictures I took." Nicole led her to the table with the pictures and donation box.

"By the way. The Great Dane went to the hospital this morning. He bloated. Dr. Meyers is doing surgery."

"Poor thing. I'll let anyone who asks about him know."

"I think Bobbi is going to adopt him. She didn't say for sure, but she's attached to him."

"Okay. We'll consider him adopted. Champagne?"

"Sounds good." Jody saw Ashley and Bill at one of the tables and led Nicole to them.

Ashley spoke before Jody could make introductions. "Great event. I'm Ashley and this is my fiancé, Bill."

"I'm so glad you could make it tonight. Help yourselves to the hors d'oeuvres and champagne. If you'll excuse me, I need to go do my hostess thing for a little while." She kissed Jody's cheek and walked away.

"So," Ashley said. "I guess you and Nicole are an item?"

Jody chuckled. "Yeah. That sounds good. We're an item."

"You like her a lot, don't you?"

"Yes. I do. I didn't realize how much until I saw that woman, Emma, touch her. She had no right!" Jody griped.

"Come on. Let's get something to drink," Ashley offered.

Jody followed her friends to one of the tables and picked up a glass. She took a sip and then finished the glass.

She picked up another glass and began to take a drink when Ashley stepped in front of her. "That won't do anything except make you sick."

Jody held the glass but didn't take a drink. "Okay. But look!" She glowered at Emma leaning close to Nicole.

Ashley grinned. "I see her. But you are the one who puts the sparkle in her eyes when she looks at you. You're the one she cares about."

Jody groaned. "Okay. I'll let *her* live. For now." She set her glass on the table and headed to where Nicole stood leaning away from Emma. As she got closer she noticed Hanna standing off to the side so she went to her. "Nice event, isn't it?"

"Yes, it is." Hanna looked to be holding back tears.

"Hey. You okay?" Jody rested her hand on her arm.

"No. I thought Emma was special. We had an instant connection that felt real to me. I think she wanted me only to get close to Nicole."

"Nicole doesn't want Emma, Hanna. Whatever Emma wants from Nicole, isn't what Nicole wants. She told me they met at Sparks.

That's it. If Emma is honest, she'll let you know how she feels. If not, she doesn't deserve you."

Hanna sniffled. "You're right. I deserve to be treated honestly."

"Come on. Let's get some hors d'oeuvres." Jody followed Hanna to a table and filled a small plate with cheese and crackers.

"So, what's with you and Nicole?" Hanna asked.

"We've been seeing each other. I told you about my dad's accident, didn't I?"

"Yes, I'm sorry to bring that up."

"No problem. Nicole's let me help her investigate, so we've spent some time together."

"Ah. Well, she seems down-to-earth. I like her." Hanna took a bite of food.

"Did you hear about the Great Dane? He bloated and Dr. Meyers took him for surgery today."

"Oh, poor baby. He's a sweetie," Hanna said.

"Yeah. Hopefully, he'll be okay." Jody noticed Nicole search the room, land on her, and smile. "I'm going to see how Nicole is doing. Will you be all right?"

"Thanks, Jody. I'm fine. You go."

Jody walked toward Nicole and took her hand when she reached for her. "I missed you."

"I'm sorry, but I have obligations. I think we've gotten every poodle puppy adopted."

"That's great. I saw Tiny today. She's grown."

"Yep. She's going to be a big girl. Did you get some champagne?" She picked up two glasses and handed her one.

"I did, but thanks for another."

"You're absolutely dazzling." Nicole leaned and kissed her lightly. "I'm the luckiest person in this room because you're with me."

"Thank you. That's the word I used for you the first time I saw you." Jody sipped her drink.

"I guess that must mean we were meant to meet." She tapped her glass to Jody's like she had the first time they met.

Jody watched Hanna and Emma across the room. They looked to be in a serious conversation and she hoped Emma wouldn't hurt her friend.

CHAPTER TWENTY-SIX

Nicole kept an eye on Jody as she traversed the room. Her response to Emma's attention indicated her feelings matched her own. She bristled at the way many of the lesbians in the room either cruised her or made overt advances. Jody gracefully rebuffed any unwanted attention and the glances she cast her way had her looking forward to their good night kiss. She checked the time and did what she'd wanted to do all evening. She joined Jody at one of the small tables and picked up a glass. "I'm missing you," she spoke softly and leaned close to her.

"You're very good at all this, you know? I'm impressed." Jody sipped from her glass.

"Thanks. My mother would be glad to hear that."

"Will I get to meet her in June?"

Nicole laughed at her first thought regarding "bringing her home to meet her mother." "You will. I don't know who all will be there, but she most definitely will be."

"I look forward to it." Jody grinned.

"Are Ashley and Bill having a good time?"

"They are. Ashley loves to show Bill off. I'm happy for her."

"They seem well matched." Nicole lifted Jody's hand to her lips. "You're beautiful."

"Thank you." Jody leaned and kissed her. "You're a charmer."

"As long as you're the only one I'm charming." Nicole watched Jody's eyes darken and a small smile widen.

"Yeah. Only you."

Nicole took the words as confirmation of their growing mutual feelings and wrapped her arm around Jody's waist possessively. "I have a few more obligatory requirements, and I'll be back." She squeezed her gently and walked away. She made her way around the room and stopped to chat or ensure people didn't need anything as well as informing them about the animals available for adoption. She reached the opposite side of the room and spotted the woman she'd hoped never to see again. Doreen stood scanning the room. When her attention settled on Jody, Nicole clenched her teeth. Jody had no idea who she was or how dangerous. She turned and crossed the room to intercept her.

"Nicole. How nice to see you," Doreen breathed.

"What are you doing here, Doreen?" Nicole forced herself to remain civil.

"It's an animal fundraiser. I came to donate." Her feral grin belied her real intention.

"Welcome, then. The donation box is on the table along with pictures of the dogs and cats available for adoption." Nicole pointed to the table and watched Doreen walk in that direction, but she had no illusions of her aim. She kept an eye on her as she continued her hostess duties. Nicole had no idea how long Doreen had been in the room and what nefarious acts she'd already accomplished. She wanted to go to Jody and warn her, but she didn't want to lead Doreen to her. She noticed Ashley and Bill coming her way and moved to intercept them.

"Hi, Nicole. Great turnout." Ashley smiled.

"It is. I'm glad you two made it. Could I ask you a huge favor?"

"Sure." Ashley looked serious. "Is everything all right?"

"Yes. But, there's an untrustworthy reporter here, and I think she's on her way to intercept Jody. This woman is after any sensational story she can get regardless of the truth. She targets members of wealthy and prominent families to make headlines. She's made up dreadful lies about me, and I need to keep her away from Jody. I'm afraid I'll lead Doreen to Jody if I go to her, so would you two mind going to check on her? Maybe Doreen will ignore her if she doesn't know she's with me."

"No problem. We were going to see if she was ready to leave anyway."

"Thank you. If she doesn't want to leave yet, tell her I'll give her a ride home." Nicole watched Doreen go to the donation table. She knew she never went anywhere without a camera, so she expected the event would be front page news for her. She didn't care as long as she left Jody alone. She checked the spot she'd seen her last and didn't see her, and hoped she'd gotten away with Ashley. She turned to take the route next to the wall and stood face-to-face with Jody.

"I missed you." Jody pulled her into the entryway and kissed her.

"I'm glad you're okay. I was worried Doreen had found you."

"She did. She gave me quite a story about the woman in charge of this event. I guess she's absolutely not to be trusted. I thanked her and told her I'd be extremely careful."

"She's the one not to trust. She enjoys making up stories to sell that rag she works for." Nicole began to pace.

"Hey. It's okay." Jody took her hand and held it to her chest. "I could see she was fishing for something, but I sure wasn't going to give her anything. She didn't admit to being a reporter."

Nicole grinned. "And I was worried about you."

Jody shrugged. "Do you need help cleaning up?"

"I'd love to have you help me clean up, and I'll give you a ride home." She looked over the room and checked the time. "Let's start putting the food away." Nicole hesitated. She wanted to pull Jody into her arms and kiss her. She took a breath and suppressed her bubbling desire before heading to begin collecting the leftovers.

"Are you saving the glasses?" Jody asked.

"I have a bin to put them in. I'll run them through my dishwasher when I get home." Nicole pointed to the kitchen.

Jody filled garbage bags and Nicole dragged them out to the garbage bin. She reviewed the room and smiled. A few people lingered to finish their drinks and she watched them drop money in the donation box before waving and leaving. "I think we're done."

Nicole gathered the flyers on the table and put them in a bin with the donation box. "Yep. I think so, too." She carried boxes and bins to her car while Jody checked the room for anything left. "All clear?" Nicole asked.

"Looks good to me."

Nicole locked the door behind them when they left and took Jody's hand as they walked to the car. She turned to Jody when they were seated. "I'm glad you handled Doreen so well. She can cause trouble for people."

Jody shrugged and smiled. "There's not a whole lot she could write about me. I don't want you to be hurt."

Nicole took her hands in hers and kissed them. "I'm glad you were here tonight. I liked looking up and seeing you."

"It was a fantastic evening. I enjoyed it and I think you collected quite a bit of money for the shelters."

"I think so, too. Thanks for your help." Nicole leaned to kiss Jody and lost herself in the feel of her lips and the heat of her hands when she pulled her closer. She leaned away when her hip kept hitting her steering wheel. "I forgot how hard it is to make out in the front seat of a car."

"Yeah." Jody sat back in her seat. "Would you like to come in for a glass of water? Or something."

"I'd love to come in for 'something' but I think I better head home."

"Okay. Be careful going home. Will I see you at the shelter tomorrow?"

"I'm planning on it."

"Good night, Nicole." Jody brushed her lips over hers and climbed out of the car.

Nicole waited until Jody was inside the building before leaving. She might be kicking herself tomorrow, but she didn't feel right accepting Jody's offer for *something.* She cared about her. More than she probably should allow herself. They hadn't completely resolved the wrongful death lawsuit and the last thing she wanted to do was hurt Jody. She tamped down her yearning as she drove and pulled into her brother's driveway ten minutes later.

"Hey, Nicole. What brings you here so late?" Caleb asked.

"I'm on my way home from one of my fundraisers. I think I've got myself into a bit of a pickle."

Caleb filled two glasses halfway with bourbon. "Here." He handed her one and sat across from her.

"Thanks." She took a sip and let the heat from the alcohol warm her stomach. "Jody and I are seeing each other. I mean beyond the being together to review her father's death case. I've developed feelings for her beyond friendship." She finished her drink in one swallow.

"Huh. Does she feel the same?" Caleb poured her another drink.

"Yes. I believe she does."

"I don't see the problem." Caleb sat back across from her.

"I think I'm scared. I don't want her to feel like I'm taking advantage of her. I've never felt so protective and possessive before. I'm used to having to vet anyone I date and be suspicious of their motives. Jody is the most honest and caring woman I've ever met."

"It sounds like she's special. I'd say go for it." Caleb smiled and finished his drink.

"Maybe I'm tired. It's been a long day, but my fundraiser went well. Doreen showed up though." She smiled at the way Jody had handled her. "I'll let you get to bed. Thanks for listening and thanks for the bourbon."

"You want some coffee?"

"No, thanks. I'm okay. I'll talk to you tomorrow. Oh. Did I tell you I'm adopting a puppy?"

"Nooo. Whatever made you do that?" Caleb looked appalled.

"She picked me. She's the largest puppy in the litter. A poodle."

"I look forward to meeting her. When she's a year old or so." Caleb laughed.

Nicole smiled as she drove home, looking forward to seeing Jody the next day.

CHAPTER TWENTY-SEVEN

Jody finished her breakfast and sat on her couch with her coffee to watch the Sunday morning news shows. A large part of her had hoped to have Nicole next to her when she woke, but relief overrode the thought. Nicole had sensed it was too soon to take their relationship to the next level, and once she pushed aside her intense desire, she agreed. She finished her coffee before taking a shower and dressing. She smiled at memories of the previous evening as she drove to her mother's.

"Good morning, honey. You're in time for hot cinnamon rolls." Her mother took a tray of rolls out of the oven and placed one on a plate for Jody and one for herself.

"Thanks, Mom." She poured them each a cup of coffee and settled in her chair at the table.

"How was the event last night?" Her mother took a bite of her roll.

"Nicole did an excellent job. It was great, and Ashley and Bill had a good time." She pulled apart a cinnamon roll and took a bite. "Did I tell you Nicole has adopted a puppy?"

"I don't remember that you did. You told me about the litter of poodles."

"She adopted one of them. She takes her home tomorrow."

"Good. I had no idea how comforting it is having a pet. I'm sure she'll enjoy a dog. A puppy sounds like a lot of work though."

"I agree. If I get a dog, it'll be an adult." Jody reminded herself to check on Bobbi and the Great Dane. "I'm going to the shelter this morning."

"Have fun and be careful." Her mom toasted her with her coffee cup.

Jody kissed her mom's cheek and left. She parked in her usual spot at the shelter and went directly to get cleaning supplies. She waved to a couple of volunteers and suppressed her disappointment at not seeing Nicole.

"Morning, Jody," Hanna called from one of the runs.

"Hi, Hanna. Have you heard anything about the Great Dane?"

"Bobbi's inside. She told me he's doing well. Dr. Meyers is keeping him for a few days, but Bobbi has officially adopted him."

"That's great! I'm happy for her. And it'll be good for him to have a permanent home."

"Yeah. Speaking of great, that was nice last night wasn't it?"

"It was. I went to Nicole's previous event, but last night's was better. I guess all the puppies have been adopted."

"Good. I have some personal news about last night." Hanna blushed.

"Yeah?" Jody suspected it involved Emma.

"Emma and I are officially dating." Hanna's blush faded and she beamed.

"That's great. I'm happy for you." Jody hugged Hanna. "I wish you both all the best. Did she give up on Nicole?"

"She did. She wasn't interested in her for anything serious, and we click, you know?"

"I do." Jody felt the same way with Nicole and hoped she did as well. She went to the next run and concentrated on her cleaning duties. She refused to believe Nicole would have kissed her the way she did and have someone else waiting in the wings. They'd both shared their feelings and it was clear to Jody that Nicole wanted more with her. She knew for sure it's what she wanted. They'd have time to talk later when Nicole arrived. She worked until noon and ignored her disappointment at no sign of Nicole. "I'm making a McDonald's run," she called to the group of volunteers. She took orders and Hanna offered to go with her. They returned within an hour and Jody's angst settled when she saw Nicole. "Good morning. You missed the lunchtime event." Jody couldn't look away from Nicole. Questions swirled between them and she took a deep breath before speaking again. "It's good to see you."

"It's good to see you, too. I had a late breakfast, so I'm okay. I'll fill food and water bowls while you eat."

"I'll help." Jody followed Nicole to the first run and took her hand. "Can we talk?"

"Sure." Nicole set the bowls on the floor and led her outside to behind the building. "I've been thinking about you all night." She lifted her hand to her lips. "What do you want to talk about?"

"Us." She took her hands in hers. "Is there an us?"

"I sure hope so. I'd like there to be." Nicole kissed her lightly. "Is this about me turning down your offer last night?"

"No. You were right about that. I care about you, but I don't think we're ready to spend the night together yet."

Nicole grinned. "Yet. I like that word. It implies maybe someday."

"I'm serious, Nicole. We may still have some difficult times ahead." Jody couldn't help but grin, too.

"I know, Jody, and I'm not pushing."

"Last night, we spoke of being the only one for each other. Did I misunderstand?" Jody tried not to hold her breath waiting for an answer.

"No misunderstanding. I don't plan on seeing anyone but you," Nicole said.

"Good, because I feel the same way and I don't like sharing." Jody held Nicole's hand.

"I don't either," Nicole said and kissed her.

Jody relaxed and vowed not to listen to anything anyone said about Nicole. She felt the truth in her words and touch. That's all she needed to know. She wasn't ready for wedding vows, but she relaxed knowing she'd be the only one Nicole would be kissing. "I'm going to finish the last two runs."

"Do you have plans for dinner?" Nicole asked.

"No."

"Would you come to my house? I have lasagna ready to bake."

"I won't say no to that." Jody hurried to get to work. She met Nicole at her car after she finished. "Ready?"

"Do you want to ride with me and I'll bring you back here, or drive yourself?"

"I'd like to ride with you." Jody relaxed in Nicole's car. "When's your next fundraiser?" she asked.

"Next month. I'm having a party planner do all the work from now on, though. It's the same company I'm using for my mother's event. I'll be able to spend more time promoting the event and following up on the adoptions. And they'll do all the setup and cleanup."

"That sounds like a good idea. I gave you the date for Ashley's wedding, didn't I?"

"Yes. The fundraiser will be two weeks after that." Nicole pulled into her garage and shut off her car. "Shall we go have dinner?"

Jody climbed out of the car impressed with how neatly Nicole kept her garage. As she followed her into the house, she remembered the living and dining room but hadn't noticed the well-appointed kitchen. "You told me you don't cook much. This kitchen is amazing."

"It is. I'm too lazy to cook, but my brother, Caleb, loves to and he's quite good. I put him to work when he comes over." Nicole shrugged and began dishing out the lasagna.

Jody stuffed a forkful in her mouth. "Mmm. This is fabulous. Did he make this?"

"He did. I told him I was going to invite you over for dinner someday, so he made this and told me to take credit if I wanted to. I made the salad."

"Thank him for me. And thank you for the salad." She continued to eat.

"You can thank him yourself in June. He'll be at whatever my mother's event is going to turn out to be." Nicole took a bite of food.

"I look forward to it." Jody took a drink of the water Nicole put on the table for her.

"Would you be interested in another movie? I've got a selection."

"Sure." Jody took her empty plate to the sink and followed Nicole to the living room.

Nicole opened a drawer in a large chest set against the wall. "You can pick one."

Jody blinked in surprise when she saw the collection of DVDs. "You must have fifty movies here!"

"Yes. About that. I got most of these from the LGBTQ center when they cleared out the library and closed a few years ago. We can watch something on Netflix if you'd prefer." Nicole pulled one out and closed the drawer. "Here. Let's watch *Claire of the Moon*."

"Okay." Jody shook her head and wondered what other surprises Nicole had. Nicole settled on the couch and wrapped an arm around Jody as she started the movie. "This is nice."

"It is," Nicole replied.

Jody moved away from her slightly when the sexy part of the movie had them both breathing harder. She clasped her hands in her lap to keep from grabbing Nicole and pulling her into a kiss. By the end of the movie, she had herself under control but took a deep breath before speaking. "That was a good movie. Thank you for sharing it with me."

"It's a classic. I like it because it's sexy as well as a love story. I have a few that are pure sex, but the sexy love stories are my favorite."

"So, you have porn?"

"I do."

"Maybe someday we can watch those." Jody grinned.

"I like the sound of that," Nicole said.

"Not tonight though. I better get home. I've got work tomorrow." Jody stood.

"Yeah. Me, too. And a puppy to bring home," Nicole said.

Jody settled in Nicole's passenger seat still struggling to keep her hands to herself. She'd never actually seen any pornographic movies, but she shivered at the thought of watching them with Nicole.

CHAPTER TWENTY-EIGHT

Good morning, Stacy." Nicole stopped at her desk on her way to her office.

"Good morning. Did you have a good weekend?"

Nicole grinned at memories of Jody at the fundraiser, with her on the couch watching a movie, and their heated kiss when she'd dropped her off at her car. "I did. How was yours?"

"Great. Mathew and I went to see that new Batman movie. It was good, and we held hands like a couple of teenagers." Stacy giggled.

Nicole hoped she'd have someone to hold hands with at the movies after thirty years of marriage. "I'll keep that movie in mind. Would you please check on our missing coroner's report again this morning?" She went to her office and took out her paperwork on the Acosta case. She'd convinced herself the final coroner's report would match what she had, but she needed confirmation. The Acostas needed confirmation. She knew Stacy would follow up with it, but she sent an email herself and planned to stop by their office after lunch. It didn't make sense it would take so long in this day and age of technology. She reminded herself of her company's data breach a year ago and the time and cost of revamping their system. She turned her attention to inventory receipts and space utilization.

She worked until lunchtime and let Stacy know she was leaving. She picked up a pizza on her way to meet Jody and settled at their picnic table to wait. She watched Jody stride toward her and took her hand when she reached for her. "It's good to see you."

"You, too." Jody sat at the table. "Is your morning going well?"

"It's been busy." Nicole opened the pizza box and put a piece on her paper plate. "Stacy and her husband saw the Batman movie this weekend. Would you like to see it?"

"I would. Maybe one Saturday?"

"It's a date." Nicole liked saying that. She liked it a lot.

"I'm glad we've had such good weather for our lunch dates. It was supposed to rain today, but it's beautiful." Jody turned her face to the sun.

Nicole stretched her legs out on the bench seat and leaned sideways on the table top. "I like taking a lunch break with you. I used to stay at my desk and end up working through lunch. It's no wonder I used to get indigestion."

"I like it, too. I know staying inside all day without an outdoor break can make for a long day." Jody mimicked her pose by stretching out on the other side of the table.

"How's your mom?"

"She's good. I'll stop and have dinner with her tonight."

"You're a good daughter." Nicole turned to sit at the table and took another piece of pizza.

"Maybe it's because I'm an only child, but we were always a close family. Dad used to call me his shining star and my mom the love of his life."

"Tell her I said hello." Nicole hoped to tell her herself when she received the final coroner's report. She checked the time, turned to face Jody, and reached for her hand. "I'll talk to you tonight." She lifted her hand to her lips, then went to her car and headed to the medical examiner's office.

"I'll check again, Ms. Bergeron, but I know we'd have sent you a copy if we found it," the clerk said before going through a door behind her.

Nicole paced as she waited and became more agitated as the minutes ticked by. She couldn't muster a smile when the clerk returned and shook her head.

"I'm sorry."

"I'm not leaving until I talk to the medical examiner. Please send him or her out here now." Nicole began her pacing again while she waited. Ten minutes passed before a tall woman in a surgical gown came through the door.

"I'm Dr. Rose, the medical examiner. Can I help you?" she asked.

"I'm here about a missing final report for one of my employees. Harold Acosta. He was killed in an accident a year ago and the family needs the final coroner's report."

"Ah. You've been here before, haven't you? If it's any consolation, the county has us on a watch list now. I'm afraid all I can do is apologize and promise we're doing all we can to straighten out this mess. I will personally make an effort to get it to you this week."

"Thank you. You can be sure I will be back if I don't get it in the next few days." Nicole left the building with a tiny glimmer of hope. She decided to stop at the animal shelter before going back to work.

"Hi, Nicole. I didn't expect you here so early," Bobbi said.

"I'm on my way back to work now, but thought I'd check on your Great Dane. How's he doing?"

"The surgery went well and he's resting and recuperating at Dr. Meyers's."

"That's great. Are you taking him home with you when he's healed?"

"I am. I have a second bedroom for him, and I bought a super large crate."

"That's great. It sounds like he'll be *super* comfortable." Nicole grinned. "I'm taking Tiny home tonight."

"Cool. She's a cutie. Good luck with her." Bobbi went back to the run she'd been cleaning.

Nicole visited with Tiny for a few minutes and left. She pulled into Dr. Meyers's parking lot half an hour later.

"Hi, Nicole. What brings you here?" Kristen stepped out from an exam room.

"I'm here to settle the bill for the Great Dane you brought in with bloat the other day."

"That's kind of you. I know Bobbi has made arrangements for a payment plan."

"I'd like to help if you'll let me."

"I'm sure she'll be grateful, but let me check with Jaylin."

"Hi, Nicole." Jaylin came out of the surgery. "I'm not charging Bobbi anything for Big Boy. I volunteer at the shelter and that's where he came from. Bobbi insisted she pay something, so I'm letting her decide what she's comfortable with. If you want to help though, you could buy her the large breed dog diet and maybe some for the shelter. We don't want him bloating again and it's expensive. I plan to send her home with a few bags when she picks him up."

"Did she name him Big Boy?" Nicole smiled at the name.

"Yep. She's attached to him, so I'm glad he came through the surgery so well."

"Okay." Nicole wrote a check and handed it to Jaylin. "Use this for her dog food." She hesitated before leaving. "Is a standard poodle considered a large breed?"

"Yes, they are. Why?" Jaylin asked.

"I'm picking up my puppy tonight."

Jaylin handed her a bag of large breed puppy food. "Good luck."

"Thanks. She waved as she left still smiling at the appropriate name. She went straight back to work.

"I'm glad you're back. I received an email from the medical examiner a few minutes ago. I forwarded it to you." Stacy spoke as she swiveled in her chair to face her.

"Thanks. I'll take a look at it now. I actually got to talk to the doctor today, so I'm looking forward to reading it." Nicole settled at her desk and opened her email.

Ms. Bergeron. We're doing everything we can to locate the file you requested. We hired a private internet security firm to review our whole system and we hope to have your lost file by the end of the week. Sincerely, Dr. Rose, County M.E.

Nicole printed the email and placed it in the Acosta file. Another piece of paper with no information. She finished her workday and didn't even try to tamp down her excitement about going to pick up Tiny. She took the note she'd written about the large breed dog food out of her pocket and read it. She stopped at the pet food store to stock up before going to the shelter.

"Hey, Nicole. Tonight's the night, huh?" Bobbi called.

"Yep." She held up her pet carrier. "She's coming home."

"I've got your paperwork all ready. Sign these and she's all yours."

"Thanks, Bobbi. I stopped to see Jaylin today. Big Boy is doing well."

"I can't wait to bring him home."

"I'll let you know how Tiny settles in." Nicole coaxed Tiny into her carrier and fastened the seat belt around the carrier in the passenger seat. "It's you and me, little one. Let's go home." Nicole drove two miles under the speed limit and stayed three car lengths away from the cars in front of her. She pulled into her garage and carefully lifted the crate from her car. Tiny sat up and blinked at her. She carried her into the house, set the carrier on the floor next to Tiny's food and water bowls, and opened the door. "You're home now."

She left the carrier door open and waited. She hoped Tiny would rush out and explore her new home, but she sniffed at the food and lay in the crate. Nicole wasn't sure what to do. She pushed the food closer to entice Tiny, but she looked at her and blinked again. "Hey, Tiny. Are you scared?" Nicole began to worry. None of this was in any of her books. Tiny didn't look scared. In fact, she looked sound asleep. She shrugged and called for a delivery from the Chinese restaurant. She watched Tiny while she had dinner and sighed with relief when she finally walked out of the crate and ate some food. She proceeded to sniff the water bowl and drink a little, and then pee on the floor before going back into the crate. Nicole quickly pulled her out of the crate and took her outside. "This is where you pee and poop. Outside!" She spoke clearly and hoped Tiny would somehow know what she meant. This puppy thing was going to be harder than she thought.

CHAPTER TWENTY-NINE

Jody had hoped to hear from Nicole by evening, but she was probably busy with Tiny. She grinned at the thought of her with a puppy. She had no doubt she'd be good with her, but she guessed Tiny would take more work than Nicole thought. She checked her phone for a call from Nicole and put it away before going to her mom's. She called to her from the back door.

"I'm here, dear. Mr. Grumbles has me trapped on the couch."

Jody laughed when she saw the big cat sprawled across her mother's lap. "I see what you mean."

"He's so peaceful that I didn't have the heart to disturb him." She stroked his side as she spoke and Jody could hear his loud purrs.

"Have you had dinner?" Jody sat next to her mom.

"I have a tuna noodle casserole in the refrigerator. I'd appreciate it if you'd heat it up for us."

"Okay." Jody put the casserole in the oven and returned to the couch. "Nicole is bringing home her poodle puppy tonight. I'm looking forward to hearing how it went."

"Have you two been spending time together?" He mother never stopped petting her cat as she spoke.

"We have. In fact, we're dating."

"That's great, honey. As long as she treats you well. She is isn't she?"

"Yes, Mom. She is. She's nothing like the spoiled rich brat I thought she'd be when we first met."

"I imagine it's hard for her. People probably judge her based on her social standing and family name. I'm glad she turned out to be someone you could care about."

Jody looked at her mother, surprised by her intuition. "How did you know I cared about her?"

"I don't believe you'd go out with her if you didn't. I want to see you happy, honey, and you light up when you talk about her."

"I do?"

"Yes. I can tell she must be special to you." Her mom stood slowly, and her cat rolled off her lap. "Shall we eat?"

"Let's." Jody set the table while her mother retrieved the casserole from the oven. "Nicole asked me to say hello to you."

"That's nice. Tell her I said hi. Did you invite her to dinner?"

"I did. Not today, but I told her you wanted her to come one day."

"How about Sunday? I'll make my usual roast with potatoes and carrots."

"Sounds good to me. I'll let her know."

Jody finished dinner and helped her mom clean up before going home. She checked her phone after she settled on her couch with a cup of chamomile tea. It rang halfway through the evening news. "Hi, Nicole."

"Hi, Jody. I hope I didn't catch you at a bad time."

"No. Not at all. I was having a cup of tea."

"Chamomile?"

"Yep."

"Is everything okay?"

"Oh yes. Mom says hello and wants you to come to dinner on Sunday. She's planning a roast."

"Sounds good."

"Did you pick up Tiny today?"

"I did. She's peed on the carpet twice already. I'm beginning to wonder if I'll be able to do this."

Jody had never heard Nicole sound defeated. "You probably need to give it more than an hour or two."

"I can hear the laugh in your voice. It's not funny." She sighed. "I know. I need to be consistent and teach her. She knows where her food and water are already." Nicole sounded like a proud mama.

"I'm coming over."

"Okay...I'll be here."

Jody wasn't sure why she needed to go help Nicole, but something she heard in her voice convinced her she did. She pulled into her driveway half an hour later. Nicole was waiting at the door for her, and she tried not to laugh when she walked in and saw doggy toys piled around Tiny's crate and three dog beds that circled it. "Well, she certainly won't be bored."

"I have a large metal crate for her to sleep in. Would you help me put it together?"

"Of course." Jody looked around unsure where they could fit this crate.

"I thought it would be best in my bedroom so she wouldn't get lonely in the middle of the night."

"Okay. Let's do it." Jody grabbed one side and Nicole the other as they carried it into the bedroom. She looked around the room after they set it down. Nicole's canopy bed against one wall took up most of the room. The nightstands on either side of the bed looked like solid mahogany and a matching chest of drawers took up much of the wall facing the foot of the bed. Closed doors on the wall opposite the entrance probably opened to a walk-in closet. A curtained off corner of the room could possibly be a dressing area.

Nicole pointed to an empty corner where Jody helped her set up the crate. "I'll be able to hear her if she whines."

Jody shook herself. She wanted to explore the closet and sit on the bed and see what kind of sheets Nicole liked. "You can always move it if it doesn't work out. Do you have a cushion for this huge crate?"

"I do. I talked to the salesperson at the store and she suggested a cushy flat flooring so I can easily clean up any messes she makes, and I have a good-sized bed for her."

"Okay." Jody took Nicole's hand and pulled her to the living room. "Sit for a minute. You look stressed out."

"I want her to be comfortable and safe, you know?"

"I do. And she is. You're going to be a great puppy mommy." Jody watched Tiny curled up asleep in her small carrying crate. "She looks pretty comfortable now." Jody finally felt Nicole relax next to her.

"Do you want a cup of tea? I didn't mean to drag you away from yours."

"I'm fine, and you didn't drag me away. I invited myself over."

"You did, didn't you? I'm glad. I appreciate your support."

"How long has it been since Tiny peed on the floor?"

"I don't know."

"Maybe you could take her outside and wait until she goes again. Then give her a treat and praise her. Hopefully, she'll get the idea soon that it's fun to go pee outside."

"I'll try it later." Nicole shifted, cupped her face, and kissed her.

Jody leaned into the kiss and her thoughts fled. She wrapped her arms around Nicole's waist and pulled her on top of her. All she could feel and all she wanted to feel was Nicole everywhere. She murmured in complaint when Nicole moved away and leaned back on the couch. She waited until her breathing returned to normal before speaking. "I think I better go home now."

"If you don't, I can't be responsible for your safety." Nicole stood and held out her hand.

Jody took it and let herself be pulled off the couch but resisted stepping into Nicole's arms. "Thanks for letting me come over and help with Tiny. I think you'll do great with her."

"Be careful driving home. I'll see you tomorrow."

Jody's raging desire settled as she drove home. She grinned at the memory of Nicole obsessing over her new puppy, and her heart rate soared at the memory of their kiss. She reheated her tea when she got back to her living room and tried to relax away her longing for Nicole's touch. The next morning, she woke before her alarm and her first thought was of Nicole. Was she awake yet? Did Tiny sleep all night? She rose to take a shower and head to work but stopped at her mother's first.

"Good morning, honey. You're up early today." Her mother poured two cups of coffee and set them on the table with two pieces of coffee cake.

"I woke up early for some reason so I stopped to say hi."

"I'm glad you did. How's Pete doing? I haven't heard you talk about him in a while."

"He's good. The store is doing well and we're getting more inventory this week." Jody took a bite of coffee cake.

"Tell him I said hello. I'll have to stop in and visit one day."

"I think he'd like that. I probably should get going. Thanks for the coffee and cake." She kissed her mom's cheek and left. Jody's thoughts strayed back to Nicole as she drove. She seemed overwhelmed by the little puppy, but Jody believed she'd settle down after a few days. They needed time to get to know each other. She didn't expect Nicole to meet her for lunch, but she'd eat at their picnic table in case. She concentrated on work until lunchtime and went outside, thrilled when she saw Nicole seated with an array of Chinese food cartons spread across the top of the table. "I'm glad you made it today. I didn't expect you."

"After all your help last night? The least I can do is bring you lunch. And I missed you."

"How's Tiny doing? Did you get any sleep last night?"

"She likes the big crate we put together. But I left her sleeping in the small one when I left."

"Won't she poop in it?"

"I don't know. She was quiet and content when I left. I did get her to go pee outside last night."

"Great. Did she know what she was doing? And why?"

"I don't know. I'll work with her more today. I've made a chart of her poop and pee schedule. When it's close to time, I'll take her outside until she goes. Hopefully, I can get her to understand what that means, and she'll let me know when she has to go."

"Let's eat and have no more talk of poo, please." Jody chuckled.

CHAPTER THIRTY

Tiny tipped her head and blinked while Nicole explained the process of using the backyard as a bathroom. Nicole sighed and considered a personal trainer for the puppy. She began to close the sliding door when Tiny walked to it and began to scratch it with her little paw. "Yes! Good girl." Nicole opened the door and waited while she bounded outside and squatted to pee in the grass. She clapped and did a little twirl as Tiny sniffed the ground and wandered a few feet away before returning and pawing the door to come in. She picked her up and twirled again with her in her arms. "Six days and you're a pro." She cuddled her for a few minutes before setting her on the floor and getting ready for work. She checked on her before she packed her lunch and found her sound asleep in her small crate. Before she left for the day, Nicole moved Tiny to the large crate in her bedroom. She had food, water, and a bed as well as a large enough area to move around. "I'll see you later, Tiny." She planned to pick an area in her office for another large crate so Tiny wouldn't be alone all day.

"Morning, Stacy." Nicole went to her office and found the perfect spot for the crate. She worked all morning and decided to stop home to let Tiny out at noon. Maybe a routine would be good for her. She gave Jody a quick call to let her know she would miss their picnic table lunch and headed home. She was on her way to her bedroom when she heard the sharp yelp. Tiny stood at the door of the crate and yelped again when she approached. "Hey, Tiny. Do you have to go outside?" Nicole repeated the question several times before opening the crate door and leading Tiny to the door wall. She opened the door while repeating the word in hopes Tiny would associate outside with potty outside. She rushed out and squatted as soon as she reached the grassy area. She looked back at Nicole and turned and ran in circles before coming back to the house. "You like this extra room and freedom don't you?" Nicole relaxed a little knowing Tiny was settling into her new home. "I'm going back to work now. You be a good girl, and I'll see you tonight." Nicole called Jody as soon as she got in her car.

"Hi, Nicole. How's the new puppy?"

"She's amazing. She's already going outside to pee. At least when I'm home."

"Are you going to be home about five thirty?"

"If you're coming over, I will be."

"I missed you at lunch, but I'll see you later."

"Yes. See you later, Jody." Nicole put her phone away and smiled all the way back to work.

She greeted Stacy and went to her office to check her email. "Finally." She opened the email from Dr. Rose, but shook her head in disappointment.

Ms. Bergeron. I wanted to give you an update on our progress regarding your missing file. The internet security firm has recovered everything that was lost. I'm reviewing every report in order of incident, and I'm certain I'll get yours to you by tomorrow. Sincerely, Dr. Rose, County M.E.

Nicole sent a thank you reply and went to talk to Roger about supplies. She finished the weekly payroll and checked the time. She planned to stop and pick up a crate for her office. "I'll see you tomorrow, Stacy," she called as she left. She picked out the crate at the pet store and bought a box of puppy training treats. She figured she needed all the help she could get. She parked in the garage a few minutes before Jody pulled into her driveway so she waited for her.

"Hi there." Jody handed her a shopping bag when she reached her. "Something for Tiny."

"Thanks." She laughed. "You think she needs anything else?" Nicole opened the door to the house and pointed to where Tiny sat in her crate which was nearly covered with dog toys.

"This one is special. She opened the bag and took out a dog food bowl with Tiny printed across it. It's her very own bowl." Jody smiled. "I had it made for her."

Nicole took the bowl, filled it with food, and replaced the one she'd been using. "Thank you." She kissed her lightly. "Watch this." She went to Tiny's crate and spoke "outside?" She opened the door to her crate and Tiny raced to the sliding door. She opened it and Tiny ran to the grass and peed. Nicole turned to Jody. "Impressed?"

"Absolutely. That's amazing for only six days. You must be working with her a lot."

"Actually, she's super smart. She started learning this after only a few days." Nicole shrugged. "Of course this helps." She gave Tiny one of her large breed puppy treats.

"Bribery I see." Jody squatted and Tiny scampered to her for petting. "She's a friendly one, too. You're doing great with her. I remember how shy she was in the shelter. I think she needed a place of her own without her litter mates competing for attention."

Nicole sat on the floor and Tiny climbed into her lap and began to chew her fingers. "No chew." Nicole squeezed her snout gently and pushed her away before giving her a chew toy. "She started this chewing thing recently. I bought her a few small chew toys so she doesn't begin on the furniture."

"Are you hungry?" Jody asked. "Because I'm starving."

"We can't have that." Nicole handed her a pile of takeout menus. "Pick one."

"Wow." Jody picked pizza. "I love that pizza."

Nicole put plates and napkins on the table. "Water, wine, beer, or Coke?"

"Water, thanks."

Nicole paid for the pizza when it was delivered and set the boxes on the table. "I'm glad you came over. I missed our lunch, too."

Jody swallowed before speaking. "I sure understand. Do you plan to take Tiny to work?"

"Yes. I bought another big crate today. Same as the one in the bedroom. I plan to try to train her to let me know if she has to go out during the day." Nicole finished her pizza and poured two glasses of wine. "Now that we have full bellies." She placed a glass in front of Jody.

"Thanks." Jody took a sip.

"Another movie tonight?" Nicole asked.

"I think maybe not if it's okay with you."

Nicole grinned. "No problem. Maybe next time."

"Let's sit on the couch. Where's Tiny?" Jody checked her crate and looked around the room.

Nicole smiled and pointed to the bedroom. "If given a choice, she chooses the big crate."

Jody peeked into the bedroom. "See what I mean," Nicole said. She didn't resist leaning toward Jody and resting her hands on her hips from behind.

Jody leaned back into her and Nicole nuzzled her neck. "Mm. That's nice." Jody turned in her arms and kissed her. Nicole wanted to walk her backwards to the bed, but she returned the kiss with her feet firmly planted on the floor.

"Maybe we should go back to the living room." Nicole nibbled on her ear as she spoke.

"Good idea," Jody said. "Are you allowing Tiny on the couch?"

"I hadn't thought about it." Nicole paused. "She's too small to jump up there yet."

"Are you sure?" Jody pointed to Tiny curled up in the middle of the couch.

"I guess she's making herself at home. I'm going to have to think about this." Nicole frowned.

"I think I'm going to leave you to it," Jody said. "Good luck."

Nicole walked her to her car and kissed her good-bye before going back inside to decide what to do about a poodle taking over her couch. She couldn't help but smile at the little dog stretched out in the middle. She settled next to her and rested her hand on her warm little body. At least she didn't shed. She'd let her stay. She finished watching the news and made sure Tiny went outside to pee before going to bed.

The next morning, she woke to Tiny whining. She got up and didn't have to say outside. She followed Tiny to the door and let her out, then went to make coffee. She put a few of her chew toys in the crate with her and closed the door before leaving for work. She headed directly for her office when she arrived and turned on her computer to check her email. Nothing from the ME yet. She worked until lunch and checked it again before leaving to meet Jody. She stopped on her way to pick up a couple of hamburgers, fries, and coleslaw.

"Hi, Nicole. I'm glad you came today." Jody smiled.

"It's another nice day. Let's enjoy it." She opened the bag and took out their meals.

"Thanks for bringing this." Jody took a bite.

"Sure. I thought we needed something different."

"It's perfect." Jody rested her hand on hers.

After they finished eating, Nicole packed up their wrappers and kissed Jody before she left. She stopped at Roger's office to check on how the new lockers were working out before she settled at her desk and checked her email again with no results. She made herself a cup of tea and set up Tiny's new crate in the corner of her office and made a note to pick up another big bed. After she finished, she decided she'd try her email one more time. She logged on and was about to disconnect when an email came through. "Finally."

The county medical examiner's office extends its sincere apologies for the delay in the final copy of the report for Harold Acosta issued one year ago. Please do not hesitate to call if you need anything else. Dr. Rose, County M.E.

Nicole downloaded the attached file and printed it. She reviewed it quickly, expecting it to match the preliminary copy. Her stomach roiled when she located the section for the toxicology results. "Oh, no. I'm so sorry, Jody."

CHAPTER THIRTY-ONE

Jody called to her mother from the door. "It's me, Mom."

"Come on in, dear. Mr. Grumbles has me trapped on the couch again." She was laughing when Jody sat next to her.

"I see who rules the roost in this house." She laughed with her mother. She immediately thought of Tiny taking over Nicole's couch. "Shall I heat up dinner?"

"Sure. I'll help." She stood and Mr. Grumbles vaulted off her lap and sat in the middle of the room grooming himself with one back leg raised.

"I passed on your dinner invitation to Nicole yesterday. She's looking forward to it."

"Good. I'd like to get to know her beyond the sadness."

"Yeah." Jody thought of Nicole and who she was besides the owner of the company where her father had worked and died. She was honest, down-to-earth, and gentle. She shook off her thoughts and helped her mother make dinner.

"Ashely's wedding is this weekend isn't it?" her mother asked.

"It is. I'll have to remind Nicole." Jody looked forward to dancing with her.

"Is she going as your date?" Her mother looked pleased.

"Yes. You're still planning to ride with me aren't you?"

"As long as you're okay with it."

"Of course, Mom."

Jody relaxed in the living room with her mom for a while after dinner before heading to the animal shelter. She waved to Hanna and picked up the cleaning supplies she needed.

"Hi, Jody," Bobbi called from one of the runs.

"Bobbi. Hello. How's Big Boy doing?"

"Excellent. Dr. Meyers let me bring him home yesterday. I'm keeping a close eye on him and he'll have a special diet for the rest of his life."

"That's great. I'll have to come over and visit him." She grinned at Bobbi's enthusiasm. She worked cleaning runs and helped feed and water animals before going home. She considered a trip to Sparks, but it held no appeal without Nicole. She poured herself a glass of wine and settled on the couch to call her.

"Hi, Jody. Everything okay?"

"Oh yes. I miss you. How's Tiny?"

"She's taken over the house, but doing well. Healthy and growing like a weed."

Jody heard a hesitation in Nicole's voice. "Are you okay? You sound...odd."

"I'm fine. I look forward to seeing you soon."

"Me, too. Mom is going to ride with us to Ashley's wedding. You're all right with that aren't you?"

"Absolutely. That'll be great. I look forward to it. Especially to holding you while we dance."

That sounded more like Nicole. "Okay. I'll see you at lunch tomorrow. Good night, Nicole."

"Sleep well. Jody."

Jody put her phone on her charger and finished her wine while watching the nightly news. Something niggled at her after her conversation with Nicole. She didn't know her as well as she'd like to, but she could tell there was definitely something bothering her. She rinsed her empty glass and put it in the dishwasher before heading to bed.

The next morning, Jody drove to work with Nicole on her mind. She was rich and beautiful, and probably had women falling at her feet wherever she went. It wouldn't be surprising if she found someone more interesting than her at Sparks, but she reminded herself of their conversation where they'd both expressed interest in only each other. By the time she got to work, her insecurity had her convinced that Nicole regretted their fledgling relationship and had moved on. She'd accepted Ashley's request to be her maid of honor with plans to go to the wedding alone but looked forward to bringing Nicole as her date. The more she thought about it, the more ridiculous it seemed from what she knew about Nicole, that she would drop her without an explanation. She laughed at herself and looked forward to their lunch. She checked the time and grabbed her lunch bag to head to the picnic table. Disappointment settled in her belly when Nicole wasn't waiting for her. She sat on the bench and lingered until the end of her lunch hour. She must've had something happen at work. She'd opened her bottle of water and checked her watch when the ring of her phone startled her. "Hi, Nicole. Everything all right?"

"Sorry I didn't call earlier, Jody. I'm not going to make it for lunch today. I'm swamped here today."

Jody forced the disappointment out of her voice. "I understand, but I'll miss you." She waited for Nicole's equivalent response.

"Take care."

Jody wiped away a tear, pocketed her phone, and went back to work. She finished for the day and stopped at the shelter on the way home. She cleaned runs and checked on the litter of kittens. All but three had been adopted and they were growing quickly. She couldn't figure out why the puppies were gone in days and kitten litters took much longer to adopt out. She played with them for a few minutes and left.

She sat in her car for a few minutes debating with herself. She finally decided she could wonder what was up with Nicole or do something to find out. She called her. Her voice mail answered after only one ring. "Hi, Nicole. I wanted to say hi and hoped maybe we could have dinner. I'm on my way home so call me anytime." She put her phone in her car's console and went home.

She made herself some soup and a ham sandwich and sat in front of the TV to eat. Nothing probably happened to Nicole because she talked to her at noon, but she definitely felt her withdrawal. Nicole was avoiding her for some reason, and she intended to find out why. She put her dishes in the sink and grabbed a bottle of water for the road as she went to her car. The first thing she heard was Tiny's puppy bark from the side fence. Then Nicole was standing in the driveway. "Hello," Nicole called.

"What's up, Nicole? I know something's wrong, and I'm not leaving until I find out what it is. I care about you too much to ignore your withdrawal."

Nicole stood quietly looking at her for a moment. "Please trust me, Jody. You'll understand in a couple of days."

"Did I do something? Do you have someone else?"

"God, no, Jody. Please give me two days." Nicole looked about to cry.

Jody hurried to her and took her hands in hers. "It's okay. It's okay." She cupped her face with her hands and kissed her. "You've got two days." She kissed her again before leaving.

She considered what it could possibly be that Nicole needed two days to work out. If she were in trouble, she'd tell her wouldn't she? She hoped Nicole would ask for help if she needed it. She'd give her the two days. But only two days. She poured herself a glass of wine when she got home and marked her calendar for two days. She tried to distract herself with her new book but read a few pages and couldn't remember what she read. She finished her wine and put her book aside. It was going to be a long two days.

The next morning, she immersed herself in work and managed to think of Nicole only a few times. She went to her favorite small restaurant for lunch and pushed away the memories of seeing Nicole with that pretty woman. She went back to work and concentrated on sales figures, accounts receivable, and accounts payable. She drove home thinking about two days. Would that be tomorrow or the day after? She shook off her ruminations and went to the animal shelter. "Hi, Bobbi. How's Big Boy?"

"He's fantastic." Bobbi beamed. "I laugh at myself when I go out to pick up his poop and remember the piles we used to pick up here."

"I'm glad he's working out for you. Do you know if anyone has adopted kittens? I would've thought they'd be long gone."

"I don't know. I think adult cats are more popular."

"Oh well. I'll feed them and scoop the litter box." Jody made sure the kittens were comfortable and went to feed the dogs. She lingered in hopes of seeing Nicole. "Hey, Bobbi. Have you seen Nicole today?"

"She was here early this morning for a little while."

"Okay. Thanks." Jody stopped at her mother's on the way home to avoid her empty apartment.

"Hi, honey." Her mother hugged her. "Is everything okay? You don't usually come by this late."

"Everything's fine. I wanted to say hello and have a cup of tea with my mom."

"Okay, dear. Anytime. I'll make the tea."

"Thanks, Mom." Jody sat at the dining room table surprised when Mr. Grumbles jumped onto her lap. "Well, hello." She stroked his back settled by its warmth and his purring. "Mr. Grumbles is getting friendlier. He's never sat in my lap before."

"He is. He did the same thing to the ladies in my book club. He's become a real love."

"I'm glad, Mom." Jody hoped visiting her mom would have taken her mind off Nicole, but it kept wandering to what she was doing and how Tiny was settling in. And what in the world was she doing for two days. She sighed.

"Are you all right, honey?"

"I am. I guess I'm tired. I worked hard today."

"It sounds like Pete's doing well. I'm glad. He and Harold were good friends. I remember when Pete and Julie had their first child."

"The store is doing well. I think their daughter, Renee, is coming on board as another salesperson." Jodi concentrated on the positive in her life. She vowed to stay grateful, even if Nicole decided to end their relationship, but she refused to believe that was happening. It wasn't who Nicole was. Two days. Whatever could happen in two days that she wouldn't talk about?

CHAPTER THIRTY-TWO

"A re you all right, Nicole?" Stacy asked. "You seem upset."
"I'm okay. Thanks, Stacy. I'll be out of the office for a few hours this morning."

"You're not sick are you?"

"No, I'm fine. I have some personal business to take care of today." Nicole stood and hugged Stacy before she left.

"Thank you, again for taking time for me, Dr. Rose." Nicole shook her hand, grateful the doctor had agreed to meet with her.

"No problem, Nicole. It's the least I can do after our huge computer issue. Come this way." She led Nicole through the morgue to her office. "These are all of my findings regarding the Acosta case." She went through each lab result explaining the process and conclusions. "This is the toxicology report I sent you yesterday."

"I appreciated it, but I've heard about cases of false positives regarding alcohol in cadavers."

"You're right. But that's if the person was deceased for over forty-eight hours. Mr. Acosta's toxicology test was done within hours of his death." She showed Nicole the lab report and noted the time and date. "I'm proud to say we have one of the best labs in the state."

"Thank you, again, Doctor. Could I get a hard copy of that lab report? I'm going to give all this information to the family tonight." Nicole put the paperwork into her briefcase and Dr. Rose's quiet, "good luck" followed her out the door. She sat in her car and closed her eyes for a few minutes. Jody's mother would be disappointed, but it was Jody's response that had her hesitating. She took a deep breath and called Mrs. Acosta to make an appointment with her and Jody for that evening. Her stomach clenched at the news she'd be delivering, but it wouldn't be fair to keep the information from them any longer. The rest of the day dragged as she checked the time every hour. She said good-bye to Stacy at five and stopped at home to let Tiny out before leaving. She parked in the Acostas' driveway behind Jody's car and reminded herself that they deserved to know what happened to Harold regardless of how difficult the news would be. She schooled her expression to what she hoped was compassionate and knocked on the front door. She nearly lost her composure when she saw Jody's puzzled expression as she opened the door and moved to let her inside.

"Please sit, Nicole. Can I get you a cup of tea or something?" Mrs. Acosta asked.

"No, thank you." She glanced at Jody and cringed at the wariness in her eyes. "I received the final coroner's report." She retrieved two copies from her briefcase and handed one to each of them and sat next to Mrs. Acosta as she reviewed it. "I'm so sorry." She rested her fingers lightly on her shoulder when she raised tear-filled eyes to her.

"This must have been difficult news for you to bring to us. Thank you for doing that." She dabbed at her tears with a napkin. "Is this point one-four a high number?"

"It is. He would have been extremely intoxicated." Nicole turned to Jody and flinched when she shook her head and glared at her. "I'm sorry, Jody, but I knew you'd want this information as soon as possible. The coroner wasn't available until today. That's why I needed the two days. I went to the medical examiner's office this morning to review and confirm everything." Nicole turned to Jody's mother, satisfied that she was all right, she reached for Jody's hand, but Jody yanked it away.

"You've done your duty. You can leave now." Jody opened the front door and stood waiting.

Nicole sat in her car to collect herself before heading home. She imagined it would be hard to find out her father's intoxication caused his accident, but Jody's reaction to push her away stung. She shook off her self-pity and considered Jody's feelings of loss. It must've felt like she was losing him all over again.

"Come on, Tiny. Let's go outside," she said as soon as she got home. She threw one of Tiny's balls across the yard and smiled when she raced after it. She hadn't quite learned the return part of the game yet so Nicole used one of her favorite treats to entice her. She sat on her couch with left over Thai food as Tiny snoozed next to her. She went to bed knowing she did the right thing by taking the information to the Acostas but wishing she hadn't had to. Jody needed time to accept the results and heal. She ignored the troubling notion that she'd lost Jody. Her frustration was giving her a headache. She couldn't let Jody go, but she'd give her time to grieve. She went to bed with a small piece of her heart broken.

Nicole arrived to work early the next day and coaxed Tiny into the cage in her office. She tossed in a few chew toys and filled her water bowl before going to Stacy's desk.

"Good morning, Nicole. You're here early." Stacy grinned and switched on her computer.

"Yeah. I brought Tiny with me today, but I wanted to let you know that last night I gave the Acosta family the final coroner's report on Harold's death."

"Are they doing okay?"

"It's been over a year, so they've already grieved. I'm sorry we had to reopen the wound, so to speak." She went to her desk and sent a note to Roger before heading to the locker area. She opened the first locker and moved aside a hanging shirt and picked up a pair of boots. She checked each locker top to bottom before returning to her office. There would be no more accidents if she could do anything about it. She updated her spreadsheet with the time and date of the locker inspection and took Tiny outside. "I'll be back in a few, Stacy." She walked along the side of the building with Tiny on her new leash. She stopped every ten feet and pushed her butt into a seated position and gave her a treat. After six times back and forth next to the building Tiny began to understand and sat automatically when Nicole stopped. She went back to work pleased with their training session.

"Welcome back, Nicole. How did Tiny do?" Stacy asked.

"Great. She's learning fast. I may skip the obedience classes if she does this well."

"Going to lunch today?"

"No. I'll stay in today." Nicole hesitated. Maybe Jody had calmed down. "Maybe I will go out." She checked her watch and left. She sat on the picnic table bench and took out the sandwich she'd brought. She began to drink her water and checked her watch again. Jody would've been there if she was coming. She finished her water and enjoyed the sunshine for a few minutes before wrestling back her disappointment and leaving.

"I'm back, Stacy." She continued to her office after speaking. "Hi, Tiny." She gave her a treat. "What do you think? Do you want to try obedience school?" Tiny tipped her head and blinked at her. Nicole concentrated on payroll and finished her day. She waved to Stacy as she left.

She considered a stop at the shelter but didn't want to make Jody uncomfortable if she was there. At the last minute, she turned and went to her brother's. "Would you like to meet your uncle Caleb?" She pulled into her brother's driveway and clipped on Tiny's leash.

"Hey, sis. This must be Tiny." He squatted and Tiny squirmed into his arms with her tail wagging. "She's friendly. That's a good thing."

"She is. She's smart, too."

"So, what brings you here tonight?"

"Got any more of that bourbon?"

"Hey. You okay?" He put his arm around her shoulders. "Come on in and tell me about it."

"Is it okay to bring Tiny inside?"

"Sure as long as she doesn't pee on the floor." Caleb poured bourbon in two glasses and handed one to Nicole when they got in the house.

"I got the final coroner's report on the Acosta case yesterday." She sipped her drink and Tiny settled on the floor at her feet. "It didn't go well when I took it to the family."

"What happened?" Caleb stretched to rest his feet on his coffee table.

"Mrs. Acosta accepted it graciously. Almost as if the results didn't surprise her. But Jody has completely shut me out." She swallowed the bourbon and poured herself another glass.

"Jody. She's the special one you really like."

"Yep. We had a standing date for lunch and she wasn't there today." Nicole resisted finishing her drink in one swallow. She placed a hand on Tiny's head and absorbed the heat from her body.

"Maybe she just needs time to accept the new information." Caleb moved to sit next to her. "If she cares about you, she'll come around."

"I hope you're right. I do believe she cares about me. She's hurting right now, and I'm powerless to help her." She swiped away a tear. "She won't let me and I don't know what to do."

"It sounds like it'll be up to her to come to you. All you can do is be available when she's ready."

"I'll try." Nicole finished her drink and hugged her brother. "Thanks for being here for me."

"Anytime. And bring Tiny with you. She's a pretty good little dog."

Nicole smiled for what felt like the first time all day. "She is." She went home and let Tiny outside before pouring herself a glass of wine, and plopping onto her couch.

CHAPTER THIRTY-THREE

Jody stood at the window at the back of the store and watched Nicole finish her lunch and check her watch. She bent to pet and talk to Tiny before collecting any food wrappers and looking toward the back door. She'd been at their picnic table every day since she'd delivered the devastating news about her father. Nicole looked so sad Jody almost gave in. Her mother had taken the news well and had returned to work at the local Laundromat. She reconnected with friends she'd worked with and had begun to smile more often. Jody had a difficult time concentrating at work, had only stopped at the animal shelter once, and missed Nicole constantly.

Her father's death had nothing to do with Nicole. She was only the messenger of the disturbing news, but Jody's pain of his loss and anger at his decision to drive while so intoxicated overwhelmed her and she shut down emotionally. It was easier to convince herself she didn't care about anything or anybody than to face the agony of losing another loved one. She watched Nicole lead Tiny back to her car and glance back once before leaving. Jody went back to work, and when she finished her day, she headed to her mother's.

"Hello, honey. I'm glad you came by. I've been worried about you." Her mother set a cup of tea in front of her on the table. "I've made homemade chicken noodle soup." She dished out the soup into two bowls and set a bowl of salad in the middle of the table.

"Thanks, Mom."

"You need to cheer up, Jody. Life goes on and I think you miss Nicole. Has she contacted you?"

Jody thought of Nicole's daily presence at their picnic table. "No."

"You probably scared her away." Her mother dished them both some salad. "And she's probably waiting for you to make the first move."

"Yeah. She isn't pushing." Jody poked at her salad. "I'm going to Ashley's rehearsal dinner tomorrow. I'll say hello to her for you."

"Thank you. I'm looking forward to her wedding."

Jody smiled at her mother's enthusiasm and wished she could muster some eagerness for it. She helped her mom clean up after dinner and stopped at the shelter on the way. She missed the animals and the friends she'd made volunteering.

"Hi, Jody," Hanna called from one of the runs. "I haven't seen you in a while. Are you doing okay? Nicole hasn't been here either. How's she doing?"

"I'm fine, Hanna. Just busy. Nicole's okay." She hoped Hanna wouldn't ask anything more. She picked up cleaning supplies and went to visit the kittens. Her disappointment surprised her when she saw the room empty. "What happened to the kittens?" she asked Hanna.

"The last two were adopted a few days ago." Hanna grinned. "I took one of them. He's a sweet little orange tabby with green eyes. I've named him M because of the M on his forehead. It's a genetic thing tied to his tabbiness." Hanna continued with all the facts she'd learned about orange tabbies.

"I'm glad you have him." Jody finished cleaning and went home to her empty apartment. She made herself a cup of chamomile tea and turned on the TV. She watched the news but didn't remember anything she heard. Her thoughts were filled with memories of her first kiss with Nicole in her kitchen. She rose and washed her cup before getting ready for bed.

The next morning, Jody made breakfast and relaxed on her couch with the morning news. She used to look forward to weekends. Endless time to shower and dress in the morning, lingering over coffee, and no thoughts of what waited for her on her desk at work. Today she felt restless and struggled to fill her time before Ashley's dinner. She attributed her unrest to her nervousness at the upcoming wedding. She'd never stood up in a wedding before, and Ashley was her best friend so she didn't want to disappoint her. She practiced a few dance steps presuming she'd have to dance with the best man. The last time she'd danced with a male was at her high school prom. That thought only managed to depress her more as she remembered dancing with Nicole. The feel of her arms around her and their bodies pressed together drove her to abandon her coffee, shower, dress, and head to the shelter. Seeing the animals and cleaning would clear her mind. She waved to Bobbi and went to work.

"Hey, Jody," Bobbi called from outside the run. "Haven't seen you lately, and Nicole hasn't been here either. "You okay?"

"I'm fine." Jody leaned on the wall and faced Bobbi. "How's Big Boy doing?" She ignored the Nicole comment.

Bobbi grinned. "He's such a love. I thought a big dog wouldn't be cuddly but he is. I don't allow him on my couch, but when I sit there, he rests his head in my lap. I love to see him relax and close his eyes when I pet him. I don't know why I never had a dog before."

"I think the time wasn't right until the right dog came along. I'm happy for you." Jody smiled at the picture in her mind Bobbi had painted. She finished cleaning and began to fill food and water bowls. She and Bobbi sat on lawn chairs to visit and enjoy the nice morning for a while before she checked the time and left. She drove home and turned her thoughts to Ashley's rehearsal event. Her phone pinged with a missed message and she set her phone aside. She'd read Nicole's fourth message later. The rehearsal was scheduled for three, so she took another shower to wash off the animal shelter and dressed before heading to the church.

"Hi, Jody," Ashley called to her from the church parking lot.

"Hi." She locked her car and followed Bill and Ashley into the church. She smiled at the young man she was introduced to as James, Bill's friend and best man. He seemed nice enough and spoke fondly of his girlfriend. She relaxed and listened closely to the instructions from the minister. They practiced the walk down the aisle and the handoff of the ring, before thanking the minister and leaving. "Are you nervous?" Jody whispered to Ashley.

"Not too much now that I know what to expect." She looked side to side and spoke softly, "I can't wait for the honeymoon." She grinned.

Jody laughed. They must be waiting for their marriage vows to consummate their relationship. She drove herself to the restaurant and settled in her assigned seat next to James. "This is nice." She looked around the room as she spoke.

"It is," James agreed. "I know Bill raves about the food here."

Jody relaxed and waited for the bride- and groom-to-be to take their seats. She grinned at James as he stood with his water glass raised. "To the bride and groom and to their many years and long life together." The few patrons nearby raised their glasses and called out their good wishes. She was thrilled for her friend as she raised her glass. She waited for most everyone to finish their meal before excusing herself and leaving. She checked the time. Her mother would still be at work. She went home, poured herself a glass of wine, and relaxed with a book. She tossed the book aside after rereading the same page several times. The wedding was in a couple of days and Nicole had been excited to be her date. She sighed. The hollowness she felt at the loss of Nicole in her life had to end eventually, didn't it? How could she ever survive if she lost her? Jody spent the rest of the weekend concentrating on the animal shelter and forced herself to ignore Nicole at the picnic table all week. She woke early the following Saturday and showered before heading to her hair appointment. The appointment was early so she put her dress and shoes in a clothes bag and went to her mother's.

"Hello, dear. You're here early."

"I am. I hope it's okay, but I thought we could have lunch. The reception and dinner are a few hours away."

"It's fine. I'm glad to see you anytime." She made grilled cheese sandwiches and tomato soup. "Your hair looks beautiful."

"Thank you." Jody pushed away the memory of the look in Nicole's eyes when she'd seen her with her hair up at the fundraiser.

Her mother checked the time and stood. "I'm going to take a shower and get dressed."

"Okay, Mom. I'll put the dishes away and get dressed, too." Jody finished quickly and went to her childhood bedroom to dress. She sat on the bed engulfed with memories of her father tucking her in at night and reading to her. She missed him. She always would. She held back tears and dressed for the wedding.

Jody led her mother to the car and drove to the church. "I'll see you later." Jody squeezed her mother's hand and went to join the wedding party. She smiled at Ashley's nervousness and at the photographer. The ceremony was beautiful and shorter than she anticipated, and she waved to Ashley and Bill as she left to meet her mother and make the short ride to the hall. "Here we are." Jody stepped out of the car and followed her mother into the room where they chose a table close to the dance floor.

"This is very nice," her mother said.

"It is." Jody tried to relax and ignore her longing to have Nicole with her.

"I want to tell you something, honey." Her mother looked more serious than she'd ever seen her.

"Okay." Jody gave her mom her total attention.

She shifted her silverware side to side before she began to speak. "Your father and I were eighteen when we met. The legal drinking age was twenty-one, but your dad showed up at my parents' house drunk several times. I didn't realize how bad his drinking habit was until he almost drove us off the road one day. I asked him if he'd been drinking and he told me he only had one beer." Her mother took her hand. "His drinking got worse over the years instead of better until I threatened him with divorce if he didn't quit." She reached into her purse and set a large coin on the table.

Jody picked it up and turned it over in her hand. "I don't know what this is."

"It's your father's one-year AA chip. He was so proud of it." Her mother looked a mile away. "He attended meetings for years and never had a slip that I was aware of. I needed to tell you this, honey. I don't know why he would have drunk that day at work, but I believe that he did."

Jody took a deep breath and handed the chip to her mother.

She pushed it back. "You keep it. Know that he loved you very much."

CHAPTER THIRTY-FOUR

Nicole picked up Tiny from the groomer's and went directly to the obedience class. She'd been attending for a week and made good progress. Her goal was to get Tiny to a place she could be trusted off-leash, and she was getting close. She concentrated on Tiny and tried to forget she'd planned to be at Ashley's wedding with Jody that night. She ignored the niggling pain that she might be dancing with someone else. She took Tiny through all of her commands and watched her perform flawlessly. "Good girl." Tiny wiggled her whole butt when Nicole talked to her and hugged her. "Let's go home."

Nicole let her out when she got home and settled on her couch with a glass of brandy. She sipped it while she watched TV and ignored thoughts of Jody in her arms as they danced. She let Tiny in and repositioned herself to make room for her on the couch. "You know this is not a good idea. You're supposed to be curled up on the floor." She wound her fingers in Tiny's hair as she spoke. "Do you think Jody's thinking about me?" She finished her brandy. "If she is, I hope they're happy thoughts." She refilled her glass. "I don't understand. She's probably upset to find out Harold was drunk and at fault for his accident, but I'm not responsible." She realized she was babbling but didn't care. Tiny listened. Nicole knew better than to waste time feeling sorry for herself, so she drank a bottle of water before changing and headed to Sparks.

Nicole wound her way through the crowd of women when she arrived and strolled to the bar. She ordered a beer and sipped as she scanned the room. Her gaze landed on Hanna and Emma at one of the small tables. Hanna waved and motioned to their table as she pulled over an extra chair. Nicole smiled and went to sit with them. "Hi there."

Emma nodded to her and smiled while she held Hanna's hand.

Nicole was happy for them as she ignored a pang of loneliness.

"Is Jody with you?" Hanna asked as she looked around.

"No. She had a wedding tonight."

"Oh yeah. Her friend, Ashley. But, she said you…" Her voice trailed off and she blushed.

Nicole drank her beer and remained quiet.

"It's good to see you again, Nicole," Emma said.

"You, too." Nicole meant it. She and Hanna made a good pair and looked happy. She sat to watch the dancers for a while and went home. She let Tiny out and checked the time. Jody would probably still be at the reception dancing with who knew who. She had to try to let her go. Somehow. She let Tiny back in and filled a glass half full with brandy. After all, she didn't have to work tomorrow.

Nicole woke to Tiny's whine and a throbbing headache. She rolled off the couch and let her out before getting a bottle of water and taking an aspirin. Tiny raced around the yard for a few minutes before returning to the sliding door to come in. Nicole took a shower, closed her eyes, and let the water flow over her head. She chastised herself for over-indulging and using Jody's withdrawal as an excuse. She knew Jody was hurting and all she'd done was feel sorry for herself instead of trying to support her. But, Jody had pushed her away. Nicole wasn't one to give up easily so she finished her shower and dressed. After breakfast, she watched the news with a cup of coffee and considered her next move. She couldn't force Jody into anything, but she couldn't let her go either. She sighed in frustration and reviewed plans for her next fundraiser to shift her thoughts away from the discomfort of her loss. She emailed the request to reserve the venue and made an appointment with her party planner before grabbing her camera and heading to the animal shelter.

"Hey, Nicole," Bobbi called. "I haven't seen you for a while."

"I've been working. How're things around here? And how's Big Boy?"

Bobbi beamed. "He's great, and things are good here. The kittens were all adopted, but we got another litter of puppies. At least they're not newborns."

"Thanks. I'm planning my next fundraiser so I'll be poking around taking pictures today."

"Let me know if you want to do a follow-up on Big Boy. He'd love to pose for you."

"I like that idea, Bobbi, thanks. Let me know when and I'll be there." Nicole wrote herself a note to follow up on the idea. She spent a couple of hours photographing the dogs and few cats before making an appointment with Bobbi and leaving. The first thing she did when she got home was phone the party planner and arrange for an extra table for her *after adoption* photos. Tiny and Big Boy would be the stars. She made another note to check with the obedience instructor. Their presence at the fundraiser might attract business and help the newly adopted dogs. She downloaded the latest photos and spent the rest of the day creating posters and flyers. The work distracted her from thoughts of what Jody might be doing. She organized her files and printed out several copies of flyers to post. She worked until dinnertime and went to her brother's.

"Hi, sis."

"Are you up for pizza, and I need a change of scenery."

"Pizza sounds great."

Nicole sat across from her brother at the tiny eatery. "It's been a long time since we ate here."

"It has. So, what's up with you?"

Nicole's first thought was to deny anything was up, but Caleb knew her better than anyone. "I gave the Acostas the final ME report. It shows Harold's blood alcohol concentration was point one-four."

"Wow. That's pretty high, isn't it?"

"It is. Jody was upset and pretty much kicked me out of the house. Now she won't return my calls or texts. I haven't seen her since, and I miss her. A lot." Nicole refused to shed her tears in the restaurant.

"Huh. Maybe she needs time to accept the results."

"Yeah, maybe." Nicole took a bite of pizza and swallowed. "I feel sort of lost." She gave up and used her napkin to wipe away her tears.

"Hey. You're a great catch. I bet she'll realize what she's losing and contact you soon." Caleb squeezed her hand gently.

"I hope so." Nicole picked up another piece of pizza and put it back. Her appetite had fled. She hugged Caleb good-bye after they got back to his house and accepted the leftover pizza to take home. She set it on the counter and chuckled at Tiny with her nose in the air trying to identify the scent. "It's called people food." She gave Tiny one of her doggy treats in hopes of appeasing her. She went to bed feeling a little more settled about her Jody situation.

The next morning, she packed the leftover pizza in her insulated lunch bag and took it to work. She refused to give up hope Jody might show up. "Morning, Stacy," she said as she took Tiny to her crate.

"Morning, Nicole. And good morning to you, Tiny. Did you have a good weekend?" Stacy stood in her office doorway.

"It was okay. I finalized plans for my next fundraiser."

"I'm going to try to make it to this one." She smiled and went back to her desk.

Nicole worked until noon and headed to the picnic table. Tiny jumped onto the bench seat next to her and sat facing her. She set a paper plate with a piece of pizza on it across from her on the table along with a napkin and put a piece on her plate. She hoped Jody was at work and would join her, but the back door never opened. "I guess we're on our own," she said. She finished her pizza and turned her face to the sun for a few minutes before finishing her water and packing up Jody's piece of pizza. "Let's go, Tiny." Tiny jumped off the bench and sat to wait for her. "You are getting to be a real expert. Maybe I'll let you show off for our fundraiser." She went back to work ignoring her disappointment at not seeing Jody. She forced her thoughts to work as she drove and spent the afternoon at her desk. She waved good-bye to Stacy when she left and sat in her car debating with herself for a few minutes before she made the decision. She parked in front of Jody's apartment building and wrote down the words she wished she could speak to Jody.

Jody, I'm sorry for the results of the final ME report, and I'm certain it had to be hard to hear. I can't do anything to change it, but I hope you let me be there for you. I care about you very much, and I miss you. Please let me know you're okay. Nicole

She folded the note and slipped it into an envelope with Jody's name on it before taping it to her door. She forced back tears as drove away. She pulled into her garage and let Tiny out into the backyard before heating up the last piece of pizza and retrieving a beer. She finished eating and took Tiny through her obedience exercises before feeding her. Then she put her phone on the charger in her bedroom and went to watch TV. She flipped through the channels until she found the movie channel and settled to watch a comedy.

CHAPTER THIRTY-FIVE

Jody walked back to her desk away from the window. She hadn't expected Nicole to come back after being stood up for the wedding. Jody wasn't proud of her behavior. It wasn't fair and it wasn't the way she'd want to be treated. She sat at her desk and tried to evaluate her feelings. She was angry and hurt. She felt deceived and frustrated. Nicole had done nothing except her job. It was her father she felt betrayed by, but she had loved her father. He was gone and Nicole was the only one left for her to lash out at. Sadness took over her anger and she went to the restroom where she broke down and sobbed. She took a few minutes to compose herself and finished her workday before leaving and heading to her mom's. "Hi, Mom," she called from the doorway.

"Hello, dear. I'm in the living room."

Jody smiled at her mother on the couch with Mr. Grumbles in her lap. "He's holding you hostage again, isn't he?"

She laughed. "He is. But I'm not struggling. Are you all right, honey?" She gently nudged her cat off her lap and stood.

"I am. I'm sad, you know?"

"Do you want to talk about it?"

"Maybe." Jody sat next to her mother on the couch. "I feel, I don't know, deceived maybe. I don't know much about addiction to alcohol, but I had a friend in college who told me one night that he was a member of AA. He called himself 'a drunk.' I'm angry at dad. Does that make any sense?"

Her mother chuckled. "Perfect sense. I was so pissed at him I filed for divorce."

"But you didn't divorce him."

"No. I loved him and he took his sobriety seriously. He worked hard at it and I trusted him."

Jody leaned back on the couch and closed her eyes. She smiled when her mother wrapped her in a hug. "We'll be okay."

"Yes, honey, we will."

"I'm going to head home. Do you need anything?"

"No. I'm good. Get some rest. You look tired."

"Call if you need me." Jody left and went straight home. She hesitated and looked side to side when she saw the envelope taped to her door. She took it inside and set it on the counter while she heated her dinner. She carried both to the living room couch and opened the envelope before eating. She held back tears and whispered, "Oh, Nicole. I miss you, too." She took a deep breath and sent her a text, *I miss you, too. Lunch tomorrow?* and put her phone down while she finished her dinner.

It was almost midnight before Jody fell asleep after checking for a reply text several times. Maybe Nicole had finally given up on her. She fixed her lunch the next morning and added an extra sandwich for Nicole in case she showed up. She checked her phone before heading to work and watched the clock all morning. At noon, she went to the picnic table and set Nicole's wrapped sandwich on a paper plate across from her and hers on her plate. She checked her watch after ten minutes and struggled to stay optimistic about Nicole's arrival as she drank her water. Nicole had waited for her the whole lunch hour every day. She could wait that long for her. She took a bite of her sandwich and watched the parking lot for her car. She was halfway finished when she saw the Mercedes race into the lot and Nicole jump out.

She held eye contact as she hurried toward her. "I didn't get your text until this morning at work." She sat next to her. "Are you all right?"

"I am, and I'm sorry if I worried you." She pointed to the sandwich. "I brought you a sandwich."

Nicole reached across the table and picked up the sandwich before shifting so their thighs met. "I missed you."

"Yeah. Me, too. I'm sorry about the wedding. It was insensitive of me to shut you out without explanation."

"I'm glad you're okay. I worried when you took the news so hard. Is your mom all right?"

"She is. Are you going to be home tonight?"

"Yes."

"Can I come over and tell you all about it?"

"I'd like that. I'll roast a chicken."

"I'll bring a bottle of wine." Jody's world righted and she grinned. She finished her sandwich and enjoyed the time with Nicole until she had to go back to work. "I'll see you tonight."

Nicole stood, reached for her hand, and pulled her into her arms. Her kiss was light, but it ignited a burning desire in the pit of Jody's stomach. She took a wobbly step back and stroked Nicole's cheek before forcing herself to go back to the building. The afternoon dragged for Jody. She finished her workday and stopped to buy a bottle of her favorite wine on her way home. They hadn't set a time, but she knew Nicole usually got off work by five thirty, so she watched the five o'clock news before leaving.

"Hi." Nicole leaned against the doorframe as Jody walked toward her, and Jody couldn't stop herself from drawing her into a kiss as soon as she reached her. She stepped into the house and realized how hungry she was when the scent of cooking chicken reached her.

"Dinner smells great," she said and handed Nicole the bottle of wine.

"It'll be ready soon. Would you like to start with the wine?" Nicole seemed hesitant. Almost nervous.

"Sure. Where's Tiny?" Jody looked out the sliding door to the backyard and laughed when Tiny raced from around the house to stand at the door watching her with her tail wagging furiously. "Can I let her in?"

"Absolutely." Nicole set two glasses of wine on the dining room table. "Want to see her newest trick?"

"Later." Jody rested her arms on Nicole's shoulders and pressed her body against her as she kissed her. "I have one of my own to show you." She walked her backwards until Nicole was trapped between her and the kitchen counter.

"Mm. I like your tricks." Nicole pulled her close and spun her around so Jody was against the counter. "I have a couple, too."

"I think we have a win-win situation here."

"And I think if we're not going to take this to the bedroom, we should have dinner." Nicole sounded breathless.

Jody took a deep breath and nodded before following Nicole to the table. "That chicken does smell pretty good." She watched Nicole take the chicken out of the oven and cut it into pieces and set a bowl of salad on the table. "You're pretty handy." She held herself back from standing and pulling Nicole back into her arms.

"Ha. Remember when I told you I didn't cook? This is an anomaly, trust me."

"So, you did this to impress me?" Jody grinned.

Nicole tipped her head sideways and looked to be deep in thought. "Umm. Yes." She laughed and sat across from her at the table.

After dinner, Jody snuggled next to Nicole on the couch with a glass of wine. "This is nice. Thanks for letting me invite myself over."

"It is nice." Nicole kissed her forehead. "I'm glad you did. Do you still feel like you want to talk?"

"I do." Jody took a moment to collect her thoughts. "Have you ever found out someone you loved and respected wasn't who you thought them to be?"

"I presume you're referring to you and your father. No, I haven't, but I think I can understand it."

"I grew up with Dad always being there for us. He went to work and brought home his paycheck. The only thing he did away from us was a weekly bowling team. Mom told me last week that those were his AA meeting days. He never did bowl. He and Mom bought a house and had friends and raised me to be a responsible adult." Jody took a sip of wine. "Now I find out he was a drunk. Mom had to file for divorce to get him to quit drinking." She reached in her pocket and took out the AA chip to show Nicole. "Mom gave this to me. It was Dad's."

"He was in AA, and he was trying to stay sober. I only knew your dad for the years he worked for our company, and he was a responsible, hard worker."

"I know he was. That's why I'm struggling to figure out why it happened. I feel deceived."

Nicole took her glass from her and set it on the end table before pulling her into arms. "I can understand that. I'd probably feel the same. I don't know why some people can have a few drinks and stop and others can't, but addiction to alcohol can ruin lives. I'm so sorry you lost your father to it."

Jody absorbed her tender words and the warmth of Nicole's body and let her tears fall. She shifted and sat up before she spoke. "Sorry. I'm certainly a fun date tonight." She sniffled.

Nicole handed her a napkin. "It all right, sweetheart. I'm sure I'd be in the same shape if it were me. Do you feel up to some ice cream?"

"Yeah!"

"Wait here." Nicole went to the freezer and returned with two small cartons of chocolate chip ice cream. "Here you go." She handed her the ice cream and a spoon.

"Did you know this was my favorite?"

"No. I asked your mom." She grinned. "But it's mine, too."

Nicole stood and pointed to the bedroom and Tiny slinked to her crate.

"I forgot about her." Jody watched Nicole give her a doggy treat.

"I've been working with her to keep her from begging, and she's doing well except when there's ice cream involved. She loves it." Nicole settled back on the couch and Jody leaned against her and finished her ice cream thinking about ice cream and love.

CHAPTER THIRTY-SIX

Nicole had hoped Jody would've stayed the night, but she couldn't push. She'd felt Jody's anguish as she spoke of her father and tried to make sense of a senseless accident. She'd done what felt right. She held her and let her express her feelings. She let Tiny out for the last time that night and went to bed. She tossed and turned trying to dispel her arousal from the feel of Jody wrapped in her arms kissing her. She'd nearly come when she pushed her against the kitchen counter and taken her lips as if she owned them. She sighed realizing she wanted Jody to own them. She wanted her to own all of her. She finally fell into a dreamless sleep and woke early to Tiny's whimpers. She let her outside and ate breakfast before showering and dressing. Her thoughts never strayed far from Jody as she drove to work, and she smiled when she thought of seeing her at the picnic table. The morning seemed to drag as she reviewed payroll and supply issues. At noon, she put a leash on Tiny and left for lunch. Jody sat at the table and smiled at her when she arrived. "I have leftover chicken." She set her insulated bag on the table and sat next to Jody.

"Thanks for bringing it. All I had at home was peanut butter and jelly." Jody leaned and kissed her.

"Your kisses may be all I need for lunch." Nicole warned herself not to push. "How are you doing today? You experienced some strong feelings last night."

"I'm a little tired." She tipped her head and looked at her. "It was good, though. I needed to talk about it all. Thank you for listening."

"Anytime, sweetheart. I want to be there for you. I hope you trust me." She set the chicken sandwiches out on a paper plate. "Help yourself."

"I had a hard time getting to sleep last night." Jody held her gaze. "I wanted you so much, I ached."

"Yeah. I had the same problem. You're all I can think about." Tiny chose that moment to try to reach her sandwich. "No." Nicole firmly pushed her nose away. "Sorry, I'll be right back." She led her to a nearby tree and tied her long lead to it.

"She's got other ideas of where your attention should be." Jody giggled.

"She does love chicken. I never should have given her a taste."

Jody took a bite of her sandwich. "Mm, this is even better the second day. So, when's your next fundraiser?"

"Saturday. It's going to be a good one, I hope. I've got shots of Tiny, Big Boy, and Hanna's kitten, M. They'll be on their own table marked *after adoption*. I also plan to have a representative from Tiny's obedience school there. She might bring one of her pupils to show off. Jaylin said she could bring Railroad if I wanted. I've never had live dogs there, so I'm a little nervous."

"I think it sounds fantastic. Do you need help setting up?"

"Nope. The party planner is doing it all. All I had to do was let her know what I wanted. Will you go with me?"

"I definitely plan to be there. You mean ride with you?"

"If you want to I'd like that. I mean like my date."

Jody took her hand. "Nicole. Remember after the last fundraiser? I told you you're the only one I wanted to be with. To be kissing. That hasn't changed except maybe the feelings got stronger. You said the same thing. Of course I'll go with you. Be with you as your date."

Nicole grinned all the way back to work. She finished out her day and stopped at the shelter to help clean.

"Hi, Nicole. How's Tiny doing?" Hanna asked.

"Great. How's little M?"

"He's settled in. I had no idea how much I'd enjoy a cat in my lap."

"That's great. I hope you bring him Saturday. I think he'd capture quite a few hearts."

"I'm planning on it. Umm, shall I ask how Jody's doing?"

Nicole grinned. "I had lunch with her today, and she'll be with me Saturday."

"I'm so glad. I worried you know?"

"It's all good. Thanks, Hanna. Say hi to Emma, and I'll see you Saturday."

Nicole drove home contemplating relationships. She'd dated many women through the years but never anyone long-term. Now she wondered why that was. There had been quite a few who wanted to be seen with her but never showed any interest in becoming serious, and she'd learned not to count on anyone sticking around except for her money. Jody couldn't care less about her money or social status, and it was a refreshing change. She smiled all the way home. "Come on, Tiny." She let her into the backyard and went to make dinner, before calling Jody.

"Hi, there."

"Hey, Jody. I wanted to hear your voice."

"It's good to hear yours, too. I stopped at the shelter on my way home and Hanna told me she saw you there."

"Yeah. I put in a little time. Tonight I plan to finalize plans for the fundraiser."

"Need some help?"

"Always." Nicole grinned. "Especially yours."

"Only mine. Remember? I don't like to share."

"Just get over here. I'll leave the back door unlocked." Nicole didn't try to contain her excitement. She printed several flyers and created a few extras of the newest animals at the shelter. She closed down her computer and went to wait for Jody.

"Hello," Jody called from the doorway.

"We're in the living room." Nicole waited for Jody to enter the room and pulled her into her arms. "I missed you."

Jody leaned into her and cradled her head with her hands while she kissed her. Her moan was Nicole's undoing. She slid her hands from Jody's waist to her ass and pulled her against herself. Jody shifted slightly and her thigh pressed against Nicole's center. She forced her knees not to buckle as she absorbed the sensation rippling through her.

"I'm having a hard time standing," Jody whispered in her ear.

"Me, too." Nicole grabbed her hand and led her to her bed. "Okay?"

"Yes." Jody sat on the side of the bed, pulled her on top of her, and rolled over. She squirmed and whimpered when Nicole slid her hand under her shirt and circled her nipple over her bra with her thumb. "Oh…wait."

Nicole instantly withdrew her hand. "What is it, sweetheart?"

"I do want this, but…"

"It's okay. We can wait."

"I'm nervous. This changes our relationship. A lot."

"How 'bout if we wait until we can spend the night together? I'd love to wake up with you next to me."

"That sounds good." Jody kissed her. "I do want you. I think I just need some time."

"I know, and it's going to be incredible whenever you're ready." She kissed her quickly and gently tugged her off the bed. "Want to see what I've got ready for the fundraiser?" Nicole hoped the change of subject helped Jody relax. She took her hand and led her to her office.

Jody sifted through the pile of flyers. "Nice. I like it. I think you'll get quite a few donations with these."

"I hope so. I think it'll be fun to have the obedience event there."

"Me, too."

"Shall we watch a movie?" Nicole asked.

"I think I'll head home." Jody stroked her cheek and kissed her lightly. "See you tomorrow."

Nicole locked the door after Jody left and decided to relax on her bed and read. Memories of the feel of Jody's body interfered with her concentration and she set the book aside, turned off the light, and went to sleep.

The next morning, she stopped at Stacy's desk on her way to her office. "Any mail for me?"

"Yes." She handed her a few envelopes. "There's one from Nancy Acosta. Maybe it's the lawsuit release."

"I'm sure it is. Jody told me the other day her mother signed it." Nicole opened the envelope when she got to her desk and reviewed the paperwork before filing it away. It was why she'd met Jody. She reflected on the rocky start to their relationship and how far it had progressed and how close she felt to her now. She saw it as a positive that had come from tragedy and hoped Jody felt the same way. She finished her weekly locker inspection and helped Roger with inventory before leaving for lunch. She sat next to Jody on the picnic table and took her hand. "How's your day going?"

"It's okay. Business has slowed since our big sale last month, but I'm keeping busy. How's yours? And where's Tiny?"

"I had all new lockers installed so every employee has their own and I've begun weekly inspections of the lockers. I left Tiny in her crate. Stacy loves to talk to her and let her out to wander around. Eventually, I'll be able to let her loose all day."

"How're your plans for the fundraiser?"

"All done. I like not having to do the setup. I'll pick you up about five and you can help me arrange the posters and flyers."

"Sounds good. I'm looking forward to it." She stood and pulled Nicole off the bench.

"I'll talk to you tonight," Nicole said and went to her car. Nicole finished her workday and started on her way home. Halfway there she took a different route. She pulled into the Acosta driveway and took a deep breath. "I hope this is a good idea." Unknowing what to expect, she went to the front door and knocked.

"Nicole. Come in. I was having a cup of coffee. Can I get you one?"

Nicole's tension eased. "Thank you, Mrs. Acosta. I'd love a cup. I came by to make sure you were doing all right."

"I'm fine, dear, but it's nice of you to check on me, and please call me Nancy." She set the coffee cup on the end table. "Jody was upset for a while, but I think she got over it."

"I talked to her the other day and she seemed to feel better about the outcome. Thank you for mailing the release papers." Nicole sipped her coffee and relaxed.

CHAPTER THIRTY-SEVEN

"Hi, Tiny. Where's your mom?" Jody looked for Nicole in her yard as she spoke to Tiny. She went to the door when she didn't see her, rang her bell, and waited.

"Hi there. Come on in." Nicole pulled her into her arms and kissed her.

"I came to help with flyers." She pressed closer enjoying the warmth of her body. "I wanted to thank you for checking on my mom. She appreciated your visit."

"No problem. I know it was difficult news for both of you. Come on, I'll show you what I have." Nicole led her to her office and pointed to a table where she had all the posters and flyers displayed. "This is my favorite." She indicated a smaller table with shots of Tiny, and Big Boy. Next to it she'd put a framed picture of Hanna's kitten. "I think these show how happy and healthy the adopted animals can be."

"It's great. I'm looking forward to it." Jody looked closer at the pictures. "You're good at this."

"Did you have dinner yet?"

"Nope."

"Good, because I made something today."

"You cooked? Again?"

"I did. Caleb dared me to make macaroni and cheese, so I did." Nicole looked so proud of herself that Jody laughed.

"I have to see this. Let's eat." Jody followed Nicole to the kitchen. "I'm impressed." Jody watched Nicole spoon out the food. "You made this from scratch?" She spoke in between bites. "It's very good." After dinner Jody cleared the table while Nicole loaded the dishwasher. The domestic scene and her ease of settling into it, took her by surprise.

"Were the flyers the only reason you came over tonight?" Nicole asked as she settled on the couch next to Jody and turned on the TV.

"I wanted to see you."

"I'm glad. I have a new movie if you're interested."

"One more thing." Jody took Nicole's hand. "I brought an overnight bag." She grinned.

"I am pretty tired from all that cooking. Maybe we should go to bed early tonight."

Jody spoke softly, "I like that idea."

"Shall we have a glass of wine first?"

"Yes, please." Jody sipped her wine, grateful for Nicole's sensitivity to her nervousness. She leaned on Nicole and shivered when she put her arm around her and pulled her close.

"I'll be right back. I have to let Tiny out." Nicole stood and left a cold space behind.

Jody finished her wine and took her glass to the kitchen. She wanted to unpack her bag but hesitated to go into Nicole's bedroom without her.

"She's all set for the night." Nicole faced her and gently pulled her close by her hips. "Sleepy?"

"Not a bit." Jody leaned into Nicole and kissed her.

Nicole stepped back and took her hand to lead her to the bedroom.

"You have a hot tub!" Jody took in the big corner of the room sectioned off by a curtain.

"It's actually a large garden tub. I love to soak in it with bubble bath. Will you join me?"

"I sure will." Jody sat on the side of the bed and took off her shoes and socks.

Nicole kissed her before speaking. "Is lavender bubble bath okay with you?"

"Oh yes." Jody would've said yes to bubble gum scented at the thought of getting naked with Nicole in the water.

Nicole added bubble bath and filled the tub before sitting next to Jody and taking off her shoes and socks. She stood, unzipped her jeans, and slowly pushed them off. Then she pulled off her T-shirt and stood in her bra and panties. Her breath caught when Jody traced her finger along the top of her bra and dipped it between her breasts.

"I want you so much," Jody said.

"Yeah, me, too." Nicole rolled her onto the bed. She lay on her side and reached for Jody's jean's zipper. "May I?"

Jody squirmed and murmured. "Please hurry." She sat up and yanked off her top and shimmied out of her jeans before she cradled Nicole's face in her hands and pulled her into an ardent kiss.

"Come on." Nicole broke their connection, took her hand, and drew her off the bed. "The tub is full."

Jody watched Nicole remove the final coverings of her body. "You're gorgeous."

Nicole stepped into the tub and stood with her hand out for Jody.

Jody stripped quickly and took Nicole's hand as she stepped into the warm water and scented bubbles. Nicole sat in one of the corner seats and wrapped her arms around her as Jody leaned back on her. She relaxed and let her legs float as she stretched out and moved Nicole's hands to her breasts. She whimpered when Nicole stroked the underside of her breasts and gently squeezed her nipples but keened when she pulled her against her and caressed her belly. Nicole nuzzled her neck as she made small circles with her fingertips and moved them as far as she could reach toward the place Jody craved her touch. Jody squirmed and rolled over to press against Nicole. Nicole stretched and Jody trembled at the feel of her naked body pressed against hers. She caressed every inch of Nicole's body that she could reach. "Can we go to the bed now?' Jody forced down her burning desire. She wanted Nicole in her arms when they both exploded with orgasms. She needed to lose herself in Nicole and feel her everywhere. Nicole released the drain and she took Jody's hand and helped her climb out of the tub.

Nicole wrapped an oversized towel around her when Jody shivered in the cool air of the room. "Thanks." She watched Nicole wrap herself with one and followed her to the side of the bed before turning back the covers. She tossed aside her towel, slid under the covers, and held out her hand to invite Jody to join her. Jody dropped her towel to the floor before she took her hand and lay next to her.

"Okay?" Nicole traced her face gently with her fingers. "You're lovely."

Jody smiled. "And you're a sweet-talker." She took her hand and kissed it. "Everything is perfect." She turned, leaned on her elbow, and kissed her. She pressed her body against Nicole's as need took over. Nicole was all she heard, saw, or felt, throughout her body and in her heart. She whimpered when Nicole teased her with her fingers and brought her to the edge of release before pulling away. "Ah...Nic, please." Jody whined and thrust her hips to meet her touch.

"Okay, sweetheart, come for me," Nicole breathed in her ear and slipped a finger inside her.

Jody bent forward and clutched Nicole's hand until her spasms subsided and she collapsed on the bed. She woke disoriented but warmly wrapped in Nicole's arms. "Mm. Nice." She stretched and rested a hand on Nicole's thigh and grinned at the tightening of her muscle beneath her caress. She began tiny circles with her fingers as she crept closer to her heat. Nicole griped when she slowed her progress so Jody massaged her upper thigh and moved her hand to her pussy to squeeze gently. She slowly stroked through her wetness and ignored her own reemerging desire while she pressed and fondled listening for Nicole's reaction. She lost her breath when Nicole sat up and pressed against her hand and shuddered before falling back onto the bed. Jody crawled back to lie next to Nicole and wrap her arms around her. "I've got you, baby."

Jody woke next to a warm body startled for a moment until memories of gentle caresses and passionate kisses reminded her she was with Nicole. She rested her hand on Nicole's arm, sighed, and drifted back to sleep. Something cold and wet tickled her neck and as Jody swiped at it, her hand landed on a fuzzy dog head. "Tiny. Go lay down." She turned over after speaking and began to drift off when she felt heavy paws weigh her down. "Tiny!"

Nicole rolled over and pulled her close.

"We have a visitor."

Nicole sat up and Tiny jumped across Jody to get to her. "Sorry. I forgot to tell you that Tiny likes to jump on the bed and cuddle in the morning."

Jody laughed. "I guess I have competition." Jody sat up and Tiny's tail began to thump on the bed. "Hello, you nosey dog." She petted her. "I suppose you were here before me."

"Okay. Down." Nicole pointed to the door and Tiny immediately jumped off the bed and went to the living room.

"Impressive." Jody wrapped her arms around Nicole and kissed her. "Good morning."

"Good morning." Nicole hugged her closer and Jody settled into her embrace. "This is nice. I like waking up with you."

"Me, too." Jody kissed Nicole's breast and ran her tongue around her nipple. She grinned when Nicole hummed and pressed her breast against her mouth. Jody would've been content to stay in bed and continue her exploration of Nicole's body, but Nicole eased away and took a breath.

"I need to let Tiny out." She kissed her quickly, climbed out of bed, and slipped on a robe before leaving the room.

Jodi stretched and enjoyed the feeling of waking in Nicole's bed for a moment before getting up and putting on a pair of sweatpants and T-shirt. She went to the kitchen surprised to find eggs and cheese in the refrigerator. "How does a cheese omelet sound for breakfast?" she called to Nicole in the other room.

"Sounds great." Nicole entered the kitchen and wrapped her arms around her waist from behind before nuzzling her neck.

"Unless you were going to make one?" Jody leaned back into her.

Nicole chuckled. "I probably could, but I like you in my kitchen." She kissed her quickly and retrieved silverware and plates to set the table.

CHAPTER THIRTY-EIGHT

"Come on, Tiny. Let's go check on things." Nicole loaded her car with the posters and flyers she wanted to arrange on the tables for the fundraiser. As she drove, her thoughts wandered to Jody. The emptiness of her house when Jody left to go home took her by surprise. She smiled at the memory of sharing the lopsided omelet and the heated kiss before she left. Jody had made her way into her life, into her bed, and into her heart. She parked next to the building and put a leash on Tiny before going inside. The party planner had set up all the tables, so it didn't take long for Nicole to arrange her materials on them. She stepped back to review everything and the planner emerged from the kitchen. "Hi, Carrie. The place looks great. Thanks for doing such a good job."

"No problem. It was fun. I'll be here later to check out the dogs available for adoption."

"I look forward to seeing you."

"Me, too. Maybe we could have a drink together. I can feed you hors d'oeuvres by hand." Carrie ran her fingers along Nicole's arm.

"Thanks for the offer, but I have a girlfriend, and she'll be here tonight."

Carrie shrugged. "She could join us. I haven't had a threesome in a long time."

"I'm going to pass on that provocative offer. You're a beautiful woman, and I'm sure you can find someone more available."

"You were certainly worth a try. Thank you for your honesty. I'll see you later."

Nicole watched Carrie leave and took one more look at the room before heading home. She chuckled at Carrie's advances, and she wondered if Jody would laugh or be pissed. She suspected the latter. She checked the time and decided she had time to take Tiny for a walk before Jody returned. Jody arrived a few minutes later.

"Hi there." Jody kissed her.

"Mm. Nice welcome. Tiny and I went around the block. Everything's ready for the fundraiser." She placed her hands on Jody's hips and pulled her close for another kiss.

"At this rate, we'll be late."

"Okay. I'm going to take a shower." Nicole turned and started for the bathroom.

"I'll help." Jody grinned and followed her.

"I can probably finish on my own." Nicole pushed Jody against the shower wall and kissed her as the water rained down on them.

"I'll make sure you're rinsed off." Jody glided her hands over her body circling her nipples with her fingers and knelt in the shower to circle her clit with her tongue.

"Ah...Jody." Nicole sucked in a breath. "At this rate we'll never get to the fundraiser."

Jody stood and kissed her quickly before stepping out of the shower. "Okay, but we're not done with this."

Nicole finished quickly, wrapped herself in a towel, and went to the bedroom. She dropped the towel and rushed to dress then noted Jody had gone to the spare bedroom to change and relaxed. She finished dressing and collected the other items she wanted to take along with Tiny. She waited for Jody by the door and her knees nearly buckled when she walked toward her wearing the same sexy green dress she'd worn the first time she'd seen her.

"Ready?" Jody took her hand and kissed it. "You look stunning."

"I'm ready, and you look exquisite."

"Thank you. I guess we're ready then," Jody said.

"Yep. Let's go." Nicole parked near the building and took Jody's hand as they entered. The room was already near capacity and they had to wind their way through the crowd. She put Tiny in the large crate she'd set up for her and looked for Jaylin and Railroad. She didn't see them and turned to Jody. "Do you see Jaylin?"

"No. I'll walk around the room and let her know you're looking for her if you want."

"Yeah. Thanks." Nicole squeezed her hand gently. "I'll be here with Tiny."

"I found you."

Nicole recognized the voice and cringed. "Hello, Doreen."

"I saw that lovely woman you came with. Jody, isn't it?"

"Yes." Nicole wasn't giving Doreen any information about Jody. "We rode together."

"It looked like you two were pretty cozy. She's quite lovely and I remember her from the last fundraiser."

"Yes. She likes them."

"You have a good time tonight. I'll see you later." Doreen sauntered away.

Nicole spotted Jody walking toward her and relaxed. She reached for her hand as soon as she got close enough.

"You all right?" Jody asked. "You look a little rattled."

"Doreen's already stopped by to needle me. I bet she'll be after you soon."

"Good. I'll let her know to mind her own business."

"Sweetheart, she'll make stuff up to make news. True or not."

Jody lifted her hand and cradled it to her chest. "I like it when you call me sweetheart." She kissed her softly.

"This must be the girlfriend you told me about." Carrie stood next to her at the table.

"It is. Jody, this is Carrie, the party planner." Nicole introduced her. "This is my girlfriend, Jody."

"It's good to meet you, Carrie. The place looks great. You did an excellent job."

"Thank you. It was a fun project and an important one. I've picked out a dog I'm adopting."

"Great. Good luck," Jody said. "I'm going to get a glass of champagne. You want one?" Jody asked Nicole.

"I'll go with you." Nicole took her hand as they walked to the small table. "There's Jaylin." Nicole pointed to a corner of the room that was set up for the obedience dogs. She led Jody to the area to watch Railroad go through her paces. She never missed a command

and several people stood clapping and cheering her on. "I'm a little intimidated to show Tiny off. She's good, but no match for that one."

"Tiny is a better example of what people need at home. A dog that will mind and be well-behaved. She doesn't need to do all that fancy stuff." Jody sipped her drink after speaking.

"You're right. Most people won't bother going through the work it takes for that level of obedience. They want to be able to control their dog," Nicole said. "I'd like to walk by the donation table and see how we're doing." Nicole kept hold of Jody's hand as they walked. "It looks like we're doing well. I think people like the before and after pictures. From puppies to dogs."

"I'm sorry Ashley and Bill missed this. I think they're thinking of getting a dog."

"Where are they?"

"They took a Caribbean cruise for their honeymoon. They'll be back next week."

"Let's get another glass of bubbly and watch the obedience dogs." Nicole picked up two glasses, handed one to Jody, and led her to the obedience ring.

Nicole watched intently as Jaylin guided Railroad through the course and made a mental note to make an appointment for her help with Tiny. She looked around the room pleased that everyone seemed to be enjoying themselves. The donation box was full when she'd checked it and the event was winding down. She took Jody's hand when she switched her glass to the opposite one and allowed herself a minute of reflection as they stood together watching the dogs. Jody had come into her life under difficult circumstances but had shown maturity and resolve as they spent time together and grown closer. She couldn't imagine her life without her now and the thought didn't scare her like she imagined it would. Jody wanted nothing from her except her. She squeezed her hand gently.

"Everything okay?" Jody asked.

"It's great." Nicole watched as Carrie and one of her employees discreetly collected empty glasses and plates before disappearing into the kitchen. She relaxed aware of a huge relief at the thought she wasn't responsible for the cleanup. She'd empty the donation box and return later to make sure everything was in order since she was the one responsible for the venue. Many of the attendees had left already, but a few people were gathered to watch the obedience demonstration. She leaned close to Jody and spoke softly in her ear. "Are you ready to leave?"

"Sure, but don't you have to be here until the end?"

"Carrie will do the cleaning. I just need to empty the donation box. We can stay if you want to."

"We have unfinished business. Remember?" Jody stroked Nicole's palm with her fingers.

Nicole shivered at the contact. "Oh, I remember." She retrieved everything from the donation box and made sure Carrie had a key to lock up before she thanked Jaylin for bringing Railroad and followed Jody out the door.

"That turned out great." Jody leaned back in the seat.

"It did. I'm glad we added the obedience dogs. It was fun." Nicole parked in the garage and turned to face Jody. The dim light from her security lamp was enough to create a sensual atmosphere. She cupped Jody's chin and kissed her.

"Mm. Making out in the front seat of your car. Is this like parking?" Jody pulled her closer and kissed her harder.

Nicole leaned as far as she could before her hip hit the steering wheel. "Ouch."

Jody instantly pulled away. "Are you all right?"

"This parking thing isn't all it's cracked up to be. Let's go inside." Nicole chuckled. "Next time we're going to the back seat." She took Jody's hand and tugged her into the house and straight to the bedroom. She unzipped Jody's dress and slowly pushed it off her shoulders. Jody reached for the buttons on her tuxedo and she slid out of it. Nicole took a deep breath when Jody stood naked and pointed to her bra and panties. Nicole removed them and pulled Jody to feel her body against hers.

Jody stepped back, took her hand, and led her to the bathroom. "Time to finish what we started." She grinned as she stepped into the shower.

CHAPTER THIRTY-NINE

Jody smiled as she drove to her mother's. Memories of the weekend with Nicole created a bubbling desire nearly as strong as when Nicole's hands had explored her body. She settled herself before going to her mother's kitchen door. "Hi, Mom."

"Hi, honey. How was your evening?" She placed two cups of hot coffee on the table and sat.

"It was great. We enjoyed the fundraiser." Jody sipped her coffee as the blush rose to her cheeks from memories of the night after they'd returned from the fundraiser.

"I'm so glad you and Nicole are getting along. I worry, you know?"

"No need to worry, Mom. We've actually gotten pretty close. I like her a lot."

"Oh." Her mom sipped her coffee.

"She likes me a lot, too. We're spending quite a bit of time together."

"Does she treat you well?"

"Yes."

"All right, then. Is she still coming to dinner tonight?"

"Yes."

"Good. I want to get to know the woman who's seemed to have captured your attention."

And my heart, Jody thought. "How's Mr. Grumbles settling in?" she asked.

"He's a love. He sleeps with me now. His purring helps me know I'm not alone." Her eyes glistened with tears as she sipped her coffee.

"I'm glad, Mom. I almost adopted a kitten a couple of weeks ago."

"Why didn't you, honey?"

"I've always planned to have a dog when I'm able to buy my own house. I guess that's still my plan." She shrugged.

"Ah. One thing I know for sure is that life's plans can change in an instant."

"That's true." Jody knew her mom was thinking of her father, but Jody's thoughts turned to Nicole and the unplanned feelings she'd brought into her life. "I'm going to spend some time at the animal shelter this morning. You want us here about six?"

"I thought we'd eat around six, but you two come whenever you want."

"Okay. I'll see you later." She kissed her cheek and left. She arrived at the shelter twenty minutes later.

"Hi, Jody. Wasn't that a great event last night?" Hanna looked excited.

"It was, Hanna."

"I loved the obedience display. If I had a dog that is what I'd be doing."

"I enjoyed it, too. How's M doing?"

"He's a lover. He sits on the couch with Emma and me, and he hasn't scratched anything since I bought him a scratching post."

"I'm glad he's got such a good home." Jody picked up cleaning supplies and began to clean cages.

"So, how's Nicole? You two looked pretty cozy last night." Hanna stood next to her to hold her attention.

"She's amazing. I never thought I'd meet anyone like her." Jody leaned against the cage lost in the feelings her memories evoked.

"Whew. I thought I was head over heels with Emma." Hanna unexpectedly wrapped her in a hug. "I'm happy for you."

"Thanks, Hanna. We're going to my mom's for dinner tonight, so let's get these runs and cages cleaned." She grinned. Nicole was picking her up at five thirty and she wanted to have plenty of time for kissing before they left. She worked for half an hour and nearly bumped into Bobbi coming out of one of the runs. "Hi, Bobbi."

"Hi, Jody. Great event last night." She grinned.

"It was. How's Big Boy doing?"

"He's bounced back nicely. Dr. Meyers says he's as good as new. I'm feeding him special food for the rest of his life, and he has a standing appointment with her every six months."

"That's great. I'm happy for you." Jody checked her watch. "I'm going to Mom's for dinner, so I'll see you all Monday." Jody waved and went to her car. She got home with an hour to shower and dress. Her mind kept wandering to the shower with Nicole, so when she arrived she pushed her against the wall and took her mouth in a hungry kiss.

"This is a nice greeting." Nicole wrapped her in her arms and pulled her tightly against herself. "I missed you when you left this morning."

"I wanted to check on Mom. She's looking forward to seeing you."

"I'm looking forward to seeing her." She held up a bouquet of mixed flowers.

"Beautiful! She's going to love those." Jody pulled out a bottle of peach juice from a gift bag. "She loves this, too." Jody settled in the passenger seat of Nicole's Mercedes. It had become a comfortably familiar event. She realized everything about being with Nicole was comfortable, and she liked it a lot.

"Hi, Mom." Jody hugged her mother when they arrived.

"Thank you for the dinner invitation." Nicole handed her the bouquet of flowers.

"And this." Jody gave her the gift bag.

"Thank you, both. Have a seat. We can eat soon." She put the flowers in a vase.

Jody grinned when Mr. Grumbles settled on Nicole's lap and she rested her hand on his back. She looked comfortable in her mother's house, and her mother seemed quite comfortable with her. She gave Nicole a quick kiss and went to the kitchen to see if her mom needed help.

"You can set the table, honey. I'm looking forward to using the dining room." Her mother took the roast out of the oven and set it on the counter.

"Can I help with anything?" Nicole asked from the door to the kitchen.

"You can fill the water glasses." Jody's mother smiled.

Jody sat across from Nicole at the table and enjoyed the easy conversation throughout dinner. Nicole helped her mother clear the table while Jody made a pot of decaf coffee.

"I'm glad you two came over tonight."

"I'm grateful you invited us, Nancy. I care very much for your daughter, so you're important to me, too." Nicole took the coffee cup Jody offered.

"I can see you two care for each other and that makes me happy."

"Yeah. Me, too," Jody said.

Nicole looked at her watch and Jody nodded. "We probably should get going. Did I tell you Nicole adopted a puppy?"

"No. You could've brought him or her with you. Make sure you do next time."

"Thank you. I will." Nicole took her cup to the kitchen and Jody followed. "What do you think about inviting your mom to my mom's gala event? Would she like that?" Nicole whispered.

"I think she would. Ask her," Jody said.

Jody followed Nicole back to the living room.

"Thank you for a lovely dinner and evening, but I should go let Tiny out. I wanted to ask you something." Nicole hesitated.

"Ask her." Jody poked her in the side.

"My mother is having a party, gala, something, a week from Saturday. It's a yearly fancy get-together she enjoys. I'd like to invite you. Jody and I will be there. In fact, my party planner is planning it."

"Oh, I don't want to intrude on your party."

"You're not intruding. I'm inviting you."

"It'll be fun, Mom," Jody said.

"If you're sure. Harold and I used to go out once a week. Either to a show or fancy restaurant. It was our date night." She wiped a tear off her cheek.

"You can ride with us." Nicole hugged her. "Thank you again for the dinner"

"See you tomorrow, Mom." Jody kissed her cheek and followed Nicole to her car.

"That was nice of you to invite Mom to the gala. She has many friends and a weekly book club meeting, but I know she misses going places."

"I like her. And she's your mom."

"Do you need to stop at home for anything?" Nicole asked.

Jody considered the question. She'd left an extra toothbrush and enough clothes at Nicole's for a few days. "No, I think I'm good. I can stop after work tomorrow if I need to."

Jody took Nicole's hand when they exited the car and walked into the house. She realized how comfortable she'd become staying with her. Their relationship had developed into a comfortable co-habitation in a short time. She waited until Nicole let Tiny out and pulled her to the couch. "Are you comfortable with me staying here so long?"

"Sweetheart, I love having you here with me. Are you tired of it?"

"No. I love being here. I think of you whenever we're apart, but I don't want to push you into anything."

Nicole wrapped her arms around her and pulled her on top of her on the couch. "I'd miss this if you weren't here" She kissed her and turned to trap her between herself and the back of the couch.

Jody let go of all her reservations as she relaxed in Nicole's arms. A few minutes later, she felt the weight of Tiny. She laughed when Nicole grunted and pushed her off them. Jody watched Tiny's tail wag furiously and heard her whine in frustration. "She wants to join the fun." Jody chuckled. "I suppose the bed would be more comfortable." She snuggled closer to Nicole.

"Let's do that," Nicole said.

Jody climbed off the couch and stood. She reached for Nicole's hand and tugged her to the bedroom. "Much more room." She lay on the bed and Nicole followed her but leaned on one elbow to face her.

"Would you consider moving in with me permanently?" Nicole traced her finger along her chin.

Jody took a minute to evaluate her feelings. "I like the idea. It feels right, but it hasn't been too long." She considered her words. How long was long enough? If it felt right, did it matter how long it took? She could always move in with her mother, and she had three months left on her lease. She landed on the decision that she'd keep her apartment until the end of her lease in case it didn't work out with Nicole. "I'll start packing tomorrow." Then she kissed her.

CHAPTER FORTY

"Come on, Tiny We need to clean out the extra closet." Nicole stood before the open closet door and wondered where all the stuff had come from. Her extra bedroom had been her storage room for extra clothes. It was time to clean out the clutter and welcome Jody into her life. She paused for a minute of reflection on how her life had changed since meeting her. Instead of feeling deprived of her freedom to date whomever she found interesting, she looked forward to spending time and sharing a life with Jody. She'd shown up unexpectedly and fit perfectly. No apprehension surfaced when she searched her feelings regarding this step of living together. She separated the clothes into a save pile and a donation pile and laughed as Tiny settled on the donation pile. "Those are going, little one." She laughed when Tiny's tail thumped on the floor but she didn't move. Nicole took her save pile to her bedroom and hung everything in the walk-in closet. "That's it for today." She took a shower and dressed before leaving for work.

"Morning, Stacy." She went to her desk and worked until noon, then shut down her computer and smiled in anticipation of seeing Jody.

"Hi, there." Jody sat at the picnic table with a bottle of water.

"Hi." Nicole sat across from her. "I brought Chinese today."

"Thanks." Jody took her hand across the table. "I'm planning to bring some things over tonight. Okay with you?"

Nicole grinned. "Extremely okay." She opened cartons and handed Jody a fork and paper plate. "I'll be home by five thirty."

"I talked to Mom this morning. She's beyond excited to be attending what she called Eileen Bergeron's yearly ball."

"Mom does have this thing every year, but I've never heard it called a ball." Nicole shrugged "I suppose it is sort of."

"You don't sound too enthusiastic." Jody tipped her head and looked at her.

"It's a big deal to her every year, and I actually don't mind helping her. My father came from a wealthy family. There are generations of landowners from New York to California. I don't remember my grandparents, but Mom told me she needed to work hard to live up to her mother-in-law's standards. I think she's still trying to do that. The event gets fancier every year, and I guess there's a part of me that hopes I can help her keep doing that."

"Now I'm looking forward to it. Thank you for sharing that with me. Ashley and Bill are home, by the way. I'm going shopping with her tomorrow."

"I can't wait to see what you wear." Nicole smiled.

Jody laughed. "Me, too. Are you wearing your tuxedo?"

"Probably not. Mom's insistent I look like her 'elegant daughter.'"

"Oh, my," Jody gasped. "I'm picturing you in a sequined gown. I'll swoon."

Nicole laughed. "It's not that big a deal. I've worn one every year."

"I can't wait to see it." Jody finished her food. "I suppose I better get back to work." She sighed.

"I'll see you tonight." Nicole gave her a quick kiss. "I'm looking forward to it."

"See you tonight, honey."

Nicole watched Jody walk to the building enjoying the sound of her endearment. She took Tiny out as soon as she got back to her office and left work early to stop for groceries. Nicole put groceries away, mopped the floor, dusted, and vacuumed when she got home while Tiny hid in her bedroom. "I think we're ready," she spoke softly and hugged her. She settled on her couch to watch TV while she waited for Jody.

"Hello," Jody called from the door to the garage. She rolled in a large suitcase and carried a dress on a hanger.

Nicole took the dress from her and led her to the bedroom. "I made room for you." She hung her dress in what Nicole now thought of as her half of the closet.

"This is definitely nicer than the teeny closet in my apartment." Jody grinned and put her suitcase in a corner.

"Can I take a peek at your new dress?" Nicole reached for the garment bag covering it.

"Absolutely not." Jody smiled as she spoke.

"Okay." Nicole pulled her into her arms and kissed her. "Welcome home."

"Mm. I'm going to like coming home to you."

"Me, too. I have more of Caleb's lasagna for dinner." Nicole set plates and silverware on the table.

After dinner, Nicole showed Jody the drawers she'd emptied for her and waited until she finished unpacking. "Tired?"

"Exhausted. I think maybe it's bedtime." Jody took her hand and pulled her onto the bed.

Nicole woke the next morning and her minor uncertainties dissolved as she snuggled into Jody's warm body. Memories of their lovemaking and subsequent drifting into sleep together reaffirmed her decision to ask Jody to move in with her was a good idea.

"Everything okay?" Jody asked.

"It's more than okay. It's special."

"It is, isn't it?" Jody turned and propped herself on one elbow and kissed her. "What time do we have to leave today?"

"I have an appointment with Carrie at two. It shouldn't take long. The event starts at six, so we can go whenever you're ready."

"I'll go back and get more of my things while you're gone."

"Sounds good. I have bacon and eggs for breakfast." Nicole laughed when Jody kissed her quickly and climbed out of bed. Nicole watched Jody scramble eggs and bake the bacon glad she hadn't asked her to cook. "I'm impressed. And grateful." She grinned. "I'll do the dishes." She cleaned up after Jody left and showered and dressed for her meeting with Carrie.

Jody was in the shower when she returned and she wished she had time to join her. She took her dress to the other bedroom and changed. She let Tiny out before calling for the car.

"Oh, my. You look exquisite," Jody said.

"You look absolutely delicious." Nicole kissed her. "Are you ready to go dancing?"

"Yes, I am. Are you driving?"

Nicole smiled. "Nope." She took Jody's hand and led her to the front door. "Your chariot awaits." She kissed her and smiled at Jody's surprise.

"A limo?"

"Only the best for you." She led her to the stretch limo and the driver opened the door for them. She gave the driver Jody's mother's address and relaxed. The hall was already near capacity when they arrived and she was grateful Caleb met them at the door.

"May I?" He extended his arm to Jody's mother.

"This is my brother, Caleb. Caleb, Nancy Acosta." She took Jody's hand and waited until Caleb introduced Nancy to her mother. She stepped close when he moved, and hugged her mother. "This is my girlfriend, Jody."

"It's lovely to meet you, Jody. And I'm so glad your mother was able to join us tonight. Please help yourself to the food and drinks. The orchestra will begin in a few minutes." She moved on to the next group entering the room.

"This is Mom's favorite part. Greeting everyone." Nicole wrapped her arm around Jody's waist and pulled her against her.

"She's welcoming. I like her." Jody kissed her quickly. "My mom looks beautiful, and I haven't seen that sparkle in the eyes in a long time."

"If she likes to dance, Caleb will keep her dancing all night. Come on. Let's see what kind of munchies we have." She led Jody to the table with hors d'oeuvres and drinks and picked up a glass of white wine.

Jody chose a glass of sparkling red wine. "This is amazing. I guessed it would be elegant, but this is amazing."

"Yeah. Mom likes to outdo herself every year." Nicole watched Caleb and Jody's mom dance as soon as the band began to play. "Shall we join them?" She pointed to an empty table where they set their glasses down and went to the dance floor. She felt Jody stiffen in her arms as her cousin tapped her on the shoulder and grabbed her into a hug.

"Hey, Nicky." She turned to Jody and hugged her. "You must be Nicole's latest fling."

"My name's Jody, and I'm her last one and only!" Jody reached for her hand and pulled her close. "Who are you?"

"I'm Nicole's favorite cousin. It's good to meet you, Jody. You two have fun tonight." She was gone as quickly as she'd appeared.

Nicole tried unsuccessfully to contain her laugh. "She can be a bit overbearing."

"Yeah, well, I am your last!"

"Yes. You are, sweetheart." She kissed her and led her to a seat at their table. Nancy and Caleb joined them after the music stopped.

"Are you having fun, Mom?" Jody asked.

"Oh yes. This is a fantastic event."

"I thank you for the dances," Caleb said.

"I thank you. I'm sure you'd rather find some young lady to dance with instead of me."

"Absolutely not." He clinked his glass against hers.

"I know I'm having a ball," Jody said.

"Hello all." Doreen stood at the end of their table smiling.

Nicole stood to confront her. "How did you get in here? This is a private, invitation only, event."

"May I have a minute to explain?"

Jody bristled next to her but rested her hand on her arm. "Maybe we should let her, love."

Nicole took her hand and nodded.

"I quit that paper I was working for. I want to apologize for any discomfort or angst I caused you. That newspaper thrives on misrepresentation, half-truths, and sensationalism. I'll leave you alone, I just wanted to say I'm sorry." She walked away.

Nicole prayed Doreen was being honest. "That was a surprise." She sipped her wine.

"I've never seen her before." Caleb said. "I only heard about her and read the awful things her paper printed."

"She seemed sincere to me," Nancy said. "Maybe she needs someone to dance with." She looked at Caleb.

"I'll be back." He smiled and followed Doreen to her table.

Nicole took Jody's hand. "Dance some more?" She held Jody close as they danced and whispered in her ear. "Will your mom be upset if we leave soon?"

"I don't think so. She's had a ball and it looks like quite a few people have left already."

"Good because I want you all to myself tonight. You are my last one and only. I love you." She raised their joined hands and kissed hers.

"I love you, too. Only you. Always."

CHAPTER FORTY-ONE

Jody smiled as she watched Nicole's bare breasts rise and fall when she stretched. She rested her arm across her waist in a familiar move developed in the two months they'd been living together, pulled her close, and nuzzled her neck. "I love waking up with you." She rested her head on her chest as Nicole wrapped her arms around her and held her close.

"Yeah. I love waking up with you, too." She kissed her and rolled over on top of her. "Are you going back to sleep?"

"Heck no." Jody pressed her thigh between Nicole's legs and rocked her hips forward. "God, I want you."

Nicole slipped her hand between them and fondled Jody's clit. Jody grasped her hand and held it against her heat as she squirmed beneath her and shuddered as she came. "Oh my God." She took a deep breath and held Nicole tighter. "It's a good thing I'm marrying you. I get to keep you forever." Jody snuggled closer.

"Forever and always, sweetheart." Nicole held her tight.

"What time do we have to get up, baby?" Jody closed her eyes.

"Not for a while." Nicole nuzzled her neck again.

"Good." Jody rolled to her side and propped herself on her elbow so she could reach Nicole's nipples with her tongue. She flicked each one while she stroked the soft skin of her inner thigh and inched her hand higher. She ran her fingers along the junction of the top of her thigh and her pubic hair and Nicole murmured and thrust her hips into her touch while fisting the sheets. She mumbled incoherently when her orgasm overtook her.

Jody held Nicole until she drifted back into sleep and sighed as sleep overtook her. She woke a few minutes later to Tiny whining next to the bed. "Okay." She rose and slipped on her robe before letting her outside and setting up the coffeepot. She let Tiny back in before she checked the time and filled two cups of coffee to take back to the bedroom.

"Mm, I smell coffee." Nicole sat up and propped a pillow behind her back.

Jody handed her a cup and settled next to her on the bed. "This is nice. Coffee in bed." She grinned.

"It is nice. Thank you." Nicole sipped her coffee. "We should probably get up soon."

"We've got time. Mom won't be here until noon. How does oatmeal sound for breakfast?"

"Sounds great." Nicole stroked her cheek. "I can't wait till tonight."

"Yeah. Me, too."

"How do you think this will work? Will we be Mrs. and Mrs.?" Nicole chuckled.

"I don't know. I only know I'm looking forward to being your wife and calling you my wife." Jody kissed Nicole careful not to spill her coffee.

"I am, too, love." Jody sipped her coffee. "I never asked you about the prenuptial thing. Don't people with money do that?"

Nicole laughed. "We can have one drawn up if you want to, but I didn't plan on it."

"Would your family want one?"

"I doubt it. I'm not a billionaire, love. And, I trust you. We'll work everything out."

Jody set her cup down and snuggled closer. "I trust you, too. Money is a commodity necessary for food and shelter. I suppose it helps having a lot of it if you want to go to Disney World every year." She yawned and drifted back to sleep in the safety of Nicole's arms. She woke to the scent of cinnamon.

"Ready for breakfast?" Nicole waved a bowl of oatmeal past her face.

"Thank you. Breakfast in bed!" She grinned and shoved a spoonful of oatmeal into her mouth.

"Only the best for my fiancé," Nicole whispered.

Jody finished eating and took their empty bowls to the kitchen before getting dressed. She watched Nicole riffle through her closet. "Just put on your jeans, love. We're not dressing for the wedding until two." She wrapped her arms around her from behind and squeezed. "Nervous?"

Nicole covered her hands with hers. "A little. I'm not sure why. I want this more than I have anything in my life. I love you and I want the world to know it." She turned in her arms and kissed her.

"I like the idea of wearing what we wore when we met. You're very sexy in your tuxedo."

"I like the idea, too." Nicole slipped on her jeans and a T-shirt.

"Does it help for me to tell you I'm a little nervous, too?"

"A little, yes. As long as it's nerves and not regret." She cupped her face and kissed her.

"No regrets, love." Jody began to giggle and it turned into full on laughing. "We're kissing in the closet."

Nicole laughed with her. "We've a lot to be grateful for. It wasn't that long ago we wouldn't have been able to legally marry. But, I kind of like being in the closet with you." She pulled her into the corner behind the line of hanging clothes and took her mouth in a possessive kiss.

Jody whimpered and melted into Nicole's arms around her, solid and sure. "We should probably get ready for my mom. She'll be here soon." She stepped out of Nicole's arms.

"Did she tell you why she wanted to come over before the wedding?" Nicole asked as she took her hand and led her out of the closet.

"She said she had something for us and didn't want to bring it to the hall."

"Okay. Shall we take her to lunch?"

"We've got half a ham left from last night. I could make us all ham and cheese sandwiches." Jody took the ham from the refrigerator and sliced it into sandwich sized pieces. She finished as her mother rang the front doorbell.

Nicole answered the door with Tiny right behind her. "Hi, Nancy. Come on in."

"Hi, Nicole." She kissed her cheek.

"Hi, Mom." Jody set the plate of sandwiches on the table and her mom set a wrapped present next to it.

"This is for you two. Have I told you how happy I am that you found each other?" She pulled Nicole into a hug first, then Jody.

"Thank you, Mom." Jody restrained herself from ripping open the gift.

"Yes, thank you, Nancy. Jody made sandwiches if you'd like to join us for lunch."

"I'd like that. Thank you. But, first I'd like you to open your gift." She smiled when Jody grabbed it and unwrapped it.

"Oh my." Jody stared at the needlepoint design and handed it to Nicole.

"Wow. This is beautiful. Thank you so much." Nicole wiped away a tear.

"Yes, thank you, Mom. It's really special." Jody ran her finger over the yarn picture of her and Nicole side by side and Tiny seated in front of them. "How did you do this?"

"I had help from my friend who's very good at needlepoint. I'm so glad you like it."

Jody hugged her mother and Nicole hung the gift on the wall.

"Are you planning to ride with us to the hall?" Jody asked.

"No, honey. You two take your time. I'll be in my seat waiting for you. I hope Caleb is up to some dancing tonight." She looked at Nicole.

"I'm certain he will be. He's my ring bearer."

"And Ashley's my maid of honor." Jody grinned.

"I'll see you both in a few hours then. Thank you for lunch." She kissed them both on the cheeks and left.

"That was really special of your mom to bring this." Nicole traced the needlepoint gift with her fingertips.

"It was." Jody stood next to Nicole and put her arm around her waist. "Shall we get ready to go?"

Nicole looked at the clock and took a deep breath. "I'm so looking forward to this." She kissed her. "I love you."

"I love you, too. Let's go tell the world."

Jody finished dressing and took Nicole's hand as they went to her car. The wedding officiant's car was parked in the reserved spot, and her nerves ratcheted into high gear when they stepped out of their car.

Nicole took her hand and kissed it before leading her into the building.

The room was half-full with guests and Caleb and Ashley were seated in the front row of seats along with her mom and Nicole's parents. Jody remembered them from the fancy gala event, but her nerves got the better of her and she faltered.

"You all right, love?" Nicole held her hand.

"I am. Just really nervous now." She stood in their assigned waiting area while the music began and they heard the cue for them to step forward. All Jody's nerves settled when they stepped next to Ashley and Caleb and listened to the officiate's words.

"May the happiness you share today be with you always."

Jody placed the ring on Nicole's finger and grinned when Nicole placed a matching one on hers. Her heart beat hard in her chest, but a sense of calm and rightness settled over her. She kissed Nicole with her heart pounding.

Nicole took her hand and walked them past the attendees to the back of the room. She kissed her again and led her to the area set up for dancing. Small tables with champagne flutes similar to the ones Nicole used for her fundraisers lined the room. The center held several larger round tables for attendees to sit and eat. The room soon filled with guests and Ashley and Bill were the first couple to congratulate them.

"So, where are you two going for your honeymoon?" Ashley asked.

"Nicole says it's a surprise." Jody squeezed her hand but smiled. "It doesn't matter to me. I just want her all to myself for a while."

"Congratulations to both of you." Ashley hugged them.

Nicole led her to the front of the room where her parents were seated with Jody's mother.

"Good luck, you two. I hope you'll come to dinner when you return from your honeymoon. We'd love to get to know the one who stole our daughter's heart," Nicole's mother spoke.

"We will. I look forward to it," Jody replied.

Jody pulled Nicole to the dance floor when the music began and lost herself in the feel of her arms. She reflected on her fear of never finding love and how wonderful it felt to have found it. Forever and always Nicole had claimed. She clung to her as they moved to the music recognizing the truth of her words in her heart.

About the Author

C.A. Popovich is a hopeless romantic. She writes sweet, sensual romances that usually include horses, dogs, and cats. Her main characters—and their loving pets—don't get killed and always end up with happily-ever-after love. She is a Michigan native, writes full-time, and tries to get to as many Bold Strokes Books events as she can. She loves feedback from readers.

Books Available from Bold Strokes Books

Before She Was Mine by Emma L McGeown. When Dani and Lucy are thrust together to sort out their children's playground squabble, sparks fly leaving both of them willing to risk it all for each other. 978-1-63679-315-3)

Chasing Cypress by Ana Hartnett Reichardt. Maggie Hyde wants to find a partner to settle down with and help her run the family farm, but instead she ends up chasing Cypress. Olivia Cypress. 978-1-63679-323-8)

Dark Truths by Sandra Barret. When Jade's ex-girlfriend and vampire maker barges back into her life, can Jade satisfy her ex's demands, keep Beth safe, and keep everyone's secrets…secret? 978-1-63679-369-6)

Desires Unleashed by Renee Roman. Kell Murphy and Taylor Simpson didn't go looking for love, but as they explore their desires unleashed, their hearts lead them on an unexpected journey. 978-1-63679-327-6)

Maybe, Probably by Amanda Radley. Set against the backdrop of a viral pandemic, Gina and Eleanor are about to discover that loving another person is complicated when you're desperately searching for yourself. 978-1-63679-284-2)

The One by C.A. Popovich. Jody Acosta doesn't know what makes her more furious, that the wealthy Bergeron family refuses to be held accountable for her father's wrongful death, or that she can't ignore her knee-weakening attraction to Nicole Bergeron. 978-1-63679-318-4)

The Speed of Slow Changes by Sander Santiago. As Al and Lucas navigate the ups and downs of their polyamorous relationship, only one thing is certain: romance has never been so crowded. 978-1-63679-329-0)

Tides of Love by Kimberly Cooper Griffin. Falling in love is the last thing on either of their minds, but when Mikayla and Gem meet, sparks of possibility begin to shine, revealing a future neither expected. 978-1-63679-319-1)

Catch by Kris Bryant. Convincing the wife of the star quarterback to walk away from her family was never in offensive coordinator Sutton McCoy's game plan. But standing on the sidelines when a second chance at true love comes her way proves all but impossible. (978-1-63679-276-7)

Hearts in the Wind by MJ Williamz. Beth and Evelyn seem destined to remain mortal enemies but are about to discover that in matters of the heart, sometimes you must cast your fortunes to the wind. (978-1-63679-288-0)

Hero Complex by Jesse J. Thoma. Bronte, Athena, and their unlikely friends, must work together to defeat Bronte's arch nemesis. The fate of love, humanity, and the world might depend on it. No pressure. (978-1-63679-280-4)

Hotel Fantasy by Piper Jordan. Molly Taylor has a fantasy in mind that only Lexi can fulfill. However, convincing her to participate could prove challenging. (978-1-63679-207-1)

Last New Beginning by Krystina Rivers. Can commercial broker Skye Kohl and contractor Bailey Kaczmarek overcome their pride and work together while the tension between them boils over into a love that could soothe both of their hearts? (978-1-63679-261-3)

Love and Lattes by Karis Walsh. Cat café owner Bonnie and wedding planner Taryn join forces to get rescue cats into forever homes— discovering their own forever along the way. (978-1-63679-290-3)

Repatriate by Jaime Maddox. Ally Hamilton's new job as a home health aide takes an unexpected twist when she discovers a fortune in stolen artwork and must repatriate the masterpieces and avoid the wrath of the violent man who stole them. (978-1-63679-303-0)

The Hues of Me and You by Morgan Lee Miller. Arlette Adair and Brooke Dawson almost fell in love in college. Years later, they unexpectedly run into each other and come face-to-face with their unresolved past. (978-1-63679-229-3)

A Haven for the Wanderer by Jenny Frame. When Griffin Harris comes to Rosebrook village, the love she finds with Bronte de Lacey creates safe haven and she finally finds her place in the world. But will she run again when their love is tested? (978-1-63679-291-0)

A Spark in the Air by Dena Blake. Internet executive Crystal Tucker is sure Wi-Fi could really help small-town residents, even if it means putting an internet café out of business, but her instant attraction to the owner's daughter, Janie Elliott, makes moving ahead with her plans complicated. (978-1-63679-293-4)

Between Takes by CJ Birch. Simone Lavoie is convinced her new job as an intimacy coordinator will give her a fresh perspective. Instead, problems on set and her growing attraction to actress Evelyn Harper only add to her worries. (978-1-63679-309-2)

Camp Lost and Found by Georgia Beers. Nobody knows better than Cassidy and Frankie that life doesn't always give you what you want. But sometimes, if you're lucky, life gives you exactly what you need. (978-1-63679-263-7)

Felix Navidad by 'Nathan Burgoine. After the wedding of a good friend, instead of Felix's Hawaii Christmas treat to himself, ice rain strands him in Ontario with fellow wedding-guest—and handsome ex of said friend—Kevin in a small cabin for the holiday Felix definitely didn't plan on. (978-1-63679-411-2)

Fire, Water, and Rock by Alaina Erdell. As Jess and Clare reveal more about themselves, and their hot summer fling tips over into true love, they must confront their pasts before they can contemplate a future together. (978-1-63679-274-3)

Lines of Love by Brey Willows. When even the Muse of Love doesn't believe in forever, we're all in trouble. (978-1-63555-458-8)

Manny Porter and The Yuletide Murder by D.C. Robeline. Manny only has the holiday season to discover who killed prominent research scientist Phillip Nikolaidis before the judicial system condemns an innocent man to lethal injection. (978-1-63679-313-9)

Only This Summer by Radclyffe. A fling with Lily promises to be exactly what Chase is looking for—short-term, hot as a forest fire, and one Chase can extinguish whenever she wants. After all, it's only one summer. (978-1-63679-390-0)

Picture-Perfect Christmas by Charlotte Greene. Two former rivals compete to capture the essence of their small mountain town at Christmas, all the while fighting old and new feelings. (978-1-63679-311-5)

Playing Love's Refrain by Lesley Davis. Drew Dawes had shied away from the world of music until Wren Banderas gave her a reason to play their love's refrain. (978-1-63679-286-6)

Profile by Jackie D. The scales of justice are weighted against FBI agents Cassidy Wolf and Alex Derby. Loyalty and love may be the only advantage they have. (978-1-63679-282-8)

Almost Perfect by Tagan Shepard. A shared love of queer TV brings Olivia and Riley together, but can they keep their real-life love as picture perfect as their on-screen counterparts? (978-1-63679-322-1)

Corpus Calvin by David Swatling. Cloverkist Inn may be haunted, but a ghost materializes from Jason Dekker's past and Calvin's canine instinct kicks in to protect a young boy from mortal danger. (978-1-62639-428-5)

Craving Cassie by Skye Rowan. Siobhan Carney and Cassie Townsend share an instant attraction, but are they brave enough to give up everything they have ever known to be together? (978-1-63679-062-6)

Drifting by Lyn Hemphill. When Tess jumps into the ocean after Jet, she thinks she's saving her life. Of course, she can't possibly know Jet is actually a mermaid desperate to fix her mistake before she causes her clan's demise. (978-1-63679-242-2)

Enigma by Suzie Clarke. Polly has taken an oath to protect and serve her country, but when the spy she's tasked with hunting becomes the love of her life, will she be the one to betray her country? (978-1-63555-999-6)

Finding Fault by Annie McDonald. Can environmental activist Dr. Evie O'Halloran and government investigator Merritt Shepherd set aside their conflicting ideas about saving the planet and risk their hearts enough to save their love? (978-1-63679-257-6)

Hot Keys by R.E. Ward. In 1920s New York City, Betty May Dewitt and her best friend, Jack Norval, are determined to make their Tin Pan Alley dreams come true and discover they will have to fight—not only for their hearts and dreams, but for their lives. (978-1-63679-259-0)

Securing Ava by Anne Shade. Private investigator Paige Richards takes a case to locate and bring back runaway heiress Ava Prescott. But ignoring her attraction may prove impossible when their hearts and lives are at stake. (978-1-63679-297-2)

The Amaranthine Law by Gun Brooke. Tristan Kelly is being hunted for who she is and her incomprehensible past, and despite her overwhelming feelings for Olivia Bryce, she has to reject her to keep her safe. (978-1-63679-235-4)

The Forever Factor by Melissa Brayden. When Bethany and Reid confront their past, they give new meaning to letting go, forgiveness, and a future worth fighting for. (978-1-63679-357-3)

The Frenemy Zone by Yolanda Wallace. Ollie Smith-Nakamura thinks relocating from San Francisco to her dad's rural hometown is the worst idea in the world, but after she meets her new classmate Ariel Hall, she might have a change of heart. (978-1-63679-249-1)

A Cutting Deceit by Cathy Dunnell. Undercover cop Athena takes a job at Valeria's hair salon to gather evidence to prove her husband's connections to organized crime. What starts as a tentative friendship quickly turns into a dangerous affair. (978-1-63679-208-8)

As Seen on TV! by CF Frizzell. Despite their objections, TV hosts Ronnie Sharp, a laid-back chef; and paranormal investigator Peyton Stanford, have to work together. The public is watching. But joining forces is risky, contemptuous, unnerving, provocative—and ridiculously perfect. (978-1-63679-272-9)

Blood Memory by Sandra Barret. Can vampire Jade Murphy protect her friend from a human stalker and keep her dates with the gorgeous Beth Jenssen without revealing her secrets? (978-1-63679-307-8)

Foolproof by Leigh Hays. For Martine Roberts and Elliot Tillman, friends with benefits isn't a foolproof way to hide from the truth at the heart of an affair. (978-1-63679-184-5)

Glass and Stone by Renee Roman. Jordan must accept that she can't control everything that happens in life, and that includes her wayward heart. (978-1-63679-162-3)

Hard Pressed by Aurora Rey. When rivals Mira Lavigne and Dylan Miller are tapped to co-chair Finger Lakes Cider Week, competition gives way to compromise. But will their sexual chemistry lead to love? (978-1-63679-210-1)

The Laws of Magic by M. Ullrich. Nothing is ever what it seems, especially not in the small town of Bender, Massachusetts, where a witch lives to save lives and avoid love. (978-1-63679-222-4)

The Lonely Hearts Rescue by Morgan Lee Miller, Nell Stark, Missouri Vaun. In this novella collection, a hurricane hits the Gulf Coast, and the animals at the Lonely Hearts Rescue Shelter need love, and so do the humans who adopt them. (978-1-63679-231-6)

The Mage and the Monster by Barbara Ann Wright. Two powerful mages, one committed to magic and one controlled by it, strive to free each other and be together while the countries they serve descend into war. (978-1-63679-190-6)

Truly Wanted by J.J. Hale. Sam must decide if she's willing to risk losing her found family to find her happily ever after. (978-1-63679-333-7)